D1364958

The praise for Susan Meissner's novels pours in from readers and reviewers everywhere.

WHY THE SKY IS BLUE

Tracy Farnsworth (roundtablereviews.com) says: "Bring out the Kleenex, you are certain to need them. Susan Meissner's debut novel is impressive and leaves me hungry for more."

A book group leader in Tennessee reports: "It was one of [our] favorites out of all the ones we have read. We discussed in depth, the characters, and how you made them so real. Only a few books have been as well received by this bunch as was *Why the Sky Is Blue.*"

A Minnesotan says: "Wow! What a brutally honest, beautifully expressed, compelling book! I simply could not put it down. I will definitely recommend it to many, since I work in my local public library. This book is so personal that I thought I was reading a diary or personal letter."

A WINDOW TO THE WORLD

Booklist Magazine: "One of the top ten Christian novels of 2005"

A high school teacher in Minnesota says: "It was amazing! I could hardly put it down and snuck it to school to finish the last couple chapters because I just couldn't wait. Thank you for writing one of the most entertaining and thought-provoking books I have ever read."

A teenager says: "I am only 14 years old but I bought your book and I couldn't put it down. I just wanted to tell you that your book doesn't only have an impact on grownups but also on teens. It really made me understand how bad things that happen to us is also a way that God is shaping us even though we may not realize it till later."

Sara Mills, at www.christianfictionreviewer.com says: "*Powerful.* When I finished the last page, all I could think was, *wow*…I highly recommend this book, and applaud Susan Meissner for writing so eloquently what is almost impossible to put into words."

THE REMEDY FOR REGRET

Kelli Standish, at focusonfiction.net says: "Meissner's incredible gift with words has never shone truer. A must for any discerning reader's library."

Publisher's Weekly says: "The novel is readable if not deeply involving, and it refrains from the high melodrama present in many contemporary Christian novels for women."

IN ALL DEEP PLACES

Mary DeMuth, author of Ordinary Mom, Extraordinary God *and the novel* Watching the Tree Limbs, *says,* "Loved *the book. Couldn't put it down. Lyrically written, sensitively wrought. Captivated me from page one."*

ArmchairInterviews.com writes "Susan Meissner has once again skillfully examined the basic truth of what it is to be alive in the world, with all the good and all the bad that is there. But she doesn't leave it at that. She gently reminds us that it is God's grace and love that will see us through the night. Meissner's books are must-reads."

NovelReviews.BlogSpot.com writes: "Ms. Meissner writes Christian fiction the way it should be written, with threads and hints and God-webs interwoven into not very rosy pictures of broken lives."

A SEAHORSE IN THE THAMES

A reader writes: "I just wanted to drop you a note to tell you how much I enjoyed *A Seahorse in the Thames.* Oh, my goodness, I loved it! I absolutely loved the story line—it was a beautiful blend of mystery and romance."

A fan in Australia says: "I have read and enjoyed all your other books but this one I found to be very special. I could not put it down! All your characters were genuine and real and I really felt I was walking alongside Alexa with her need for answers, her heartache and anxiety over what the future held—simply a beautiful story."

Ane Mulligan from http://www.novelreviews.blogspot.com writes: "This is a fast moving story, thoroughly entertaining and mesmerizing. I read it in one sitting, stopping only long enough to make dinner. Not your typical love story, Susan Meissner sweeps her readers away on a journey, beginning with the first paragraph. I found the ending just right. Satisfying but fitting. I enjoyed *A Seahorse in the Thames* so much I ordered another of Meissner's books which I will begin tonight. *A Seahorse in the Thames* receives this reviewer's high recommendation for a great read."

Pamela James from Fab Four Book Picks writes: "This is a masterfully created work of art…Her characters are so rich and real that you root for them from the get go…wonderful and gripping, get this book."

STICKS & STONES

SUSAN MEISSNER

HARVEST HOUSE PUBLISHERS

EUGENE, OREGON

Cover by Left Coast Design, Portland, Oregon

Cover photos © Jose Luis Pelaez Inc / Bend Images / Getty Images; Megumi Takamura / Dex Image / Getty Images

Susan Meissner: Published in association with the literary agency of Alive Communications, Inc., 7680 Goddard Street, Ste #200, Colorado Springs, CO 80920.

This is a work of fiction. Names, characters, places, and incidents are products of the author's imagination or are used fictitiously. Any resemblance to actual persons, living or dead, or to events or locales, is entirely coincidental.

STICKS AND STONES
Copyright © 2007 by Susan Meissner
Published by Harvest House Publishers
Eugene, Oregon 97402

ISBN-13: 978-0-7394-8341-1

Printed in the United States of America

ACKNOWLEDGMENTS

To my editorial team at Harvest House—especially Nick Harrison and Kimberly Shumate—for your keen insights and steady encouragement.

To my agent Don Pape at Alive Communications—for believing in me.

To the professionals who answered my early questions, my deepest thanks. Any liberties taken within these pages regarding Minnesota law and police procedure were my decision alone.

To Judy Horning, my mother, friend and fellow bibliophile—for being the best proofreader a writer could ask for.

To my wonderful colleagues in the ChiLibris writers group—for your collective wisdom so freely shared.

And to those who described to me what it's like to live as the victim of a bully—for dredging up the not-so-great past so that I could feel what you felt. I couldn't have written this book without you.

Where, after all, do universal human rights begin?
In small places, close to home
so close and so small that they cannot be seen
on any maps of the world.
Yet they are the world of the individual person;
the neighborhood he lives in…
Unless these rights have meaning there,
they have little meaning anywhere.

ELEANOR ROOSEVELT

My thoughts trouble me
and I am distraught at the voice of the enemy,
at the stares of the wicked;
for they bring down suffering upon me
and revile me in their anger.
My heart is in anguish within me;
the terrors of death assail me.
Fear and trembling have beset me;
horror has overwhelmed me.
I said, "Oh, that I had the wings of a dove!
I would fly away and be at rest."

PSALM 55:2–6 NIV

ONE

Rachael Flynn stepped out of her car, stepping gingerly onto the gathering snowflakes, pressing them into the asphalt at her feet. Above her, the sky was a swirling whiteness. Four to six inches were in the forecast. It looked more like eight to ten, to her seasoned eye. Rachael had grown up with the peculiarities of Minnesota springs, she had hunted for Easter eggs in fresh powder more than once in her childhood.

She wished she could've picked a different day to visit her brother. But her return to part-time work after the move back to Minnesota left her with fewer days for personal agendas. And there were, after all, only certain days the prison allowed visitors. She might've been able to sneak in a weekday visit if she were Joshua's attorney, but the fact was, Joshua hadn't allowed Rachael to defend him when he confessed the previous fall to killing a man. Not even when she begged him. She had been certain that he was innocent. And in a way, he was—morally, if not legally.

She closed the car door and the padded air quickly absorbed the sound. Her husband Trace had tried to talk her out of driving the 100-mile round trip from their loft apartment in downtown Minneapolis. They had both watched The Weather Channel that morning and saw the forecast, though it had been accidental that they were watching at all. Their eight-month-old daughter, McKenna, had a fondness for the station and its colorful, moving weather maps. The Weather Channel had become a part of McKenna's morning routine as much as rice cereal and apple juice.

"I think I can make it back before it gets too bad," Rachael had said when Trace suggested that she could wait until next Saturday to visit Josh. "It's not supposed to start until early afternoon."

But the snow began to fall just after she left the Twin Cities. It followed her south to the prison and was now fully committed to its task. Didn't seem fair. It was mid-April already. In Manhattan, where she and Trace had lived until five months ago, New Yorkers were walking the sidewalks in shirt sleeves and open-toed shoes.

The only thing she could credit the snow with was the way it added a touch of elegance to everything it fell upon.

It made even the prison look good.

Rachael walked tentatively across the lot, noting that many others had braved the weather to visit the errant people they loved nonetheless. The lot was full.

She made her way to the visitors' entrance and began to mentally prepare herself for her visit with her younger brother. Rachael had seen Joshua only twice since his sentencing, mostly because life had taken on a rather hectic pace since she and Trace moved from New York back to the Twin Cities. Her new job as an assistant prosecutor for the Ramsey County Attorney's office was somewhat of an experiment for both her and her employer. She had negotiated a workweek that amounted to three days instead of five so that she could spend Thursdays and Fridays with her daughter. The arrangement had translated into a challenging blend of court preparation and appearances on the trio of days that defined the front half of the week.

Rachael had found it odd to be at the prosecutor's table instead of the defendant's. For the past five years she had represented juvenile delinquents. Now she spent her days representing the local human services agency and partnering in the county's effort to end parental neglect—a trigger for juvenile delinquency as much as anything.

Rachael stamped her feet onto the floor mat just inside the prison entrance and then turned to walk down the long hallway to the registration area. The visiting commons was full of people—parents who had come to see wayward children and children who had come to see wayward parents. Wives and sisters waited in the chairs. Brothers and girlfriends. She signed in and took a seat near a window to wait for Joshua to be led into the room.

Her brother had tried to talk her out of moving back to the Twin Cities. It took a bit of convincing to assure Josh it wasn't merely pity for his circumstances that brought Rachael and Trace back to Minneapolis. And it wasn't pity that drove her to visit him at the prison as often as she could. Josh was five years younger than Rachael but she had always been in awe of his insights into human character. That talent had always made him seem older. He saw far more than she did. He always had.

That was precisely why she had braved the storm and come in spite of the forecast. Josh knew what went on in the minds of hurting people. Despite what he had done, Josh was still the most compassionate man she knew. And she was in need of his insights.

Rachael wondered if Joshua had heard what had happened to her several weeks earlier in the Ramsey County courthouse parking lot. She could scarcely believe it had been real herself. Some days she woke up unconvinced that she had indeed had a gun held to her head for a few fleeting minutes. It had happened at the end of a long day in court. Rachael had gone out to her car and unlocked it, and then she had run back inside the courthouse to make a last-minute phone call. In these brief moments, a distraught mother whose children had been ordered into long-term foster care at Rachael's recommendation had slipped into her backseat. When Rachael returned to her car, the barrel of a gun had been thrust at her head and a rush of angry words had been leveled at her. Of course, she had been afraid at first, but then the fear had given way to pity.

The woman didn't want to kill anyone; she wanted her kids back. By the time her attacker had been subdued, Rachael was strangely certain her life had never truly been in danger. Rachael was sure of it, but no one else was—especially her friend and colleague Will Pendleton, the police detective who saw her sitting in her car in the icy twilight as he also left the courthouse and who had come to her aid. The mother never would've pulled the trigger, Rachael had told Will. Will had told her gently that

that was something she couldn't know. But somehow she felt she did. She wondered as she waited if Josh would understand this. Surely if anyone would, it would be her brother.

A woman twice her weight and seemingly half her height now took a seat across from Rachael, interrupting her thoughts. Rachael smiled at her and the woman smiled back.

"Rotten day for visiting," the woman said, adjusting her body in the foam-padded chair.

"Yes," Rachael answered.

"I didn't even bring my windshield scraper. Took that out of the car three weeks ago."

Rachael nodded. "Me, too."

"You here to see your husband, too?" The woman looked dubious. Rachael knew her expensive clothes gave her away every time she came here. She didn't look like the type to have a family member in prison.

"No. My brother actually."

"Oh. Caught selling drugs?"

Rachael shook her head. She looked toward the doors where Josh would emerge. "No," she answered.

"So many fine young people get caught up in those drugs. Happened to my Douglas. He's not here though. He's in treatment. Clyde, my husband, got off them a long time ago. But he's here just the same."

Rachael smiled and said nothing.

"Your brother rob a bank or something?"

Rachael sighed but the woman didn't seem to notice. Clearly, Clyde's wife wanted to know what Joshua had done to land him in a place like this. Was it as bad as whatever it was Clyde had done? Or did it place Josh and Clyde in a fraternity of some kind and thus bind their women as well? Rachael doubted she would adequately be able to describe how Josh ended up in prison for killing a man. She decided she'd give the woman what she wanted and hopefully gain her respect and silence.

"My brother is here for voluntary manslaughter. He killed a guy who was running a prostitution ring in Frogtown."

The woman's mouth opened a little. "He killed a man in Frogtown? In the Cities?"

"Yes."

"And it wasn't about drugs?"

"My brother was trying to save two teenage girls from forced prostitution, but he was too late. And when my brother realized what this man had done—not only to those girls but other girls, too—he lost it. He killed him. He crushed the man's skull."

The mouth was now open wide enough for a dentist to have a peek inside.

"The judge ruled it voluntary manslaughter because my brother hadn't meant to kill him," Rachael continued. "But he did kill him, of course."

The door across the room opened and several inmates entered the room—Josh was among them. Rachael stood up.

"Nice talking with you," she said quickly and moved away before the woman could respond. If indeed she was planning to.

Rachael waved to her brother and walked quickly over to the visiting tables and took a seat. Josh smiled and met her there. They clasped hands across the table. Rachael saw that Clyde's wife was staring at them both from across the room. She knew what the woman was thinking. Josh didn't look like a violent man.

"Is that snow in your hair?" her brother said, giving her hand a squeeze before letting go.

"Can you believe it? They're expecting half a foot."

"Gotta love Minnesota."

Rachael studied his face, searching for a sign that underneath the prison jumpsuit and the stress of the last five months Josh was still the same person she had grown up with. Compassionate, quirky, and utterly devoted to helping the helpless. The truth was, he *wasn't* a violent man.

"Are you doing okay?" she asked.

Her brother, lean, tall, and pony-tailed, shrugged. "Other people have it worse off than me," he answered. "Food's not bad. Company's a little hard to please sometimes. The chaplain here is a nice guy, though. He wants me to help him lead a Bible study."

"That's great, Josh," Rachael said, reaching across and squeezing his hand.

"Yeah, I guess that's something I could do."

"You'll be great at it."

Josh smiled. "Perhaps."

"So, you're sure you're okay?"

"I should be asking you that," he replied, the smile never leaving his face.

"Me?"

"We get newspapers in here, Rachael. And cable."

Rachael sat back in her chair. So he knew. He knew what happened to her in the parking lot. She was glad he knew. One less thing for her to have to describe for him. "The newspaper made it seem so much worse than it really was."

"How much worse could it have gotten, aside from getting shot?"

"She wasn't going to use that gun. She was just mad. And frustrated."

"I heard your friend Sgt. Pendleton say she had every intention of using that gun. He said on the news that he believes that woman had planned on shooting you as you walked across the parking lot, without even talking to you. That she had been waiting around the side of the building for over an hour. You changed your mind about getting into your car and went back inside. But you had already unlocked your car. That's when she got inside it. 'Cause she wanted you to know who it was that pulled the trigger."

Rachael stiffened. Josh had been afraid for her. He still was.

"But she didn't pull it," Rachael said softly. "She wasn't going to. I'm sure of it."

"Yeah. I read that in the paper," Josh continued. "That that's what you thought. Like it was an unfortunate mishap that she climbed in your car with a gun."

"I really don't think she was going to pull the trigger, Josh. She was just desperate and calling out for help. She was like all the people you yourself have reached down to help. I thought you would understand that."

Josh studied her face and said nothing. She wondered what he was thinking. It wasn't the first time in the past few months Rachael had told him she was sure of things she couldn't actually prove.

"Will Pendleton saved the day, I hear," he said.

"Yes. Will saw me sitting in my car. He was able to convince her to give up her gun." Rachael said it all as if there were no weight to the words, but Will had drawn his own weapon and there had been several tense seconds when there were two guns within inches of her body. She should have been terrified. What consumed her tangled thoughts in that awful moment was only that Will would shoot first.

"God was watching out for you, I think," Josh said.

"I'm not saying he wasn't."

Josh held her hand and stroked it. "Sometimes he lets the bad stuff happen, Rachael."

"Look, I'm not going to do that again, Josh. I won't ever leave my car unlocked again. I promise. But I'm telling you, I knew somehow that I wasn't truly in danger."

Josh was silent for a moment. "What does Trace say about all this?"

Rachael smiled ruefully. "At first, Trace wanted me to quit my job."

"Maybe you should."

Rachael held his gaze for several long seconds. "That's not what you would do."

Josh said nothing.

"Can you stop being who *you* are?" she said to him. "Even in here, can you stop being *you*, Josh? Are you telling me you don't look at every guy in this place who got dealt a heavy hand and don't find yourself looking for ways to help him?"

Josh looked away. When he brought his gaze back to her his smile had softened. "You always were the smart one."

A moment of silence passed between them. Rachael was ready to change the subject. She could tell Josh didn't particularly like what she had told him. But he at least understood that she was not imagining things. He too, had been gifted in ways that defied explanation.

"I don't want you staying if we're going to get that much snow," he said a moment later. His voice was kind, but authoritative.

"I'll be all right, Josh."

"You should head back. The roads will be slick."

"I can stay a little longer," Rachael countered.

But Josh stood up. "I want you to be safe," he said. He reached for her hand and she held it out to him. He kissed it.

"Bye," he said.

"Josh, I'm sure another half hour won't make a difference."

But her brother had turned and was walking away. He raised up a hand in farewell.

There was nothing Rachael could do except sign out and leave.

The drive back to Minneapolis wasn't terribly perilous but it wasn't easy either. Rachael eased up on her speed when she passed two cars that had slid into a ditch. She drove the rest of the way on I-35 well below the speed limit, as did almost everyone else.

While she drove, Rachael's thoughts tossed and turned. Part of her was still contemplating that what happened in the courthouse parking lot two months ago could happen again. But part of her knew that what she was doing with her life career-wise mattered to every neglected child in Ramsey County whose name crossed her desk.

The world, even clothed in the bridal white of an ill-timed April snowfall, was still an unkind place for far too many people. And everyone had to find a way to live with that.

Trace had his art as an outlet. He painted and drew beautiful things to counter the ugliness. But her way to counter it was the only way she knew. She couldn't just quit her job with the county and sit at home watching The Weather Channel. Being a lawyer was the only way she knew to eke a little justice out of a crazed world. And if God had decided to start nudging her now and then with perceptions that didn't make sense, who was she to question it? Besides life had again taken on the comfortable if not predictable pace of managed demands.

She switched on the radio and listened to a few tunes before the latest news on the weather made her grimace. More snow was expected on Sunday. Monday's commute was already expected to be a slushy snarl of blocked roads. She decided to swing by her office and get Thursday's and Friday's mail and messages. If she couldn't make it in until noon Monday, she'd never get caught up.

A few minutes later Rachael eased into the Ramsey County courthouse parking lot. The lot was empty except for a few cars. She double-clicked on her power lock button.

The halls were dim and strangely quiet in the county building. No surprise for a Saturday afternoon. She smiled at the deputy manning the entrance and then hurried to the attorneys' offices. She just wanted to get in and get out. Her work area was tidy but a tiny pile of phone messages lay on her blotter as did several interoffice envelopes and mail from the outside world. She grabbed the messages and mail, locked the door behind her and made her way outside into the falling snow. Rachael hurried back to her car and tossed the mail and messages onto the passenger seat. A small envelope fell away from the rest of the mail and landed on the floor of the car. It was the only envelope that wasn't business-sized.

Curious, Rachael bent down, retrieved it and turned it over. It was addressed to her in typed lettering. There was no return address but Rachael could see that the postmark was St. Paul. In the lower left hand corner were the typed words "personal and confidential." Rachael turned the envelope over. It was still sealed.

Rachael ran her finger through the flap and opened the envelope. A single folded sheet of paper was inside. She drew it out and unfolded it.

Four typed sentences stared back at her. There was no name or signature below them.

Rachael read them and then read them again. And again.

A body is going to be found at the River Terrace construction site.

He deserved what he got, but it was still an accident.

You understand about accidents; I've read the papers.

You need to know it wasn't supposed to happen.

Several minutes passed before Rachael remembered she was sitting alone in the courthouse parking lot. She put the key into her ignition and drove away, her head burning with questions, the "managed calm" forgotten.

TWO

Rachael tried to concentrate on the flow of traffic leading out of downtown St. Paul. It wasn't terribly busy for a Saturday afternoon but the falling snow was obscuring her visibility. She willed her eyes to stay on the road, but every few seconds they wandered of their own volition to the seat beside her and the open note.

She kept seeing the words "a body is going to be found" and feeling her own body prickle with the knowledge and fear that there probably *was* a body at the River Terrace construction site, wherever that was. And the writer knew whose it was. And how it got there. Who would write a note like that if it wasn't true? The writer sounded contrite if not straightforward. Why would anyone alert her to a body if there wasn't a body? What was to be gained by fabricating such a claim?

And why on earth did she get the note? She wasn't a cop. She wasn't even a trial lawyer. She wouldn't be the one to prosecute if there was indeed a body and it was evident there had been a wrongful death.

You understand about accidents; I've read the papers.

A chill swept across her as she considered that she had been especially singled out to receive the note. Maybe someone had read the news account of Joshua's confession and the part she played in uncovering the truth behind his admission. Maybe someone knew Josh didn't mean to kill anyone and that she had helped the police sort out the truth from the lies. Perhaps this someone also knew she had been accosted in her car, threatened with her life and yet she didn't think the attacker meant her any true harm. The news coverage of both incidents had been on the front pages of the Minneapolis *Star Tribune's* and St. Paul *Pioneer Press'* metro sections.

Someone had taken note of her name and where she worked. *And how,* she thought. Someone believed she would do the right thing with this information.

Rachael sat back in her seat. She had been sitting forward, tense and troubled. And what was the right thing? What did the writer truly expect her to do?

Her cell phone rang at that moment and she fumbled in her purse for it while keeping the steering wheel steady. Rachael's home phone number blinked back at her in the phone's tiny screen.

"Hey, Trace," she said.

"Hey. Where are you at?" His voice was laced slightly with worry. Rachael smiled.

"I'm almost home. I just stopped at the office for messages and stuff. Something tells me I may not get into the office by 8:00 on Monday."

"So you've heard we're supposed to get more?"

"Yes."

"Visit with Josh went okay, then?"

"Short, but nice. He's doing okay, I think. He didn't want me to stay long because of the weather, so I was only there maybe fifteen minutes. Say, Trace. I got a really weird letter in the mail and I…"

"What do you mean a 'weird letter'?"

She needed to be more careful with what she said. Trace hadn't gotten over what had happened to her two months ago.

"It's nothing bad, Trace. Really. Just very odd. I'm bringing it home. I was wondering if while you're waiting for me you could Google this name for me? River Terrace. I'm thinking there should be a construction project somewhere around here with that name."

"Is this about the letter?"

"Yes. I'm thinking I'll need to call Will maybe. Once I find out what River Terrace is."

"Will." The name sounded frosty and harsh when Trace said it. Trace liked Will. Trace liked Will a lot. But Will was a cop. Will had been the one to save the day when Rachael was being held at gunpoint in the parking lot. Her wanting to call Will meant whatever was in the letter *was* indeed something bad. She could sense the resistance in his voice.

"Really, Trace. It's not…it's not that bad," Rachael said. "I just think he'd want to know about this."

Silence.

"Okay?" she said.

"All right. River Terrace."

"Yep, River Terrace."

"Okay."

Rachael itched to change the subject. "So is McKenna awake?"

"I heard her stirring just before I called you. She'll be up when you get here."

"Okay. I'll see you in about ten minutes."

"Rachael, be careful. The snow's really starting to pile up." Rachael caught the shift in his voice. Frustration had given way to concern.

"I promise. See you soon," she said.

Rachael sat on the wrap-around sofa in a room that had once been part of the secondary manufacturing floor of a textile company. The room was now the living area of a converted loft in Minneapolis' rein-vented warehouse district. Snow continued to fall outside tall windows that stretched to the twenty-foot ceiling. A cup of coffee was on the table in front of her and her daughter was in her lap. In her right hand she held a printout of a web page for River Terrace Condominiums, a seventy-five-unit towered complex under construction in St. Anthony Park and set for completion in December. The developer was already taking buyers for individual units even though grading of the site had only just begun. People were already buying the luxury units based on pictures and a scale model. Rachael studied the photo of the site, her eyes searching the pixels of brown dirt and native grasses.

A body is going to be found...

"Da!" McKenna announced, picking up a toy elephant in Rachael's lap and directing its plastic trunk to her mouth.

Trace sat next to her, leaning forward. He held the strange note in his hand.

"Could be a hoax," he said.

"Yes," Rachael said, as she placed the printout on the cushion next to her and readjusted McKenna's weight on her lap. "But even a hoax has a purpose. There's usually an ulterior motive when someone concocts a hoax. I just don't see what the benefit is in sending this to me if it's not true."

"What's the benefit of sending it to you if it *is* true?" Trace said, turning to her. His finely spiked hair was tinted a faint teal at the tips; a new shade he was trying out after tiring of the melon-hued tint he had worn for the past year. Rachael had long since embraced the notion that having an artistic husband meant becoming comfortable with the exotic.

"Well, I'm not sure. It almost seems like a plea for understanding," Rachael said, peering at the note in Trace's hand, though she had the four lines memorized.

Trace turned back to the note. "I don't want you going down there," he said.

"Going down where?"

"To that construction site. You give this to Will like you said you would. Let him handle it. It's his job." He turned his head back to look at her. "Okay?"

"Well, Trace, I hadn't even thought that far ahead yet. I wasn't planning on going there."

"So you'll give it to Will and let him handle it?"

"Um, yeah," she stammered. "Of course."

"You going to wait until Monday?"

"I think I'd better at least call him now and tell him about it. It should be his call to decide what should happen next."

Trace stood. "I'll get the phone." His bare feet made only the slightest sound on the polished wood floor as he walked over to the open kitchen.

A cordless phone lay in its cradle atop a charcoal gray granite counter-top. Trace picked it up and brought it back to Rachael and then lifted McKenna out of her arms.

"I suppose you know his number," he said as he placed McKenna on a rug nearby where baby toys were spread about.

"Yeah, I do." Rachael punched in Will's cell phone number and waited. After four rings Will's voice mail kicked in. When the recorded message was finished, Rachael cleared her throat and spun together a hasty message.

"Hey, Will, it's Rachael. It's about two-thirty in the afternoon on Saturday. Say, I stopped by my office today to get my mail and I got a very strange unsigned letter that I think you should know about. I'm not quite sure what to make of it. It can probably wait until Monday, but I didn't think that was my call to make. I should be home the rest of the day. Bye."

Rachael clicked off the phone and set it on the coffee table in front of her. "We're planning on being home the rest of the day, aren't we?" she asked Trace.

Trace, who was lying on his side next to McKenna and propped up on an elbow, turned his head toward her. "Actually," he said. "Fig and the guys are coming over tonight, so yeah, we'll be home. It's Brick's birthday."

Rachael tried not to betray her slight annoyance at having to play host-ess on the spur of the moment. She should be used to this by now. Fig, Brick, and Sidney were Trace's art school classmates from days gone by and still his closest friends. They were always coming over at the last minute—especially Fig, who lived in a loft similar to theirs only one block away. It was actually Fig who'd told them about the loft they were now living in when she and Trace first discussed moving back to Minneapolis. Fig and Trace shared an art studio in Fig's building, which had turned out to be the perfect arrangement for Trace. He could work on the illustrations for his new contract with the publications arm of Mayo Clinic pretty much anytime he wanted, day or night. And Figaro Houseman, strange as he was, was good company for Trace. Fig's highly eccentric ideas and surpris-ing antics kept Trace motivated, on schedule, and wildly entertained.

She had to admire Fig. For all his weird ways, he was a sought-after sculptor who had already made his first million. Alphonse Brick, who tended to describe himself as neo-Impressionist exiled to the public school system, taught high school art. Fig and Brick, both single, were over at their place at least once a week. Sidney, a cartoonist for the *Star Tribune* came less often, since he was married and the father of a toddler. Having the guys over that night really wasn't that big of a deal, except that she now knew it was Brick's birthday. She would have liked to have at least made a cake or bought him a birthday present.

She said as much to Trace.

"You don't need to worry about a gift. Guys aren't that way, Rach. He won't care."

"And a cake?" Rachael said, intimating that guys do, however, have a fondness for food.

"Brick doesn't like sweet stuff so Fig's bringing some smoked octopus. He says it's Brick's favorite."

"Of course it is," Rachael said wryly, rising from the sofa and slipping the note back in its envelope. Saturday chores beckoned.

Fig and Brick arrived at the loft a little before eight, just as Rachael was putting McKenna to bed. She tiptoed out of the nursery, switching on the baby monitor and closing the main door to the hallway that led to the bedrooms. The guys tended toward volume. She walked down the open staircase to the main floor of the loft.

"Rachael! Kumquat!" Fig exclaimed as she came down the stairs. Fig, dressed in decidedly deconstructed jeans and a madras shirt, sailed over to her. He grabbed her by the shoulders when she reached the bottom step and kissed her on both cheeks. He had been to the hairstylist since she had seen him last. His salt-and-pepper shoulder-length hair had been neatly cornrowed, and his goatee trimmed.

"Hello, Fig," she said. Rachael turned to Brick and walked over to him. His brown-black hair was doused in snow, making his Mediterranean features even more pronounced. "Happy birthday, Brick," she said.

"Thanks, Rachael," Brick answered, bending down from his six-foot-seven frame to kiss her cheek.

"Wow, Fig," Trace said as he closed the front door and took their wet jackets. "That's a new look for you."

"Ah, yes, the cornrows! Well, Jillian got me these lovely beads on eBay and I didn't know how better to use them." Fig pointed to the tiny, odd-shaped blue and green orbs that dangled on the end of each braid.

"Jillian couldn't come tonight?" Rachael said, inquiring about Fig's current love interest.

"No, no," Fig said turning to her. "She's off to Peru tomorrow, you know. Some kind of weaving convention or whatnot. Hey, I brought fried plantains, too. Didn't think you'd care for the suckers on the octopus tentacles, Kumquat."

He handed her a brown bag that was warm to the touch. As she took the bag, the buzzer rang from within the lobby downstairs.

"That'll be Sidney," Fig announced. "I'll let him in."

Rachael took the bag into the kitchen and as she set it down, the phone rang. Rachael reached for it.

"Hello?" she said.

"Rachael, it's Will. What's this about a letter?"

"Just a sec, Will," Rachael said. She covered the mouthpiece and turned toward Trace. "I'm taking this in our bedroom. It's Will."

Trace nodded.

Rachael grabbed the letter from the kitchen counter and made her way back up the stairs to the master bedroom, waving to red-haired and stocky Sidney as he crossed the threshold into the loft. Once inside the master bedroom, she closed the door and sank onto a plush area rug, resting her back on the footboard of the bed.

"Okay, I'm back. I picked it up today at the office. I just went in to get Thursday's and Friday's mail. There's no return address and the postmark is St. Paul." Rachael removed the letter from the envelope and read it out loud.

When she was done, there was a momentary silence on the other end. "No signature, nothing?" Will finally said.

"No. It's typed. Looks like it was printed off your basic computer printer."

"What the heck is River Terrace?"

"It's a condominium complex that's being built in St. Anthony Park. I looked it up on the Internet."

"Being built?"

"Well, the pictures make it seem like they're just now starting to excavate. The site is a wooded area off a set of residential streets."

Will sighed into the phone. "Well, there hasn't been a report of a body being found in St. Anthony Park the past few days, so either no one's dug it up yet or we've got a nut case on our hands. I don't know which is worse."

"I don't think it's a joke, Will."

"And why is that?"

Rachael had no answer. It was a gut feeling. She'd been having a lot of them lately. "I don't why. I just feel like whoever wrote this is being truthful. And they're feeling some kind of remorse."

Will was quiet for a moment.

"Well, we'll have to treat it like whoever wrote it is being truthful regardless. I'm glad you called me," he finally said. "Okay. No one is working at that site tomorrow. It's Sunday. And with this lovely new snow we've got it could be four or five days before it all melts away and they do start back at it. It'll give me some time to get a team together, check Missing Persons and schedule some hounds. I'll come by your office Monday and get the letter. All right?"

"Okay."

"And Rachael?"

"Yes?"

"Please don't go down there."

Rachael clucked her tongue. "You sound just like Trace."

"I like Trace."

Rachael grinned in spite of her annoyance. "I'm not going there," she said.

"Good. See you Monday."

THREE

Monday morning dawned partly sunny and breezy, an interesting mix when paired with the near-foot of snow that lay heavy on the streets of downtown Minneapolis. Street crews began tackling the messy drifts before daybreak, but at 7:00, local morning news anchors were still agog with traffic reports of spinouts, fender-benders, and blocked lanes.

Rachael sipped her coffee and contemplated her options and the snow outside her window. Actually, she realized had no options. The fact was, she desperately needed to prepare for court the following day. She was typically in court all afternoon on Tuesdays. That meant she simply had to ease her way onto the slushy, congested roads—along with all the other commuters whose work would not wait for them. Next to her, McKenna banged the tray of her high chair with a chunky, plastic spoon, sending tiny squares of toast to the floor and rousing Rachael from thoughts of tangled traffic.

"An-ga!" McKenna burbled.

"Easy, girl," Rachael said, setting her coffee cup down and touching her daughter lightly on the arm. "Don't toss your food, McKenna."

"Nnnn," McKenna happily replied, grabbing a half-circle of sliced banana and stuffing it in her mouth.

Trace sauntered into the kitchen, stopping to kiss McKenna on his way to the coffee pot.

"I'm going to call my mom and tell her not to come, Trace," Rachael said. "The roads are nasty. Do you think you and Fig can keep McKenna with you at the studio today?"

Mondays were her mother's usual day to watch McKenna. Tuesdays and Wednesdays, Trace kept McKenna with him and Fig at the studio. Between the two of them, McKenna was kept fed and entertained, and apparently the men seemed to get enough work done. At least they hadn't complained.

"Yeah, I guess," he answered, sidling up to a chair next to her. "I'm actually kind of ahead today. Just don't make any changes for Thursday. I've got a meeting in Rochester and I can't bring the Princess to that."

She patted his knee under the table. "No changes to Thursday, I promise."

Rachael stood and walked over to the counter across from the open eating area. She picked up the phone and pressed the speed dial for her parents' home in St. Cloud. Her father answered the phone.

"Hey, Dad," she said.

"Rachael. How's it going?"

"Not bad, except for this weather. Mom hasn't started out yet, has she?"

"No, I haven't even gotten to the driveway yet. I'm on my way out right now to start on it."

"Well, tell her not to bother. The roads are terrible. I don't want her coming."

"Here. You can tell her yourself."

A second later Rachael heard her mother's voice on the other end of the phone.

"So, you don't want me to give it a try?" Eva Harper said.

"The roads are a mess, Mom. It'd probably take you a couple hours just to get here. It's not worth it."

"Well, I can see if I can get tomorrow off and work today instead," Eva offered. "Mondays are usually busier than Tuesdays at the library anyway. So then I could come watch McKenna tomorrow."

"Trace would probably appreciate that, Mom," Rachael said. "If you don't think it will be too much trouble."

"Not at all."

"Okay. Thanks, Mom."

"Sure. Say, Rachael?"

"Hmm?"

"You saw Josh on Saturday?" Eva's voice was suddenly soft and pensive, as if she were speaking among the stacks of the library where she worked.

"Yes, Mom."

"Was he all right? Did he seem okay?"

Rachael walked over to the kitchen table and picked up her coffee cup. "Mom, you just saw him yourself the week before. You told me he seemed fine to you." She brought the cup up to her lips and sipped it. It had cooled and she winced.

"I know. I just thought maybe he was being brave for me. He's…well, seven years is such a long time. He's got so far to go."

"It's not going to be seven years, Mom. I can almost guarantee you that. We talked about this before. Remember?"

Eva sighed on the other end. "Yes."

"So don't worry about it. And yes, I think he's doing okay."

A moment of silence hung between them.

"All right," Eva finally said and then she added, "So are you doing okay?"

Rachael didn't acknowledge from where the question had sprung. She knew why her mother was asking it. It wasn't the generic "hi-how-are-you" conversation-starter traded daily between the masses. Her parents, especially her mother, had begged her to quit her job with the county after the incident in the parking lot. They were disappointed that she hadn't even considered it.

"Sure, Mom. I'm doing great."

No way was she going to mention the letter.

At twenty minutes after nine, Rachael pulled into the courthouse parking lot. Giant piles of snow had been shoved to one side by plows and now glistened in the mid-morning sunshine. She reached for her briefcase on the seat next to her and checked one more time to make sure the letter was inside.

She got out of the car, picked her way across the sloppy lot and stepped inside the courthouse building, stamping her wet shoes on the thick, rubber-lined mat just inside the double doors. The mat was already saturated, no doubt from dozens of other wet shoes.

"Gotta love Minnesota," she mumbled under her breath. She entered the lobby and then made her way through the security checkpoint and to the prosecutors' offices.

"Hey, Pendleton's looking for you." Kate Markham, her administrative assistant, waved a tiny fan of phone messages at Rachael as she walked past the reception desk. Rachael reached for them.

"Are all these from him?" Rachael said, astonished.

Kate shook her head. "Nope. Just one. He's called twice since leaving the first one, though."

Rachael walked past Kate's desk and toward her own office. "He does know there was a foot of snow on the roads this morning, doesn't he?" Rachael murmured light-heartedly.

"He's got that four-wheel-drive thing and actually likes driving in a foot of snow," Kate called out to her. "Hey! Don't forget you've got that task force meeting at Human Services at eleven. They called to tell me they haven't cancelled it."

Rachael nodded. "Right, right. I'm going to call Will."

Fifteen minutes later, Sgt. Will Pendleton was sitting across from her reading the letter looking every inch like Morgan Freeman's younger brother. His brow was furrowed but not with concern. He looked annoyed. After several minutes and presumably several readings, he looked up at Rachael.

"Did you get anything in today's mail?" he asked her.

"Just the usual."

Will peered down at the letter again. Then he suddenly stood, grabbed the envelope and placed the letter back inside it. He stuck it in his shirt pocket. "If you get another one, I want to know about it the minute you get it. If you get a strange call or you think someone's tailing you, I want you to call me. Day or night, all right?"

"Sure, Will. But do you think this person means me some kind of harm? Because I don't think they do."

"Yeah, I know what you think. But you'll call me, right?"

"On one condition," she said.

Will smiled and waited.

"You keep me in the loop," Rachael continued. "I want to know where this goes and I don't want to have to find out from Sidney's co-workers at the *Star Tribune*."

"C'mon, Rachael…" Will began.

"I'm serious!" Rachael said, half-laughing. "I'll call you the second I have new information if you call me the second you have it. Deal?"

Will cocked his head. His grin was lopsided. "Deal," he said. He turned and started to walk out of her office, but then he stopped and turned his head back toward her.

"So, you're doing all right?" he said and the lopsided grin was gone.

Rachael exhaled heavily. "Why do people keep asking me that?" she said.

"Because people care about you, of course," Will's tone had lost some of its usual authoritative edge.

"It's been eight weeks. I'm fine."

"It's been eight weeks and I still wake up in the middle of the night thinking about it."

His comment surprised her. For a moment, Rachael struggled with a suitable response. She had no idea Will was still troubled by what happened in the parking lot. "But this kind of thing must happen all the time in your job, Will," Rachael finally said, haphazardly dismissing his concern.

"Not to people I know. Not to friends."

Rachael couldn't come up with a second comeback. She didn't want to think too hard about what Will was communicating to her. His concern on top of everyone else's was both bothersome and gratifying. "I'm okay, Will," she said. "Really."

Will smiled, turned his head back around and continued walking away.

"So you'll call me?" Rachael called after him.

He didn't answer verbally, but he stuck his hand out, closing his fist and extending his thumb.

Thumbs-up.

By Wednesday afternoon, Rachael had heard nothing from Will. At 3:00, when she could stand the wait no longer, she called him.

"Well?" she said when he answered his cell phone on the third ring.

"I keep my promises," Will said good-naturedly.

"So you've found nothing?"

"We found a lot of snow at the site, as I'm sure you can imagine. Between plowing that away and assuring the developer we'll do everything we can not to tube his construction schedule, I've been pretty busy."

"So now what?" Rachael asked.

"Tomorrow we bring in the dogs and our own earthmovers. We've started to attract some attention so I hope you don't say anything to anyone about this."

"I've told Trace only. No one else," Rachael replied.

"Well, tell him not to leak it to his artsy friends. The longer we can keep this under wraps the better. I don't want to compromise the site more than it already has been."

"All right."

Will paused for a moment. "Now you'll stay away tomorrow, right?"

"*Yes*, I'll stay away! I'll be with McKenna all day, for Pete's sake."

"Good. I'll call you if we find anything."

"All right. Bye." Rachael hung up the phone and stared at it for several long moments. She couldn't help wondering what she would do if she didn't have McKenna with her all day.

Will called Rachael Thursday evening, just as she was laying McKenna down in her crib for the night.

"It's Will," Trace said, bringing the phone to her.

Rachael grabbed it from his hand and made for the living room. "Will?" she said.

"Relax. The dogs found nothing. Not a thing."

Rachael was unsettled by the disappointment she felt. "Really?"

"Yeah. Really. We had a crew digging there all day. And they didn't find anything either."

"So…now what?"

"Well, we're going back tomorrow. But I don't know, Rachael. I'm thinking maybe someone's messing with you. And us. I mean, the dogs picked up *nothing*."

Rachael sank into the sofa. "I just don't see what the point was in sending the letter if it's not true."

"Wackos don't need a point."

Rachael shook her head. "I don't think whoever wrote it is 'wacko,' Will."

"It's not my first inclination to think they are either, but where's the body? The site isn't that big, Rachael. We had the best hounds in the state traipsing across not only the site but also the wooded area surrounding it. They didn't find anything."

Rachael leaned forward and ran a hand through her hair. "You're going back tomorrow, though, right?"

"We're going back tomorrow."

"And you'll call me if you find anything?"

"Scout's honor."

She hung up.

Rachael slept in stages on Thursday night, waking up every few hours with needling thoughts. Was she being tricked? To what purpose? What was the letter-writer really trying accomplish? If it was a hoax, what was the benefit?

The following day Rachael was distracted and on edge. She took McKenna for a long walk, washed all the bed linens, made cookies, watched The Weather Channel with her daughter and read three magazines. But thoughts of the letter, the construction site and cadaver-sniffing dogs intruded on her day. Every time the phone rang, she dashed to it, think-ing it was Will with news. And every time it was someone else.

At 4:30 in the afternoon when the phone rang for the sixth time that day, Rachael answered it with detached interest.

"Hello?" she said.

"Rachael." It was Will. His voice sounded…different. He was outside; she could hear the wind whipping around the mouthpiece of his cell phone.

"What? What is it?" Rachael exclaimed as she walked toward the dining table. "Did you find the body?"

"Yeah, kind of."

Rachael felt behind her for a chair and sat on it. What on earth could Will possibly mean? How do you "kind of" find a body? Unless the body was dismembered and only a part of it had been found…Her long-ago lunch began a slow dance in her stomach.

"Kind of?" she whispered. "You mean you found just a part of a body?"

"Oh, no. We found the whole thing."

"And?"

"Rachael, we found a skeleton. Male, probably a teenager. There isn't so much as a shred of flesh on it. It's been here a long time."

Rachael's eyes widened in surprise. A teenager? Her mind sailed to the memorized sentences in the letter. *He deserved it.* What could a kid have done to deserve death? "How…how long?" she stammered.

"Forensics is down here. They'll be able to give me a more exact figure after lab tests. But you're not going to believe what their best guess is." The wind hushed his words as if to confirm Will's prediction.

"Tell me," Rachael murmured.

"Rachael, it's…" The wind swallowed his voice and it disappeared. A second later it returned. "…guessing at least twenty."

"Twenty? Twenty months?" Rachael gasped.

"No," Will replied. "Years. Twenty years."

FOUR

The Sunday paper lay strewn about the living room like torn wrapping paper on Christmas morning. McKenna had single-handedly dismantled five inside sections in the minutes it took Trace to get the espresso machine going. Rachael had barely noticed their daughter's achievement: She was absorbed in the story on the front page detailing the discovery of a human skeleton at a construction site in St. Anthony Park.

"I'm going to put McKenna down for a nap," Trace said to Rachael as he came back into the living room from the kitchen and surveyed the wreckage.

"Mmm," Rachael replied, not looking up from the paper.

A moment later he stood by her with their daughter in his arms. "Think I'll get this ink off her fingers with a little Lime-Away, whaddya think?"

Rachael grinned and looked up at him. "I'm not totally ignoring you two," she said.

Trace smiled back. "Just checking." He disappeared down the main hall and Rachael started at the top of the page and read the article a second time:

St. Paul—A human skeleton was unearthed Friday afternoon at a construction site in St. Anthony Park after a Ramsey County assistant prosecutor received a tip that a body had been buried there.

The remains were discovered in roughly four feet of earth at the site of the River Terrace condominium complex currently under construction in this northeast St. Paul suburb.

Forensic experts called to the site reported that the skeleton, which appears to have been underground at least twenty years, belonged to a male, probably between the ages of fourteen and eighteen.

At a press conference early Friday evening, St. Paul homicide detective Sgt. William Pendleton stated that foul play is suspected, based on information contained within the tip. He would not elaborate on how the tip was relayed or to which county prosecutor it was directed.

"We really can't comment on the tip at this point as doing so could negatively affect our investigation," Sgt. Pendleton said. Pendleton said the forensics team would be working on identifying the remains by comparing dental and other distinguishing criteria with missing person reports. He said the team would begin with reports that date as far back as 1980.

The undeveloped construction site, located off Como Avenue, is adjacent to a neighborhood of homes built in the 1940s. Residents in the neighborhood began to gather at the perimeter of the site Friday afternoon as the number of police vehicles on the site continued to increase. Police resorted to yellow police tape to keep the spectators off the lot.

"We didn't know what they were looking for," said Carole Beilke, who lives near the construction site on Willow Ave. "We saw the dogs and the bulldozers so we figured out they were looking for something that was in those woods."

Bielke said she was as "shocked as anyone" when the skeleton was uncovered.

"I've lived on this street for 34 years and I've always felt safe here," Bielke said. "I never would have guessed a body had been buried so close to my house."

Police plan to return to the site on Monday to search for additional clues.

Anyone with information regarding the discovery of the skeleton is asked to contact the St. Paul Police Department.

Rachael folded the paper and set it on the coffee table, her thoughts a tangle of guesses. She rose from the couch and starting picking up the strewn sections of newspaper. As she worked to make sense of the jumbled pages, Trace returned to the living area with two tiny white cups of espresso.

"So," he said, handing her one of the cups and reaching for the front page. "Did Will manage to keep your name out of this?"

"He did."

Trace sank into the sofa with the newspaper in his hand and took a sip of espresso. "And here I thought I was bringing you back to the Midwest where it was safe," he said. His tone was casual at the surface, but an unmistakable under-layer of unease rested just below it.

Rachael retook her place on the sofa and cuddled up next to her husband. She wanted to tell him there was no place that was completely safe but she knew such a thing was better left unsaid.

She also didn't tell him that Will had kept her name out of the paper for reasons beyond protecting her identity: Will wanted the letter-writer to feel comfortable with writing to her again.

Monday morning found Rachael's immediate co-workers abuzz with the skeleton's discovery. A few of the other attorneys in the office were flummoxed that she had been sent the tip, some were curious, a couple were concerned for her safety. One was clearly annoyed: If the letter-writer had any brains, he or she would have sent the tip to one of the trial or charging attorneys; someone who would actually handle a case against a suspected murderer, if indeed the skeleton belonged to a victim of a homicide. If the letter-writer was expecting leniency from the state, he or she had sent it to the wrong prosecutor.

After a morning spent fielding questions, comments and suggestions from both the well meaning and the frustrated, Rachael took her lunch break and decided to visit Will.

"Look. I really don't have anything concrete to tell you," Will said, when she was sitting across from his desk a few minutes after 1:00.

"But surely by now you know how many male teenagers went missing in the 1980s," Rachael said. "I mean, there couldn't have been that many."

Will shook his head. "In this area, there weren't. There were far more missing girls than boys. Our best count is that there were five missing males. Two of them we can dismiss from the get-go; one kid was 13 when he disappeared and small for his age and the other had a missing digit. Our guy has all his fingers and toes."

"So you're down to three."

"Well, three from the Twin Cities area. We're still looking within Minnesota and the rest of the nation."

"You really think this kid was from another state?"

Will reached for his coffee cup. "One of the first things I learned in homicide is that anything is possible."

Rachael pondered his words. But her instincts were whispering to her that there was no need to consider missing teenagers from other states. "What does your gut tell you?" she said.

Will sipped his coffee and then set the mug down again. "That he was from around here."

"So you're down to three," she said again.

"Yeah, I think so."

Rachael sat back in her chair, signifying she was ready to listen.

"All right," he said. "I'll tell you who we're looking at." Will moved some papers on his desk, opened a file and withdrew a typical, school-portrait photo of a blond-haired youth. "This is Sam Greenstow," Will continued. "He disappeared at the age of fourteen in Cottage Grove. He was riding his bike home from his grandmother's place two miles from his own house on July 7, 1983. Never made it home. Hasn't been heard from since."

"Cottage Grove isn't that far away," Rachael said.

"Close enough to raise my suspicions, yes."

"And what kind of kid was he?" Rachael asked.

"You mean was he the kind of kid to deserve an accidental death? It's difficult to say. We've only just begun this investigation."

"Well, what do you know about him?" she said.

"He was the youngest of three boys, got A's and B's in school, played Little League, sang in the youth choir at his church."

Rachael frowned. "That can't be him."

"Of course it could," Will countered. "Appearances can be deceiving."

"Who else?" Rachael said, wanting to move on.

"There's this kid," Will continued, extracting another file from the array of papers on his desk. He opened it and handed her a wallet-sized photo of a somber-faced teen. "This is Jason Garber. Sixteen. Disappeared October 21, 1981."

Rachael studied the image in the photo. The youth wore the face of defiance.

"Jason lived with his father and stepmother in a duplex in Shakopee. Was a known drug-user. Had been in court-ordered treatment twice before his disappearance."

"Shakopee is what, twenty miles from here?" Rachael said, fingering the teenager's frozen face on the photograph.

"The kid could drive. He didn't own a car but he knew how to drive one. I don't need to tell you there were at least a dozen stolen cars in the fall of 1981."

"He had a record, then?" Rachael asked.

"Truancies, under-age consumption, possession, that kind of thing."

Rachael looked up at Will. "Was he ever in trouble for hurting anyone?"

Will shook his head. "No. He never was."

Rachael handed the photograph back. "And the last one?"

Will cleared his throat as he rummaged for the final file. "Now, look, Rachael, I don't want you to jump to conclusions when I tell you about this next kid," he began.

"Why?" Rachael replied. "Why would I jump to conclusions?"

"Because initially I wanted to. But until we can get some dental records and make comparisons, we don't have a match, okay?"

Rachael nodded. She could feel a tiny pulse of adrenaline wanting to speed its way through her body. Will handed her a photograph of a dark-haired teen with muscular features, intense eyes, and obvious facial hair. In the photo he was sitting next to a portly man with a scraggly beard. The man with the beard had a can of beer in his hand. The man was smiling; the teen was not.

"That's Ronald Buckett, fifteen, nicknamed Bucky. He disappeared

April 2, 1982. He had run away a couple times before, when he was fourteen, so his disappearance was eventually catalogued as runaway. His family was textbook dysfunctional. Domestic abuse charges were filed against the stepdad a couple times by Buckett's mom, but she never let it go to court. Bucky was also known as quite the bully around the neighborhood where he lived. Two different families had contacted the police on two different occasions—both families alleged that Bucky had harmed their kids. Charges were dropped both times, though."

Will stopped and Rachael looked up from the photo. "Where did he live?" she asked.

Will cocked his head. "St. Anthony Park. On a street adjacent to the River Terrace construction site."

The adrenaline that had been threatening to invade her veins pulsed its way through her body.

"Will! This has to be him!" she exclaimed.

"Not necessarily, Rachael. And may I remind you that you're jumping to conclusions after I warned you not to."

Rachael looked back down at the photo in her hand. This was him, she was sure of it. "Sorry, Will, but I don't think it's much of a jump," she said.

"I actually agree with you, but we can't ID the remains based on this picture and a hunch. We need to contact the family and get some dental records. So stop jumping."

"Jumping? It's more like standing on tiptoes, Will. This is *him*."

"Well, we'll soon find out, won't we?"

Rachael handed the photo back to Will. "Call me," she said.

She left Will and hurried out to her car. She wanted to write down the name lest in the exhilaration she would forget. She grabbed a pen and a Taco Bell napkin from the floor of her car and quickly scrawled three words across it:

Ronald "Bucky" Buckett.

Rachael had just returned from an afternoon in court the following day when Will called her. She slid into her office chair and kicked off her shoes as she picked up the phone. She felt like she had been standing all day, even though she had been able to sit down between cases.

"Thought you might want to hear the latest," Will said.

"It's Bucky, isn't it?" Rachael interrupted.

"We haven't been able to locate his family yet, Rachael."

"Sorry. Go on."

"The guys in the lab have found no evidence as to how this kid died. Skull was intact, no visible fractures, major bones were all okay, too. But he broke his right arm when he was little. He had a chipped front tooth, too. And we've not found anything else at the site, Rachael. We're going to let Mr. Donavan get back to building his condominiums."

"I bet he's happy," Rachael replied.

"Elated. Although he's ticked there was news coverage of this. He's not had any interested buyers the past two days."

"The poor fellow," Rachael said, injecting a bit of venom in her sarcasm. "So where do you think his parents are? Bucky's, I mean."

"We've followed the mom as far as Florida and then she kind of drops off the radar. Stepdad died in 1992 of cirrhosis of the liver."

"Mom may have remarried," Rachael suggested.

"Yep, we've got someone scouring the registrars in every county in Florida. Buckett had a sister, too, but we can't locate her anywhere. She married young, divorced young, moved away, got married again and who knows where she is now."

Rachael rubbed her toes into the fabric of the carpet. "Thanks, Will. Call me if anything comes up."

"Yep," he said.

Rachael was putting away the last of her court files Wednesday in preparation for her four-day reprieve from work when she was aware that someone was standing behind her. She turned. Will tossed a bag of M & Ms onto her desk.

She looked at the familiar brown and white bag. "What are those for?" she said, unable to squelch a grin.

Will slid into the chair opposite her desk. "I always hand those out when a colleague and I positively ID a victim of murder and mayhem."

"Bucky," Rachael said, sinking down into her desk chair. "It's Bucky."

"Yes."

"Murder and mayhem? M & Ms?" she said, grinning wider.

"I like to reward myself for hunches. And others."

Rachael reached for the bag and opened it. She spilled a dozen colored candies onto the desk in front of Will. She did the same in front of her own chair. "Well, then, here's to us and our hunches," she said.

"*Salud,*" Will said. He grabbed a few M & Ms, gestured toward her and then tossed them into his mouth.

"So you found the mother?" Rachael asked.

Will inclined his head while he chewed. "We did. Her name's Irene Buckett Siebel. Twice widowed and presently living in a trailer park outside Tallahassee. She directed us to the location of her son's pediatric dental records here in St. Paul. And she also told us Bucky had broken his right arm falling out of a tree when he was ten, which was also how he chipped his front tooth."

"Wow," Rachael breathed. "And so how did it go with her?"

"Telling a mother her kid is dead is never easy, even when he's been missing for 25 years."

"She took it hard?"

Will leaned forward and grabbed a couple more M & Ms. "I don't know. She seemed more angry than sad. I guess I can understand that. All this time she thought her son had just run away. I think she'd been nursing a 25-year grudge because he up and left her and never had the decency to let her know he was okay. Well, now she finds out she has no basis for that grudge. Bucky hadn't run out on her. He'd been dead. Maybe the victim of a homicide. And someone had buried him to cover any tracks. She's not mad at her kid anymore. She's mad at whoever killed him or let him get killed and then buried him like garbage."

Rachael's elation at being right about Bucky was immediately tempered as she considered how Irene Buckett's life had been shaped by the disappearance of her only son. And would now be reshaped by the discovery of his remains.

"So is she coming here?" she said.

"Definitely not," Will answered. "She had some choice words for the life she led while living in St. Paul. She won't come back. But she wants the remains sent to her, like yesterday."

"How long will she have to wait?"

"Maybe not very long. I don't think our boys are going to find any more clues on those bones. They're too old, they've been buried too long and there's just nothing substantial to indicate what killed him."

Will paused for a moment before continuing. "We've called a press conference for 4:30 today. We're releasing Bucky's name. And we've also decided to announce that the tip was sent in the form of a note, and that the note suggests the writer has information that would lay this case to rest."

"But you're keeping my name out of it, right?" Rachael said.

"Absolutely. We just want to give this person the opportunity to come forward. Someone out there knows how Bucky ended up dead and buried in the woods."

Rachael fingered a red M&M, absently pushing it around in a tiny circle. "Do you think he ended up there because he was a bully?"

"Well, I can tell you we're tracking down those two sets of parents who reported abuse by Bucky and then dropped the charges. If they were angry enough to contact the police about it in the first place, who knows? Maybe one of them was angry enough to take matters into their own hands."

"What did Irene say about those two police calls?"

Will popped a brown M&M in his mouth. "That it was a bunch of bull. And that's why the charges were dropped."

As Rachael spun the little red candy disk, she became aware of an inkling revealing itself within her. It was as strange and unexplainable as the notion that Penny Duggin wouldn't have pulled the trigger on that cold February evening. And as strong.

Bucky had hurt people. Someone wanted him to stop. Things went too far.

He ended up dead.

Rachael looked up and saw that Will was waiting for her to respond.

"But you're not taking her word for it, I'm sure," she finally said.

"Not hardly." Will stood. "I've got to run. I need to sit in a quiet corner for a few minutes. Cameras and microphones make me nervous."

Rachael smiled. "You'll do fine."

He turned to go.

"Thanks for the M & Ms, Will," she said.

"Thanks for jumping," he replied as he walked away.

FIVE

The melodic tones of Andrea Bocelli filled the open spaces in Fig's enormous art studio. In the far left corner behind a clear plastic curtain, Fig stood on a ladder, sculpting with a motorized chisel an eight-foot pillar of Kansas limestone. What had started out as an obelisk of creamy stone two weeks earlier was now taking the form of a young woman: Joan of Arc on the morning of her execution. The bowed head and slender neck were now clearly defined, and the hood of the French maiden's robe was just beginning to crinkle from the imagined weight of the heavy fabric.

Rachael sat a few feet away on a thick area rug on the other side of the curtain while McKenna crawled and played about her. She watched through the plastic as Fig shaped the doomed girl's clavicle, and winced as Fig's voice soared every few seconds to the Bocelli CD playing at peak volume. Fig matched all of the celebrated tenor's intensity and none of his talent. Every now and then McKenna would glance in Fig's direction and sound off as well, appreciating without awareness the acoustics of the high-ceilinged room.

Friday afternoons often found Rachael and McKenna in Fig and

Trace's studio. The guys didn't seem to mind McKenna's constant babbling or Rachael's audience-of-one as both artists forged beauty from nothingness. To Rachael, lazing around the studio was cathartic in a way that was hard to adequately describe. The distressing daily reports she read of abuse and neglect, coupled with the sad monotony of seeing the same scenario over and over again, left her needing to see something graceful and serene at the end of the week. Even Trace's illustrations of the musculature of an unfleshed human hand spoke peace to her. Trace and Fig seemed to understand this; at least they never asked her why she and McKenna ended up at the studio most Friday afternoons.

Next to her, McKenna was crawling over to the diaper bag at the rug's edge. The child poked at the bag with a pudgy fist.

"You hungry, sweetie?" Rachael said, moving on her hands and knees toward her daughter. She pulled out a container of Cheerios, scooped up McKenna and placed her in her walker a few feet away. Rachael opened the container and placed a handful of cereal on the tray. "There you go."

"Trace!" Fig yelled over the swelling notes and the whine of his chisel.

"He's out getting some cappuccino and bagels," Rachael called back.

"For me, too, Kumquat?"

"Of course, Fig. Do you need something?"

"There's a little flat-blade file on the table by the window…"

"I can get it."

Rachael walked over to a wooden table, the top of which was littered with mallets, awls, picks and other instruments she couldn't identify. An assortment of files was strewn about. She picked up the smallest one, walked over to the curtain and pushed it aside. Fig, in a cloud of white dust, looked down at her. His cornrowed hair was confettied with white powder. The mask he wore over his face made him look eerie and alien—and totally un-Fig-like. He shut off the chisel and placed it on the top of the ladder. The CD ended and the room was suddenly quiet.

"Is this it?" she said.

"*Bueno, chiquita!*" he said, reaching down and taking the file. He began to work a rough spot off Joan's emerging shoulders.

Rachael peered through the curtain to make sure McKenna was content and then stepped back to watch Fig work. As she did, she noticed the wall in front of Fig was covered at eye level with 8 x 10s of a young teenage girl wearing a hooded cloak. The cloak was navy blue and fell about the girl in rolling folds that gathered at the floor where she stood. Her hands were clasped to her chest, but the fingers were open; they clutched at nothing. The girl had a haunting, yet perceptive look in her eyes. Rachael wondered if Fig's model knew the story of Joan of Arc. Did she know Joan had walked without a struggle to waiting flames?

"Your model is beautiful, Fig," she said. "Who is she?"

"Oh, that's Jillian's niece, Kayla."

Rachael stepped closer to the photographs, zeroing in on the girl's face. "She has such convincing eyes. Did you pay her extra to pretend she *was* Joan of Arc?"

Fig laughed. "Those are actually her angry eyes. She was mad that I made her wear the cloak. No one would be able to see her hair. That bugged her. She said the robe made her look like a monk. I told her she looked great and that I was going to make copies of the pictures and give them to all her friends. The newspaper, too. Well, then she totally freaked out. Told me if I did, she'd just as soon be dead. Hence, the look. I apologized, and told her I was only kidding. After I shot the photos of course."

Rachael stared into Kayla's frozen eyes—the eyes of someone imagining the horror of being teased, belittled, mocked.

An invisible cord seemed to pull at her as she stared at the girl. Drawing her in, tugging at her thoughts, reminding her that childhood for the victimized can seem as close to hell as a person will ever know in this life. As she contemplated the photos, Rachael began to consider more deeply what had been weighing on her since Wednesday afternoon when Will was in her office: Whoever sent the letter knew Bucky; knew Bucky bullied people. That person believed Bucky had been cruel enough to deserve death as well as his private interment into unhallowed ground. Will wanted to talk to the parents of the kids Bucky had supposedly terrorized, which certainly made sense. She knew that if anyone dared to harm McKenna, she might possibly resort to desperate means to stop him.

But Bucky's victims hadn't been the adults, if indeed the rumor that he had been a bully was true. The victims of a teenage bully are no doubt other teenagers.

Which meant the person who wrote the letter could easily have been a teenager when Bucky died. Could have been one of Bucky's victims.

…could have been the one who watched Bucky die.

…could have been the one who caused Bucky's death, even if it was an accident….

"Rachael, I really was only kidding. I didn't send those to pictures to her friends."

Fig's voice made her jump. "Oh! I'm sure you didn't, Fig. I was just… I was thinking…" She didn't know how much to divulge to Fig about the case, but she suddenly wanted his input on it. "Fig, were you ever teased as a kid?"

"Weren't you?" He laughed her question away.

"I mean really teased, like bullied," she said.

Fig stopped filing and brushed away dust from Joan's left shoulder. He waited for a moment before answering. "Oh, there was this one kid in junior high who had it out for me. Geoffrey Linder."

Fig said the name like it was a cough stuck in his throat.

"Why did he have it out for you?" Rachael continued, smiling.

Fig looked up at the rafters above them as if nailed there was a list of the reasons why Geoffrey Linder had hated him. He shrugged his shoulders. "I guess he liked picking on people and I was available, unattached to any other bullies. You know. Open."

"But why did he do it? What did he get out of it?"

Fig pulled his mask away and looked down at her. "I can tell you he got enjoyment from it. He liked the rush it gave him. Made him feel pretty powerful, I think."

"What did he do to you, if you don't mind me asking?"

Fig scraped the file against the stone. "Well, he found all kinds of ways to ridicule my name. It's hard to be the only Figaro in your school, you know."

Rachael grinned.

"And he assumed because I liked art and dance and sewing that I was, you know, not a *real* guy, so he had some inventive words for that, too. Fig sounds a lot like fag, I'm afraid. And he loved that it did."

The grin fell away from Rachael's face.

"One time, we were outside after lunch and I was minding my own business. Geoffrey came up from behind me and grabbed me by the hood of my sweatshirt," Fig continued. "It was October and I had it zipped up almost all the way. Well, he started dragging me around by the hood. And the teeth of the open part of the zipper bit into my neck like razors. Felt like I was going to die of course. I pulled at it, but that only made the pain worse and Geoffrey pull harder."

"And no one did anything?" Rachael said, barely above a whisper.

"You mean the other kids? Of course, not. You didn't want a guy like Geoffrey to know you existed. It would've been suicide to intervene."

"The teachers did nothing?"

"Well, it was noon break. There was a monitor outside with us but she couldn't see everything happening out there. She would've stopped it if she had seen it. That time."

"But no teacher got involved?"

"Kumquat, I didn't tell any of the teachers. Or my parents."

"Why not?"

"Because," Fig said, starting to climb down the ladder. "That also would have been suicide."

"Oh, Fig," Rachael said looking up at him.

But Fig just waved it off. "That was ages ago, Kumquat. I'd nearly forgotten all about it."

"But you hadn't forgotten it," Rachael replied. "Look how quickly you remembered it."

Fig stood at the bottom of the ladder, a half-puzzled, half-amused look on his face. "Why are you asking about this, Rachael?" he said.

"It's…it's about that skeleton that was uncovered a few days ago. The police ID'd him, you know. His name was Ronald Buckett. And he had been a bully." She said nothing about the note.

"Ah," Fig said, leaning forward and shaking the dust out of his hair. "So you're wondering what killed him. Or who."

"Yes, I am."

"You want to know if one of his victims just couldn't live with it anymore and took him out."

"Something like that."

Fig stood upright again. "Well, since I was an artistic little wimp I was able to make a voodoo doll of Geoffrey, and I stuck him with every sharp object I could find, even though I didn't believe in any of that stuff. Dull objects, too for that matter."

"You wanted to see him get hurt."

"I wanted to see him stop. I didn't care how."

"So did it stop?"

Fig shrugged. "I guess." He pushed aside the plastic curtain and moved past it.

"It did?" Rachael exclaimed as she followed him, hopeful.

Fig turned back to her. "My dad got a job transfer and we moved. I never saw Geoffrey again." Fig turned back and headed toward the wooden table by the window, laying the file down and then brushing his hands against his pant legs.

"Fig," Rachael said, as she walked over to McKenna and put another handful of Cheerios on the tray. "What if you hadn't moved? What do you think would have happened?"

Fig didn't turn around. He looked out the window onto the reinvented warehouse district along the river. "I don't know, Rachael. I was just about at the end of my rope, I can tell you that. I was only thirteen, but it really did feel like my life was over."

Rachael was silent for a moment as she considered Fig's long ago misery. It scared her to imagine him that way. "What do kids do when they reach the end of their rope and their dad doesn't get a transfer?" she finally said.

Fig turned to look at her. He shrugged. "I can guess," he said.

"Do...do you think it's possible for a kid to...to..."

"To kill the bully?" he finished for her.

"Accidentally."

"Accidentally? Yeah, maybe. I think most kids bullied to the point of despair don't have the guts to become killers, although the school shootings of late make me think there are exceptions. I don't think the majority of them have the strength to plan and execute the bully's death. They would more likely plan someone else's."

Rachael sighed. "Their own?"

"I think so."

"Would...would you have considered that?" Rachael said, sensing a wavering in her voice.

"I never had to. Dad got a transfer. I got a new rope."

The main door to the studio opened and Trace breezed in with a paper sack of bagels in one hand, a cardboard carrier of frothy cappuccinos in another and the day's mail under his arm.

"Hey!" he called out to Rachael. "Want to grab our mail? I'm losing it."

Rachael closed the distance between them and grabbed for the loose collection of mail under Trace's arm. An art magazine, a catalog and two nondescript envelopes fell to the cement floor despite her rush to help him.

"Oops," Trace said.

"I got them," Rachael said, grasping what was left under Trace's arm and then bending down to pick up what had fallen.

She reached for the envelopes, turned them over and then froze.

"Oh," she breathed aloud.

One of the envelopes was a utility bill. But the other was white, square-shaped, and typewritten to her home address.

No return label.

Marked "personal and confidential."

SIX

As Rachael held the envelope in her hand, a maddening and sudden realization began to somersault in her brain: the letter-writer knew where she lived. He or she knew where she went at the end of the day, where she lived her private hours, not as an assistant county prosecutor but simply Trace's wife and McKenna's mother. Rachael was somewhat surprised she sensed no accompanying fear for her safety, but she was nonetheless immediately shaken by the notion that a possible killer, albeit a contrite one, knew where she lived.

She hadn't noticed she had dropped the rest of the mail.

"Rach, what is it?" Trace's voice sliced through the moment and she looked up at him. He was placing the cardboard carrier and the bag of bagels onto a long table he and Fig used for consultations, meals and Texas Hold 'Em.

"It's another one," she replied, noticing that the rest of the mail lay at her feet. She reached for it and stood.

"What do you mean, 'another one'?" Trace's voice was edged with irate concern. He knew what she meant. "Are you telling me that person wrote to you at your home address?" he continued. "To *our* house?"

Rachael wordlessly walked over to the table. Three pairs of eyes watched her—even McKenna seemed to sense something was amiss.

"Yes," Rachael answered, barely giving the word any volume at all. She set the rest of the mail down on the table. But not the letter.

Trace looked down at the envelope in her hand.

"What's going on?" Fig said, looking from Trace to Rachael and back to Trace.

Trace turned his head back to Rachael, obviously waiting for her to explain to Fig what had suddenly sucked the afternoon calm out of the sunlit room. She wondered if Will would expect her to simply pick up the phone and call him without explaining anything to Fig. And without opening the envelope.

But as she stared at her name, typed across the front of the envelope in an ordinary Times New Roman font, she knew she would open it first and then call. She might as well tell Fig, too. She wasn't a cop; she didn't have to respond like one.

And Fig might be the one to help her understand what it might have been like to be one of Bucky's targets. She raised her head to Fig.

"You know that skeleton that was found at the construction site the other day?" she began. Fig nodded. "The police were tipped that it was buried there."

"Yes. I heard about that on the news," Fig replied.

"It was me who received the tip," Rachael said calmly.

Trace turned his head away from her again. He lifted one of the covered cups out of the carrier and set it on the table. Drops of hot liquid splashed out of the tiny opening meant for a mouth.

"You?" Fig said.

"I got an anonymous letter the week before last, Fig. One like this." Rachael waved the letter in her hand. "The writer told me a body was going to be discovered at that construction site. They didn't say anything at all about how long that body had been there. The writer also told me it was an accident that the body was there but that the person who died deserved what he got."

"That person had been a bully," Fig said, understanding evident in his eyes.

"Yes," Rachael answered. "That person has been identified as Ronald

Buckett. He was nicknamed Bucky. He disappeared from his home, which was incidentally right next to that site, twenty-five years ago. Everyone thought he had run away. Even the police."

"But why did you get the tip?" Fig said. "Why didn't the writer just tip the police, if they felt they had to tip someone. I don't get it."

"You're not the only one," Trace grumbled, pulling out another cup and sending another mini-fountain of cappuccino onto the tabletop.

"I don't know exactly," Rachael said, fingering her name on the front of the envelope. "The writer thought that I would understand that accidents happen. That sometimes someone gets killed in the process of trying to mete out a little justice."

"Ah, the writer read about Josh," Fig said the name tenderly. "That terrible mess with your brother."

"The writer said they'd read the papers. Not just from last fall, but recently, too."

"Oh, when that crazy woman nearly…when you almost got…"

But Rachael broke in. "She wasn't going to pull the trigger."

Trace grabbed the last cup and slammed it onto the table. A splash of cappuccino baptized his hand and he winced, swallowing a cry of pain. "I think you should call Will," Trace said quickly, wiping his hand on his jeans. "Don't even open it, Rachael. Just call Will."

Rachael slipped into one of the chairs around the table. McKenna scooted over to her in her walker. "La-na," her daughter intoned, as if to offer her own snippet of advice. Rachael looked up at her husband and then Fig. She sensed that even Fig was thinking she should just pick up the phone and call Will.

But she knew she wouldn't call first. Curiosity was a strong pull, but stronger still was the feeling that she was being entreated, that the writer hadn't been merely trying to clue the authorities, he or she was rather reaching out to her—to someone who understood. It was incidental that she worked for county law enforcement, which would explain why the writer had chosen to send the second letter to her home address instead of the courthouse.

"I have to know what it says," she said to Trace.

"Why? Why do you have to?"

"Because this person believes I will understand how…how…"

"How Ronald Buckett ended up dead," Trace finished for her.

"Trace, this person doesn't want to harm me. I'm sure of it!"

"Do you think they want to get caught? 'Cause that's what Will is trying to do. Catch them. You think they don't know that?"

Rachael paused. She didn't really want to contemplate at the moment what Will would do with this second letter. She knew the moment she called Will the letter would cease to be hers and would become state's evidence. And that Will and a colleague at her own office would use it against the writer in a court of law.

Within her spirit she sensed no inward pull to leave the letter untouched. She felt no direction to open it, either. The choice seemed to be hers.

She turned the letter over.

"And aren't you the least bit bothered by how they got our home address," Trace said. "We got an unlisted number for a reason."

Rachael ran her finger over the flap. The seal was loose. Only the point of the flap still held to the back of the envelope. The writer had been in a hurry. Or careless.

"What if it's a bomb?" Fig said, taking a step backward.

"It's not a bomb," Rachael said. "It's practically unsealed. Get my phone, Trace. I'll call Will while I'm opening it."

Trace sighed, stepped over to his main drawing table where Rachael usually set her keys and phone when she visited the studio. He picked it up and began to scroll through Rachael's menu of saved phone numbers while he walked back to the table.

Fig stepped back toward her and took a seat at the table.

She poked away the sealed part of the envelope with one finger and drew out the single, folded piece of paper. The text was a little longer than that of the first letter, but not by much. It was also unsigned:

Dear Mrs. Flynn:

After all this time, everything's happening too fast. I don't know what to do now. You had to tell the police, I guess. But I don't think they will understand. They never understood. I don't know what to do. I shouldn't have told anyone. I thought you would understand. Someone needs to understand it was an accident. It was only supposed to teach him a lesson.

As Rachael read, she was aware that Trace was at her shoulder peering over her, talking to Will on her phone.

"She got another one, Will…Yeah, at our home address. Of course she opened it. She's reading it right now." Trace handed her phone to her. "He wants to talk to you."

Rachael reached for her phone.

"Do I need to get a unit over there?' Will sounded intense. And annoyed.

"No, you don't," Rachael answered. "There's no death threat, no implied malice, nothing that would justify sending a unit over here, Will. This person is not dangerous. They're scared."

"Scared people do dangerous things, as if I should have to remind you," Will said coolly.

"I know that, Will, but there's nothing here to indicate I'm in danger. None."

"Except that this person is now writing to your home address."

"That doesn't necessarily mean I'm in danger."

"I don't like it. Read it to me."

Rachael read the note aloud. When Will spoke again his voice was even and controlled.

"I'm coming over to the studio."

Rachael, Trace and Fig sipped cooling cups of cappuccino as Will sat at the long table. McKenna banged a set of plastic keys on her walker tray and listened as the sound reverberated around the plaster walls.

When he was done, Will folded the letter, placed it back in the envelope and started to rise from his chair.

"The next time you get one of these—if there is a next time—can you at least call me before you open it?"

Rachael looked up at him. "Will, there's skin cells from who knows how many mail handlers on that envelope, plus mine and Trace's, and I bet you anything the writer didn't use his or her own saliva to seal it. So it's not like I'm destroying evidence. Besides, it's addressed to me."

Will put the note in his inside pocket. "Look, we're starting to find out a lot more about Buckett. He was indeed a kid with a nasty mean streak."

"Tell me," Rachael said.

Will eyed Fig and Trace and cocked his head. "Let's just say this kid was bad news. In a lot of ways. It ain't a pretty picture."

"Can I come down to your office and see what you've got so far, Will? I can help you with this. I want to help you with this."

Will shook his head. "You don't have to do that, Rachael. We've got a team of people working on this. And it's not your responsibility to figure out how Bucky died. It's mine."

"Will's right, Rach," Trace interjected. "Let the cops figure this out."

"I know it's not my responsibility," Rachael countered. "I'm not trying to make it mine. But I have…well…a hunch about this writer. I want to help you. And them. You like my hunches," Rachael said, attempting a slight grin.

"You have admirable hunches," Will said. "And you are free to share them with me anytime. Just call me."

Rachael rose, too. "Will, I just want to see what you've found out about Bucky. I just want to better understand this person who is writing to me. They're reaching out for some kind of exoneration, I think. They want absolution. And eventually they're going to have to come forward to get it. You know I'm right about this. If we keep this second letter—and any others—out of the media, we'll give the writer the opportunity to continue coming forward a little bit more each time."

Will studied her face as she spoke. "Rachael…" he began, but she cut him off.

"I'm someone this writer trusts. And this writer is currently the only person we know who knows how Ronald Buckett was killed."

Behind her, Rachael heard Trace sit back heavily in his chair. She didn't look at him.

"If you release the right kind of facts about Bucky, facts that show the level of his abuse to other children, don't you see how that could draw our writer out?" she continued.

"I take it you're assuming the writer was one of Bucky's victims," Will said.

"I know it! Look at that line in the letter, Will!" Rachael said. "The writer said something like the 'police won't understand. They never did.' Doesn't that sound like a child who thought surely the police would help them and didn't?"

"It could also be a parent who'd called the police and didn't get the results they wanted," Will replied.

Rachael sat back in her chair. She knew the writer was a victim. She just couldn't explain how she knew.

"Look, Rachael," Will said, and his voice took on a kind tone. "I appreciate everything you're trying to do here. And I do have respect for your hunches. But you don't have to do anything about any of this."

"C'mon, Rach. Let Will do his job and you do yours. This has nothing to do with you," Trace said, and his tone was kind, too, but also anxious.

"I have to agree with Trace. I don't want you involved with this," Will said.

Rachael looked from one to the other. "Are you guys missing the obvious? I *am* involved with this. I already am. And I'm not saying I want a police uniform so I can start taking statements. I'm just saying this person trusts me. They've started a conversation with me, and yes, I know it's only one-sided. But if you really want to find this person, doesn't it make sense to keep me in the loop? I'm the only person they've been in contact with."

Will rubbed his temple with his hand. His movement exposed the holster wrapped around his torso and the gun strapped within it. Trace saw it, too. Rachael could sense his breath had quickened behind her.

"You can come down on Monday," he finally said. "I'll brief you on what we've got. But only because I think it might help the case to get your insights and there is apparently no risk to you at the moment. The minute that changes—if it changes—that's it."

"Okay. I'll see you Monday, then," Rachael said, standing as well.

"See you, Trace, Fig," Will said as he turned to walk toward the door.

Trace nodded and Fig waved as Rachael saw Will to the door.

"So can we keep this one out of the media, you think?" she said, pointing to his shirt pocket.

Will turned the knob on the door and opened it as he answered. "I wasn't planning on going public with this one," he said. "Unless it was a tip to another body. But it's not. Your instincts are right about keeping this one quiet. It invites more interaction from the writer."

Rachael nodded in relief.

"You should have been a cop, Rachael," Will said.

She inclined her head. "But I have a tendency to jump to conclusions."

"Yeah," Will said stepping over the threshold. "But there are worse character flaws."

Rachael smiled. "You agree it's one of Bucky's victims that wrote the letters don't you, Will?"

Will turned his head toward her. "Could be anybody, Rachael."

Rachael said nothing in response at first. There was no point in arguing with Will this early in the investigation. Besides, she knew she was right. "Okay, then," she said. "I'll see you Monday?"

"Yep," he said.

She closed the door behind him and turned back toward the inner workings of the studio. Trace had moved from the table and was standing at one of his drawing tables, staring at his current, half-completed illustration. McKenna had scooted in her walker to stand beside him. Fig was changing the CD in the stereo.

The bag of bagels sat forgotten and untouched on the long table.

SEVEN

Moonlight and a wash of drifting streetlight bathed McKenna in a milky glow as Rachael stood over her sleeping daughter. The phone had rung moments earlier as she was placing McKenna in her crib; Trace had answered it. She heard his voice now and again as he paced the long open room on the other side of the bedrooms.

He had been pacing a lot over the weekend, saying little, but expressing much nonetheless. The second letter had interrupted their lives more acutely than the first, even though it said nothing new. Rachael knew they had to talk about it, not just about the letter, but her part in the investigation and his reluctance to let her be a part.

The last 24 hours had been awkward for them both. She and Trace had never had much to disagree about. In the six years they'd been married they had seriously argued only twice. The first time, early in their marriage, was a disagreement about where to attend worship together. She preferred traditional services with a robed minister, stained glass windows, an organ with pipes that stretched to the heavens and a choir of singers whose voices swirled about a vaulted ceiling. Trace felt at home only in a gathering of less than a hundred, with a trio—at the most—of

musicians and singers, gourmet coffee at the ready, and where a variety
of ways to express devotion to God were available including art, dance
and poetry. They had compromised, alternately attending services that
met the other's need and desire. The second argument was so trivial she
could not now remember what it had been about.

So Rachael felt unskilled in the mechanics of disagreement when it
came to Trace.

"Sure. I don't think we have plans," Trace was saying. He was near the
entrance to the bedrooms. "I'll let you know if we can't make it. Okay.
Catch you later."

She heard the phone click off. Seconds later, Trace came up behind
her, but he said nothing about who had been on the phone. Nor did he
say anything else. She was about to turn around when he placed his arms
around her waist and pulled her toward his chest.

Rachael closed her eyes and leaned into him. For several moments
they stood that way, neither saying a word.

"I love it when you're in moonlight," he whispered. "I love it more
when you're looking down on McKenna at the same time."

She smiled.

"I'd be lost without you," he continued, his voice softer still. "I don't
mean to be a pain in the butt about all this, but Rachael, I just can't help
it. I don't like what's happening. I don't like this person writing to you.
I don't like it."

Trace had nuzzled his face to her neck. The little cross earring he was
wearing brushed across her cheek.

"I know you don't," she whispered back.

"At our wedding I told a church full of nicely dressed people and God
himself that I would always look after you. That I'd lay down my life for
you if I had to."

Rachael stroked his hand across her waist, feeling the cool metal of
his wedding ring. "And I like knowing you're watching out for me, I do,
Trace. But I know this person doesn't want to hurt me. I know it."

Trace was silent for a moment. "How can you know that?"

Rachael turned her head to look up at him. Trace knew her better than
anyone. He knew she was a pragmatic thinker, someone who respected
order, not only in the courtroom but also in the rest of life. And she loved

his art because she saw beauty in the perfection of his creations, not the creativity of the art itself. Abstract art like Brick's didn't resonate with her and Sid's cartoons were too satirical to be real, but Trace's artistic grasp of the human body spoke flawlessness to her, as did Fig's sculptures of people. She was drawn to them because they were *real*.

What had been happening to her lately defied reason. The truth was, she was finding herself perceiving things that had no tangible evidence of their authenticity. And she knew when it had begun. It had started after she gave birth to McKenna, when Joshua had confessed to a murder she knew he couldn't have committed. She had been certain there was another person involved and that there had been more to it—and she had been right.

She was certain that she had been right about Penny Duggin: The woman would never have pulled the trigger.

She was also certain the letter-writer was one of Bucky's tortured victims.

But she could not explain how she knew.

"Something happened to me after McKenna was born," she finally said. "I don't know how, but I sense things, Trace. Like when I told you there had been another person in the room with Josh when Vang Thao was killed, that was something I somehow knew. And after Will told me to get out of the car, and I was standing there looking at Penny, I knew she wouldn't have gone through with it. I wasn't in real danger that night."

"That doesn't make any sense. Especially coming from you," Trace said.

Rachael looked back down at McKenna sleeping in the pearly hues of diffused light. "I know it doesn't. But coming from me, don't you think I would know if something is real or not? I think maybe God has gifted me somehow, like he did Josh with his passion for helping hurting people. Or maybe I've always had this ability and I just didn't know it. You know, Trace, my grandmother prayed over me just like she prayed over Josh. She wanted us both to make a difference in this world. Everyone could see that Josh was making a difference. I thought he was the only one who was. And could."

"But Rachael, look where Josh is right now," Trace said.

"Josh is where he is because he took matters into his own hands. I still believe he is a gifted person, Trace. But he blew it. And now he's paying the consequences. When he's done paying, he'll be back where he's supposed to be. Out here, where desperate people need someone like him."

Trace was silent for a few moments. "Promise me you won't take matters into your own hands," he finally said. "That you won't make the same mistake."

Rachael rubbed her head against his chest. "I promise."

"I'll still worry about you. I won't be able to stop," Trace continued. "But I won't nag you about it. Much."

Rachael grinned and reached up with a hand to touch his face.

Several seconds of calm silence hovered in the room.

"Trace?" Rachael said.

"Mmm?"

"Do you believe me? I mean, do you think I'm being irrational about... you know, about what I think is happening to me?"

Trace kissed her right temple. "I don't understand it," he said. "But I believe you."

She closed her eyes again. "Thanks."

They stood there for several long minutes before Rachael remembered the phone call.

"So who was on the phone?" she said.

"Fig. Jillian's home from Peru and he's asked us all over for dinner tomorrow night. Sid and his wife, and Brick, too. I told him I thought we could come."

"Maybe my mom can stay overnight and we can leave McKenna here at home with her."

"Sounds good."

"So what's on the menu?" Rachael asked, as she contemplated what kind of odd cuisine Fig would serve.

"Yak."

Rachael slumped against him. She'd have to resort to peanut butter and jelly before they left.

"Just kidding," Trace said. "He's making tamales. Beef."

Monday morning at the loft bordered on chaotic. Rachael's mother arrived in plenty of time for Rachael to get to work before 8:00, but Rachael made the mistake of telling her mother she had been the one to receive the tip on the location of Ronald Buckett's body. She had hoped to casually alert her parents that she was involved in that investigation, but in such a way that would not make them worry.

But Eva had taken the news with the same shock and fear as Trace had initially. It took Rachael a full fifteen minutes to assure her mother that the police were on top of things and that the letter-writer appeared to have only one thing on his or her mind—the desire to be understood.

"This is what happens when you live downtown," Eva said sternly, holding McKenna close to her body—as if the letter had contained a threat that her granddaughter would be abducted by nightfall.

Rachael grabbed her briefcase and keys. "Mom, if I lived in the suburbs I still would've gotten the letter. I would've gotten it if I lived in a farm-house in Anoka County. Where I live is inconsequential."

"Well, how did they get your address? You told me you had an unlisted number. And I sure haven't given your address to anyone."

Rachael shook her head as she reached for her filled travel mug of coffee. "I don't know, Mom. It's not that hard to find an address these days if you know where to look. I'm late. I've got to go." She walked over to her daughter and kissed the back of McKenna's head. "Don't let Trace sleep past nine," she continued to Eva. "He told me he has a meeting at eleven." She hurried to the door of the loft.

"Lock your car the moment you get in it!" Eva called out to her.

"I will, I promise, Mom. Oh, did you call Dad to tell him you're stay-ing here tonight?"

Eva nodded and waved.

Rachael decided to forgo the ancient gated elevator and instead sailed down the stairs to the garage below ground. She hurried to her car, unlocked it and tossed her briefcase and purse inside. She got in and set her travel mug in its holder as she started the engine.

Moments later, as Rachael was merging into the rush of morning traffic, she saw with fresh eyes the sea of people in and outside of cars, stores and garages. She was suddenly mindful that the writer could be just about any one of the dozens of people all around her—in surrounding cars, on the sidewalk, or maybe even gazing at her from a storefront window.

It hadn't occurred to her until just that moment that the letter-writer might be watching her; could have his or her eyes trained on her even as she considered it, staring at her as she left her apartment building and joined the morning commute.

She took a tentative sip from her travel mug, assessing her response to such a notion. Rachael had the distinct impression the writer felt terribly alone and plagued with an equally terrible secret. And that more than anything, that person wanted release. He or she longed for relief and believed Rachael could somehow help. Rachael frowned and placed the cup back in the holder on the dashboard. The writer was begging for someone to listen to his or her side of the story. She was ready to hear it.

The moment she arrived at the courthouse, Rachael was swept up in the flurry of details that defined the day before court proceedings. The remainder of the morning was a blur of activity. Phone calls from public defenders, emails from human services, files to review, orders to draft. It was nearly lunchtime before she had a moment to herself to call Will.

"I was wondering when I'd hear from you," said Will, when she called him a few minutes before noon.

"You busy for lunch?" she said. "I thought I'd get us some sandwiches and meet you at your place. Reubens. Your favorite. And Kettle Chips."

"And a peach Snapple?" Will replied. She could tell he was smiling.

"Of course." Rachael answered easily.

"Deal."

"See you in fifteen."

EIGHT

Will Pendleton's office quickly took on the aroma of sauerkraut, melted Swiss and toasted rye within minutes of Rachael's arrival. They had each just taken a bite when Will's partner, Samantha Stowe, poked her head into his office, apparently on her way to grab a bite as well, but with a piece of paper in her hand. "Yuck!" she said, wrinkling her nose. "What's that smell?"

"Lunch," Will said, saluting her with half a sandwich.

"Gross! Rachael, is that sauerkraut?" Samantha asked, turning toward Rachael.

"You can't have a Reuben without sauerkraut," Rachael replied.

"You can have a lot of things without sauerkraut." Samantha paused for a moment. "So, are you going to tell her everything?" She directed this comment to Will.

"Well, if I wasn't before I would have to now, wouldn't I?" he said, crunching on a Kettle Chip.

"Yes, he is," Rachael said. "That's why I'm here smelling up the office."

"Why? What did you find out?" Will asked Samantha as he crunched another chip.

"Those kids and the parents mentioned in Buckett's school records and the old police reports?"

"Yes?" Will said.

"All but one still live in Minnesota. And the lone pilgrim isn't that far away. The Valasquez kid, the older one, lives in Eau Claire, Wisconsin. Most of the others are nearby. One of the parents is dead, the others are all still around the Twin Cities. April Howard's parents still live on that street, actually." She handed Will the piece of paper. "The Downing kid is now a meteorologist and works for the National Weather Service in Chanhassen, so he's pretty close by. Valasquez's sister Elena lives in Cloquet. Her last name is Brighton now. April Howard is married now too; her last name is Madden. She's in Coon Rapids—real close. And there's one girl who also lived on the same street as Bucky but apparently wasn't one of his targets, at least her name doesn't appear in any civil complaints or in Buckett's school records. But we looked her up anyway. Her name is Stacy Kohl. She lives in Edina."

Will chewed and gazed at the sheet. "This is good, Sam. Great work." He looked up at her. "Thanks."

"No prob. Okay, no offense, guys, but that smell is making me ill." Samantha turned and walked out.

"Bye, Sam," Will called after her.

"Five people?" Rachael said as soon as Stowe was gone. "Did I count right? You guys have leads on five different people?"

Will wiped his mouth with a paper napkin. "Bucky was a busy kid."

"I'm listening," Rachael said.

Will reached for a file, opened it and pulled out a sheaf of papers. "Mom let us have carte blanche with Bucky's school records," he said, patting the thick file. "He was a classic underachiever and troublemaker. Lousy grades, lousy attitude, spent a fair amount of time in the principal's office, starting as early as first grade. And he and his family weren't even here yet. They moved from northern Minnesota to St. Anthony Park when Bucky was nine. He beat up his first classmate when he was ten."

"Ten?" Rachael echoed. "Who was it? What happened?"

"Well, it happened after school on the playground. Kid's name was…" Will studied the report. "Joey Pickert. Bucky broke his nose and gave him a concussion."

"A concussion?" Rachael said, incredulous.

"Actually Joey Pickert, who was twelve at the time, started the fight. Threw the first punch. Gave Bucky a rip roarin' black eye. But I think Bucky got a taste for power with that first altercation. He probably didn't think he could win a fight against someone older than himself. It probably made him feel pretty invincible when he did, despite the fact that he was suspended for three days. I don't think Mom knew his records would say his home life stunk; the teachers' notes in here are full of comments about how uncooperative his parents were, how they would blame Bucky's learning problems on the school but then would openly insult their kid in front of the teachers. He probably enjoyed life for the first time after he exercised a little muscle, found out he could easily instill terror and win the respect and fear of the other kids at school."

"So that's how it started?"

"Well, that's my best guess. There's nothing in here from the school psychologist, anyway. He was seen as a discipline problem, not a troubled kid. There's also nothing in here that indicates Bucky committed extreme acts of bullying on school grounds. But that's pretty typical. Bullies do their best work when adults aren't looking and victims don't always report it because they fear it'll just get worse. There are a few exceptions here, though."

"You mean some kids reported it," Rachael said.

"Yes."

"So who were these five kids?" Rachael said, wanting to hear their names again. Wanting to imagine one of them typing her a note...

Will paused for a moment and looked at her. "No jumping?" he said.

"Both feet firmly on the ground," she said.

"We got a court order and were able to gather some information from the kids' school records. We also borrowed this from the high school where Bucky last attended. It smells like they had to unearth it from the catacombs." Will grimaced and reached for an over-sized, bound book on his desk. "This is the high school yearbook from the year Bucky disappeared," Will said, flipping open the book to the freshman class, perusing until he came to the D's and then placing it on the desk in front of

Rachael. He pointed to a boy with a shy smile, unremarkable brown hair and soft features.

"That's Andrew Downing. Everyone called him Drew. He was born in Des Moines in 1967, moved to St. Paul at age ten and lived next door to Bucky. He was the oldest of three kids, had two much younger sisters. He was fourteen at the time of Bucky's disappearance and a year younger than him. Mom and Dad are Lyle and Ginny Downing. I think you might've heard Sam say just now that they still live in the area and that Drew is a meteorologist with the NWS in Chanhassen."

"Yes," Rachael said, studying the tiny photo. "What happened to Drew? What did Bucky do to him?"

"School records show Drew had a fairly significant stuttering problem. His file is full of session reports from the school's speech therapist. And there are indications in here from more than one teacher that he was teased about his speech troubles, primarily by Bucky. And then we have a copy of an initial civil complaint filed by Lyle and Ginny Downing alleging that Bucky slammed Drew up against a set of lockers, that he attempted to shove a pencil down Drew's throat and then bent Drew's left arm back until their son thought it would break."

"This happened at school!" Rachael exclaimed.

Will shrugged. "After school. No teacher saw it happen. When the Downings reported it to the school and didn't get the response they wanted, they called the police. But a few days later they dropped the charges."

"Why?"

"You can probably deduce it for yourself. But I want to talk to them about it. My guess is Drew thought things would just get worse for him if his parents took Bucky to court. He probably begged his parents to call it off."

"When did this happen, Will?"

Will looked at her for a moment before answering. "A few weeks before Bucky disappeared."

Rachael's eyes widened.

"No. Jumping." Will enunciated each word separately.

"I'm not," Rachael returned.

"I'm thinking that wasn't the only time Bucky went after Drew

Downing. It looks like Bucky started in on him as soon as Drew moved in. He put up with it for four years. I'm going to need to talk to him. And his parents."

"Who are the others?" Rachael said. She pushed the rest of her sandwich away.

Will leaned forward, turned the yearbook toward himself and flipped to the sophomore class, stopping at the V's. He turned the book back around and pointed to a Latino teen with intense eyes, wavy hair and a wide neck.

"That's Santos Valasquez, the one Sam says is now living over the river in Wisconsin," Will said. "He's Guatemalan, but a first generation American. He was born in Florida in 1966, moved to Willow Street when he was five, which means he lived there before Bucky did. Has one sister, Elena; she's the one Sam says is married and living in Cloquet. She's not in that book. She was in junior high when Bucky disappeared. Santos however, was the same age as Bucky and in his class. He lived two doors down from Drew Downing."

"Bucky bullied both Santos and his sister?" Rachael said.

"We're not sure. We need to talk to them both. Santos and Bucky definitely didn't get along. But I get the impression that Santos was the only one who ever stood up to Bucky. Or tried to. Santos and Bucky were both sent to the principal's office several times for fighting, and although it appears Bucky was always the instigator, Santos didn't hesitate to defend himself. He was short and stocky, though. Bucky was tall and stocky, so Santos was outmatched every time. There's nothing in Elena's records that indicates Bucky hurt her, but her name came up in one of the disciplinary actions against Santos for fighting Bucky on school property. He apparently told the principal he was defending his sister's honor. And that he'd do it again in a second. He and Bucky were both suspended for three days that time. They broke a window, which they both had to pay for. Santos' mother, Marisol Valasquez, called the police once, too, to report Bucky's abuse against Santos but apparently the police got the impression Santos was as much at fault as Bucky. Marisol Valasquez dropped the charges."

Rachael fingered the image of Santos Valasquez. "And April Howard?" she asked.

"April lived directly across the street from Drew Downing," Will continued. "We got her name from Carole Bielke, the lady quoted in the first news story—she's lived on that street for thirty-odd years, right next door to the Howards. Samantha talked to her on Friday; was planning on talking to April's parents—who still live in that house—but they weren't home. Mrs. Bielke said they're gone until next Wednesday. Anyway, April's not in the yearbook, either. She was twelve when Bucky disappeared. We haven't contacted the elementary school where she attended yet, but Mrs. Bielke told us she saw Bucky tease April numerous times. She even told him to knock it off a couple times."

"What did Mrs. Bielke see Bucky do?" Rachael asked.

"April was overweight I guess. Mrs. Bielke said she was a very pretty girl but plump. Kind of shy. Nice manners, though. A bit dreamy. Mrs. Bielke said she often saw April in her backyard talking to birds, flowers, butterflies—that kind of thing. Anyway, Bucky called April "Ape," among other choice names. And he'd make gorilla sounds around April and drag his arms around like an ape, usually when April was outside and her parents weren't home from work yet. Mrs. Bielke thinks Bucky heaped verbal abuse on April more than anything else. Although, she did see Bucky push April once. She told him if she ever saw him lay a hand on a girl again, she'd call the cops."

"Did she ever do that?" Rachael asked.

Will shook his head. "No. But I have a feeling that Bucky just made sure she just never saw him lay a hand on a girl again."

"Is torturing people really that enjoyable?" Rachael said, crossly.

Will shrugged. "I think it's the power derived from it, that bullies are addicted to not the pain they inflict."

"Did Mrs. Bielke not see what Bucky did to Drew and Santos?" Rachael asked, clearly annoyed.

"She said she knew that Bucky didn't get along with the other boys on the street. She saw Bucky taunting them from time to time. She just thought it was a bit more than just boys being boys."

Rachael shook her head. "And the last girl? Stacy someone?"

"I don't know anything about her. We got her name from Carole Bielke, too. She lived two doors down from the Howards. Stacy was significantly younger than the other kids. She was eight when Bucky disappeared. Mrs. Bielke said she never saw Bucky tease Stacy but that he really wouldn't have had a reason to. Stacy was too young to be a peer, and too normal—not short, not fat, didn't stutter and didn't have a name that lent itself to ridicule. But we want to talk to her. She might have seen what went on."

Rachael closed the yearbook and handed it back to Will. Her mind felt weighed by all that he had shared with her. She felt tired. Wearied by the new information. "Too bad it's not Friday," she said drearily.

"Friday!" Will exclaimed, as he took the yearbook from her. "We're only halfway through Monday."

Rachael stood and gathered the remains of her lunch. "Yes, but on Fridays I get to spend the afternoons with my husband in his art studio, surrounded by pretty things. I could use a little loveliness right now. But instead I have to go back to my office and read reports of parents neglecting their children, while you sit here and figure out which one of these tortured kids knows how Bucky died."

"Rachael."

She tossed the lunch remains in a trash receptacle by the door. "And don't even tell me we don't know that it's one of those kids. It *is*."

"Maybe. And let's remember they aren't kids anymore. They are older than you."

"I know they're not kids anymore," Rachael said, making her way to the door of Will's office while an image of Fig filled her thoughts. "But I bet you a bag of Murder and Mayhem that those people still remember everything that Bucky ever did to them. And exactly how it made them feel."

Will grinned at her pun. But the grin was thin and weak. She could tell he knew she was right.

"Keep in touch?" she said, from his doorway.

"I'll keep in touch."

"Promise?"

"Promise."

NINE

"We won't be late," said Rachael to her mother as she knelt down on the living room rug to wiggle one of McKenna's toes. "Jillian's probably tired from her trip and I have court tomorrow anyway."

"Won't matter to me if you are," Eva replied. "I turn into a pumpkin during the ten o'clock news. I'll be asleep by ten-thirty."

Rachael stood and lingered for a few moments, watching her daughter lift and lower chunky plastic flaps that revealed animal faces underneath. Her thoughts strayed to the conversation she had had earlier in the day with Will, in those moments when she had her first glimpse into the world Ronald Buckett lived in and created. It didn't escape her notice that Bucky had been a baby like McKenna once. So had Drew Downing, Santos and Elena Valasquez and April Howard. They had all once been unaware of cruelty, untouched by the hand of violence. Even Bucky, who apparently excelled at lavishing abuse on other kids, had been a victim. She wondered when Bucky made the internal switch from innocent child to victimizing bully. Was it really when he broke Joey Pickert's nose? Or was it several years before—when he was still young and expectant, ready to receive love, but denied it.

"Ready?" Trace's voice from behind startled her.

"Yes," Rachael said, looking away from her daughter. "Just let me grab my purse and cell phone." She shook away the troubling thoughts and walked over to the dining room table to where her purse and phone lay.

"'Night, Princess," she heard Trace say to McKenna as she walked back. "Want us to bring you back a tamale, Eva?"

"Not if Fig's making them," Eva replied quickly. "Most likely it would be stuffed with ostrich feet or goat livers."

"Or yak," Rachael said under her breath to Trace. "Thanks again for staying, Mom."

"Have fun, kids," Eva said.

Rachael and Trace rode the elevator down to the lobby in silence, though Rachael was only half aware of it. They stepped out onto the street. A late April twilight had doused the sun and infused a gauzy violet hue over the redeveloped warehouse district.

"Bad day at the office?" Trace said as he reached for her hand.

Rachael let Trace's fingers close around hers and she leaned in close to him. Fig's building loomed a block ahead; the walk to his place would take less than five minutes. She wished they could just keep walking for a while.

"Not bad," she said. "More like sad. I see so much across my desk, Trace, you'd think I'd be used to it. But I'm just starting to realize there are kids who put up with considerable abuse from other kids; the kind of abuse that if it was their parents dishing it out they'd be in court. And if the abuse didn't stop, we'd remove the kids from the home until those parents learned how to treat their kids like human beings and not dirt. I can't stop thinking that Bucky was just one of a million bullies who've preyed on vulnerable kids."

Trace squeezed her hand. "You can't save them all, Rach," he said. "You told me that yourself once."

"I know," she replied, and her voice fell away as if there was more to say but the words wouldn't come.

A moment later they were inside the foyer of Fig's building. As Trace pressed the intercom to Fig's loft, the doors behind them opened and Sidney and his wife and son joined them in the lobby.

"Hey, Sid. Molly," Trace said.

"Hey guys," Sid replied.

"Molly, how are you?" Rachael said warmly. "Hi, Braden," she added, speaking to the three-year-old holding Molly's hand. The boy had red curls like his father and Molly's gray-blue eyes.

"Our sitter stood us up," Molly said, nodding toward her son.

"You can take him down to our place," Rachael said. "I'm sure my mom wouldn't mind."

"Nah. Thanks anyway. I don't want to stay late. He'll be okay. Of course I did decide to feed him before we came, if you know what I mean."

Rachael smiled. She knew what Molly meant.

"Where the devil is Fig?" Trace said, pressing the intercom button a second time.

"He probably decided to tattoo his left earlobe at the last minute," Sid offered.

The inner doors that led to the lofts opened at that moment and Brick appeared with a bottle of green chile sauce in his hand.

"Hey! You're all here," he said. "Fig's decided to have the get-together in the studio."

"Well, let's go then," Trace said, producing a key ring from his pocket. He opened a door just off the intercom wall that led to two flights of concrete steps and the mezzanine where Fig and Trace had their art room.

The group made their way up the stairs and entered one of the two rented spaces in the mezzanine located over the original, main manufacturing floor. Festive music was blaring from the stereo, and Jillian—wearing a long cape of peacock colors—and Fig were dancing in the middle of the room. Jillian's long blonde hair was bound by a leather strap studded with tiny silver bells. Her hues in her cape accented her unusual eyes, one blue eye and one green one.

"Amigos!" Fig yelled when he saw that the rest of his guests had arrived. "Come in! Come in! Look who's back from the Andes!"

A chorus of hellos to Jillian filled the room. The couple stopped dancing.

"That's a beautiful cape, Jillian," Rachael said.

"Yes! I just love it," Jillian gushed. "I've got this gigantic project in Chicago I'm working on and the lady in charge there will just flip over this. I can see fabric just like it for the window treatments in her salon. Can't you just see a whole wall of it?"

"Sure. Lovely," Molly said, but turning toward Rachael and crossing her eyes.

"I'm sure it'd be wonderful," Rachael offered.

"I don't think windows should ever be covered with curtains or drapes or *treatments*," Brick said, heading to the long table where Fig had set up a selection of drinks and a plate of sliced jicama. He set the hot sauce down.

"So you just get undressed in front of God and everyone, eh Brick?" Sid said. "Wait until you're married and have put on a few extra pounds. Then we'll see if you feel comfortable putting on your nightie in front of an open window."

"How hard is it to get undressed in the bathroom?" Brick countered, and then he abruptly turned to Fig. "Where are the tamales? I thought we were having tamales. Isn't that why you sent me upstairs for hot sauce?"

"Actually, I changed my mind about the tamales," Fig replied as he helped Jillian remove her flowing cape. "Go put this on Joanie, Jills," he continued motioning toward the emerging image of Joan of Arc in the far corner of the room. "She'll look divine in it."

"So, we're having raw potato instead?" Sid asked, looking at the plate of sliced jicama.

"Sidney, you need to get out more. That's jicama."

"Is that dinner?"

"Of course not. It's our hors d'ouevres. I've ordered in. It should be here any minute. I should probably go see if they're downstairs trying to ring me."

"What will be here any minute?" Molly asked cautiously.

"The yak," Trace whispered to Rachael.

"Cornish pasties!" Fig replied. "I found this great place in uptown. They make them the way they're supposed to be made. These people are from Devonshire, which is next door to Cornwall, so they know what they're doing."

"Then why did I bother to get the hot sauce?" Brick grumbled.

"Because I like green chile sauce on my Cornish pasties," Fig replied calmly, as if it were the most natural thing in the world to serve Mexican hot sauce with British meat pies.

An hour later, the pasties were gone and a plate of marzipan cookies had been consumed for dessert. Fig had replaced the rumba music with soft jazz. Trace, Sid and Brick were relaxing and chatting on a trio of tan leather couches. Fig called them Idea Couches but Trace had confessed to Rachael that they were more napping couches than anything else. Molly was sitting on the area rug next to Braden as he colored in shapes that Jillian drew for him on a piece of art paper. The two women were discussing the latest issue of *Elle* magazine.

Rachael sat on the floor with her back against Trace's legs. She was a part of neither discussion. Fig sidled up next to her and handed her a cup of Irish coffee.

"You look like you could use a jolt of caffeine," he said.

She took the mug. "Thanks, Fig."

"You're awfully quiet tonight, Kumquat."

Rachael sipped her coffee and shrugged. "A lot on my mind, I guess."

"No more letters, though?"

She shook her head. "No. But I've been learning some things about what Ronald Buckett did to other kids. You weren't the only one who was treated like garbage by another kid. Not by a long shot."

"Yeah, well, it happens."

"It shouldn't. I mean, it shouldn't happen to the same kid over and over again."

"No, it shouldn't. But it does," Fig said, sipping his own mug.

"What shouldn't happen?" Sid interjected. The conversation on the couches had suddenly hit a lull.

Fig opened his mouth to answer but Rachael hadn't told him to keep quiet about the letters and Will's investigation. She rushed in to answer.

"Kids shouldn't be allowed to bully other kids," she said quickly.

Sid frowned. "McKenna's not even a year old. Who could possibly be bullying her?"

"We're not talking about McKenna!" Fig exclaimed.

"Well, who, then?"

Before Rachael could say a word, Fig was answering Sid. "That dude whose skeleton the cops found at a construction site had bullied a bunch of kids."

Rachael inwardly cringed. She wished she had told Fig not to mention anything about her involvement with the case.

"Oh yeah. I read about that in the newspaper," Brick said.

"Rachael thinks one of his victims did him in," Fig continued.

"Fig!" Rachael exclaimed.

"What?"

"I really don't think we should be talking about Will's investigation," she said through her teeth.

"What investigation? Who's Will?" Sid asked.

Rachael didn't know how to stop the runaway train. She faltered and Trace stepped in.

"Rachael's friend Will Pendleton at homicide is working the case. So Rachael's kind of in the loop."

"I didn't think they had charged anybody yet," Molly said from across the sitting area.

"No. No one's been charged," Rachael said, wondering how the conversation had so suddenly shifted to include the whole room.

"Do you really think he was killed by one of the kids he bullied?" Jillian asked.

"Well, I think it's highly possible," Rachael answered, as she felt herself getting sucked into the conversation. If nothing else, she could end it by becoming a part of it. "He got away with too much for too long. A victim desperate enough for it to stop might've gone too far."

"But why couldn't it have been some psychopathic pedophile that killed him?" Sid asked.

"Because the police got a tip somehow," Brick said. "The police said on the news that they were led to believe it was accidental, that the tip was some kind of anonymous confession."

Rachael shifted her weight nervously. She did not want to get on the subject of the tip. Trace leaned forward behind her.

"Anyone care for more coffee?" he said. But no one took the bait.

"I tell you what. There was this one kid in seventh grade who made my life hell," Sid said, ignoring Trace completely. "And he was easy on me compared to what he did to the real nerds at my school. You know, all that 'sticks-and-stones-will-break-my-bones-but-names-will-never-hurt-me' mumbo jumbo is nothing but a load of…"

"Sid!" Molly interjected, nodding toward Braden.

"Okay, is nothing but a load of significant barnyard waste," Sid finished. "You get called Squidney and Carrot-Brain and moron and dufus and dork often enough and you may as well just point a gun at my head and pull the trigger. You can only take so much of that."

"That's just what I told Rachael the other day," Fig said. "I had a kid like that after me in junior high, too." He turned to Rachael. "I think you're on to something, Rachael."

"I'm really not *on* to anything," Rachael replied quickly. "It's just a suspicion I have. That's all." She looked up and over her shoulder to her husband. It was time to end the discussion. "Trace, we'd better go. I have court tomorrow."

"Sure." Trace stood and offered his hand to help Rachael up.

"Hey!" Fig exclaimed as he stood also. "You should let us help you and your detective friend, Rachael, like we did with Josh and his case. You know, the drawings?"

Rachael's thoughts immediately flew to the collection of sketches Fig, Trace, Sidney, and Brick had done of Josh and the crime scene last fall. Those drawings had enabled her to envision what really happened on the night Josh took a man's life. Trace and his friends had filled the drawings with possible scenarios based on the police reports and Josh's confession—and her own burgeoning intuition. The sketches had been instrumental in Rachael's discovery of the truth.

Fig's idea was crazy.

But not that crazy.

Still, it was too soon. She didn't know enough.

"Perhaps, Fig," she said. "I'll think about it."

"Okay, but this time I don't want to get stuck drawing the least likely suspect," Sid interjected, apparently oblivious to what Rachael had just said.

"And I want to use charcoal," Brick chimed in. "I don't like sketching with pencils. Especially smooth-barreled ones. They're useless to me."

"Slow down, guys!' Rachael said. "I don't even know if I need you to do that."

"Don't even think of trying to rein them in now, Rachael," Molly said, as she stood and helped Braden gather up his drawings. "You may as well just let them have at it."

"But I don't know enough," Rachael said. "Hardly anything really."

"Well what do you know?" Fig said to her. "Tell us and then we'll crash your place on Friday night like we usually do and show you our homework."

Rachael glanced at Trace and he lifted his shoulders as if to say, "Your call."

If she could count on them to keep what she knew a secret the effort might prove helpful. Will wouldn't approve. But Will didn't have to know.

"You guys can't breathe a word of this to anyone," she said. "Sid, that means no one. None of your buddies in the newsroom at the paper."

"Cross my heart," Sid said stoically.

"Our lips are sealed," Fig said and Brick nodded.

"Okay. Ronald Buckett's remains were found a couple hundred yards from where he lived. There were at least five other kids living on the same street when he disappeared. Two boys about his age and three girls, all younger. The girl who was twelve was definitely one of his victims. So were the two boys. We don't know about the other two girls. One of them is a sister to one of the boys. Cause of death is unknown. And you should know that the parents of the two boys both called the police on two separate occasions to report Bucky's abuse but both charges were dropped before they went to court."

"How come?" Fig said.

"We don't know."

"So it could've been one of the parents," Sid said.

"Yes."

The room was silent, all ears waiting for more.

"That's it. That's all we know."

"Well, there's the tip, too," Brick said.

"Someone out there knows how Bucky died," Fig agreed, but he gave Rachael a cautious look, as if to suggest he knew he should say nothing about who it was who got the tip. "And how he got buried in that lot."

"You know, if it was one of his victims that killed him, then that means that person was a...was a kid when they did it," Jillian said solemnly.

"We really should go." Molly poked Sid in the shoulder and nodded toward their son. Braden's eyes were wide. There was no question that he had heard the word "kid." And "killed."

"Right," Sid replied, grimacing. "Thanks for the chow, Fig. Jillian, welcome home."

Rachael and Trace moved toward the door as well.

"Okay, so it's Trace and Rachael's place on Friday then," Fig said as his guests headed for the door. "I'll bring the food."

Rachael glanced at Trace.

"Why don't you let us get this one, Fig," Trace said casually. "You deserve a break."

TEN

Will Pendleton appeared deep in thought as Rachael poked her head into his office on Wednesday afternoon and saw him leaning over his desk, his forehead creased and half-covered by one hand. She followed his gaze to a collection of photos that lay in front of him. From her vantage point several feet away the only distinguishing feature she could make out in the photographs was blood. Lots of it. Crimson splashes covered the images.

"Am I interrupting something?" she said from the doorway.

Will looked up. "Hey, Rachael. What brings you here?"

She took a step inside. "Just chatting with the arresting officer in a maltreatment case I'm working on. I don't think I want to ask you what you're working on," she said, gesturing toward the photos.

Will gathered the photos and placed them in a large envelope. "You don't. I'm only too ready for a break. Have a seat."

Rachael walked over to the chairs in front of Will's desk and sat down in one.

"So are you here to say hello or to get an update on Bucky's case?" Will's tone was genial.

"Can't it be both?"

The detective smiled. "I'm actually glad you stopped by. I've been thinking it's probably wise to keep you in the investigative loop. I think we're going to shake things up a bit as we start talking to the people who knew Bucky."

"You think I might get another letter," Rachael said.

"Perhaps. Or they may stop altogether *because* we're talking to people."

Rachael could see Will's point. If Will or his partner Samantha should unknowingly interview the letter-writer, that person could possibly confess, or become motivated to write again. Or stop writing completely.

"Can I ask who have you talked to so far?" she said.

"Stacy Kohl, the neighbor Carole Beilke, April Howard's parents and the principal who saw a lot of Ronald Buckett and remembered more about him than he probably would like. We're holding off interviewing primary potential suspects until we've talked with everyone else."

"And your primary suspects are?"

"Primary *potential* suspects."

"Okay. Your primary potential suspects are?"

"At this point they're Drew Downing, Santos Valasquez and their parents."

"But not April Howard and her parents?"

"No. April at twelve, even overweight, had a sizeable disadvantage when it came to body mass. I don't see how she could have accidentally killed Bucky and then had the fortitude to drag his body to the lot and bury him. Plus, I don't think she possessed the needed motivation to do something so drastic. The neighbor, Mrs. Beilke, said April was not harassed near as much as the two boys were."

"Not as much that she could see," Rachael corrected.

"Yes, but I don't think April's own parents even saw that much. And they never contacted the cops, either. Not like the boys' parents did. Actually, I didn't get the impression the Howards were aware of much at all when it came to their daughter. They're not suspects at all in my mind."

"What did they say?"

"It's more what they didn't say that convinced me. I don't think they had a clue to what their daughter had to put up with. Carole Bielke provided more info than they did regarding April." Will reached for a portfolio and opened it. Inside was a sheaf of papers, which he shuffled through. He unclipped a wallet-sized photo and handed it to Rachael. The face in the picture belonged to a plump-cheeked girl with mousy-blonde hair and easy smile.

"When was this taken?" Rachael asked.

"That's her sixth-grade school photo. It was taken six months before Bucky disappeared, at the beginning of the school year." Will lifted out a sheet of notes. "Here we go. Joseph Howard, that's her dad, is a retired pharmaceutical salesman. He was on the road a lot when April was a kid, which explains why she's an only child, I guess. Glennis, that's her mom, was a dedicated real estate broker—full days, long hours, yada, yada. Good thing April was such an easy-going kid who could fend for herself."

"Except she couldn't fend for herself," Rachael said.

"But Joseph and Glennis weren't home often enough to know that."

"So they knew nothing about Bucky? Nothing about him calling their daughter 'ape' or teasing her about her weight. Or shoving her? None of it?"

"They knew who Bucky was; remembered him as the disrespectful kid across the street who they thought ran away when he was fifteen. They were surprised when they saw on the ten o'clock news that he had spent the last 25 years decomposing in the vacant lot at the end of the street instead."

"How could they not know about any of the abuse?" Rachael said.

"They knew Bucky liked to tease kids on the street; they even knew that April was singled out now and then, but all they witnessed was a little name-calling."

"And they never told Bucky to stop?"

"The best way to get a person to stop paying attention to you is to not pay any attention to them; that's a direct quote from Joseph Howard. They ignored Bucky's occasional taunts and encouraged April to do the same."

"Did you ask them if they knew how Bucky made April feel?" Rachael said, feeling anger swelling inside her.

"April never talked about Bucky, Mom said. But Mom added that they were in fact very concerned for April; not because of Bucky's bullying, but because she was overweight. They did all they could to encourage her to watch what she ate, to exercise, all that. Did I mention Joseph and Glennis Howard are members of an athletic club and are avid golfers?"

Rachael sank back in her chair. "No wonder April never said anything to them. She probably thought they would just tell her if she wasn't so fat, Bucky would have nothing to say to her."

"That's my guess, too."

"Have they talked to April since Bucky's body was discovered?"

"They've talked, but not about Bucky. Glennis said she and April talked last week, by phone, and that Glennis mentioned all the activity at the vacant lot—the discovery and all that—but that she and April didn't spend more than a couple minutes in conversation about it."

Rachael wrinkled her forehead in thought. "How did they describe their daughter to you?"

Will glanced at the notes. "A good student, mostly A's, quiet, compliant, loved books and animals—though they couldn't have pets as Joseph has allergies. Never gave them any trouble, except for the weight issue and yes, they lumped that in there with trouble. She didn't have a lot of friends, none to speak of in junior high. She wasn't friends with Stacy, who would have been too young, really. Stacy's four years younger than April. And of course she didn't hang out with Drew and Santos across the street, either. Mom and Dad did say she seemed to come out of her shell some in high school when she joined the drama club."

"She was on stage?" Rachael asked.

"No. Backstage. Props mistress. She did it all four years of high school. But her weight continued to be a problem."

Will said the last sentence with a mocking undertone. One of the Howards had said that—just like that.

Rachael sighed. "I just don't get some people."

"I don't get them either, but I see them every day. Just like you do."

"Okay, so what did April do after high school? How did she meet the man she married?" Rachael continued.

"She went to a community college for a little while, undeclared major. She quit school when she got offered a job in the children's section at a Barnes and Noble. She knows a lot about children's books, apparently that's one thing about their daughter the Howards are proud of. She moved out of the house at age twenty, met Jay Madden at the bookstore when he came to work on the store's computers—he's a self-employed computer repair guru—and got married at twenty-one. Joseph and Glennis like Jay very much, by the way. He's very well-off and a very nice man but he has a bit of a weight problem, too."

Rachael grinned cynically. "These people are amazing. Such wonderful judges of character."

"Yep. Nice to know we're not the only ones, eh?"

Rachael let the grin slip away. "April and Jay have children?"

Will shook his head. "No. Joseph and Glennis aren't real happy about that. They've mellowed in their retirement it seems and are eager to invest their lives in the nurture of little ones."

"Better late than never, I guess."

"Glennis volunteered that April has always wanted children, but after fifteen years of waiting they say she's pretty much resigned herself to being childless. She also said that April has been open to the idea of adoption after the first year of trying to conceive, but Jay doesn't want to go that route and Glennis says that's probably just as well because you just don't know what you might get."

"I think I've heard all I can stomach from April's parents," Rachael murmured.

"Good. Because that's all there is." Will placed the sheet of notes back in the portfolio. Rachael handed him April's photo. "When are you going to talk to April?" she said.

"Actually I called her house this morning to set something up but Jay's out of town and she doesn't like to entertain strangers when he's not home."

"Is that what she said?" Rachael exclaimed.

"No. But that's what she meant. She won't talk to us until he gets home and that won't be until this weekend. I can live with that. If she does know something I don't want to scare her into silence."

"So how did she react to you wanting to talk with her?"

"I'd describe her as amiable but cautious. When I asked her if she remembered Bucky she said, 'Of course I remember Bucky,' but then she kind of clammed up after that. She really didn't want to discuss him or his disappearance or the discovery of his remains over the phone and without the master of the house at home."

"But you did talk to Stacy Kohl?"

"Samantha did. She's pretty much a non-player in this as far as having motive and opportunity. She was too young to pose much of a threat to Bucky's safety and he never targeted her. But she did see what he did to others."

"Like what?"

"She saw Bucky making life miserable in general for Drew and Santos; not at school but when the boys were outside. She played on occasion with Elena, but Santos' sister was two grades ahead of her. It wasn't often that they did things together. The interesting thing is Stacy never saw Santos and Drew playing together, either, even though Drew was only a year younger than Santos and they had a common nemesis. Anyway, Stacy saw Bucky doing the ape thing often around April and ridiculing her about her weight. On more than one occasion he crossed over to April and Stacy's side of the street, probably only when he was spectacularly bored, to threaten to kill the neighbor's cat in front of April. April liked the cat and Bucky knew it. Stacy said one time she overheard Bucky tell April he was going to bash the cat's head in with a baseball bat and then tell the neighbor April killed him by sitting on him."

"Was there really nothing better for him to do with his time than make threats like that?" said Rachael crossly.

"Apparently not. Stacy did mention something to me that concerned me, though. She said April developed early, that when Bucky was at his worst, April already had a bust line. She said she realized later that some girls do develop at that age, but at eight Stacy thought it was weird. Here's the thing: She said one time she saw Bucky grab April's breasts while April was walking home from school. Stacy was under her porch, retrieving a doll's shoe. Bucky had been walking behind April, but he ran up to her just as they were in between Stacy's house and a house that no one had lived in for quite awhile. Stacy figures Bucky thought no one would see him because the house they were in front of was empty. Bucky said something to April when he grabbed her, but Stacy doesn't remember what it was. April ran home in tears. She only saw Bucky do this the one time. But she remembers feeling very embarrassed for April. She never told anyone about it."

"She never mentioned to April that she had seen Bucky do that?"

"No. Never. They weren't friends, really. She said April was kind to her, but they didn't play together or spend any time together."

"And did she think April seemed different after Bucky disappeared?"

"She stopped noticing April after Bucky disappeared. She said the same thing about the two boys across the street. There was nothing to notice about them when Bucky ran away, as they all thought he did, because the thing that made them noticeable to her was the abuse Bucky heaped on them."

Rachael was silent as she pictured Bucky's victims suddenly becoming unnoticeable after months and years of being obvious targets of torment.

"Want to hear what the principal said?" Will continued.

"Sure," Rachael replied, exhaling heavily.

"Gordon Kennick's still at the same school, been there for twenty-eight years, plans to retire next year," Will said, as he turned to a second set of notes. "He remembers Bucky primarily because he was a runaway, or so everyone thought, and because the police had been called because of the incident with Drew and the pencil-down-the-throat. He told me Bucky was suspended for a couple of days based on what Drew said had happened to him. There were no witnesses, but Kennick said he didn't doubt that Bucky had roughed Drew up because Bucky had long been a discipline problem and had a hard time getting along with his peers."

Rachael narrowed her eyes. "Mr. Kennick called what Bucky did to Drew 'roughing him up'?"

"Kennick didn't see it happen. No one did. And Bucky didn't leave any marks or draw any blood."

"Will!" Rachael's sensitivities for the plight of unprotected children wheeled madly within her.

"I know, I know. I'm just telling you what he told me," Will said. "Now Kennick did tell me there were a couple times when Bucky did draw blood and plenty of people saw him do it. The time that interested me was when he lit into Santos one day, about a month before he assaulted

Drew, on school grounds. Kennick doesn't remember what it was about. He said he does remember Santos threw the first punch."

"Because he was provoked, I'm sure," Rachael said.

"No doubt. In any case, Bucky pummeled him. He was suspended a week that time."

"And what about Santos? What was done for him?"

"He was given a day of in-school suspension for fighting on school grounds."

Rachael bolted forward in her chair. "This is nuts! Did the school offer any kind of counseling to Drew or Santos? Anything? Any assistance of any kind?"

"Bucky was referred to the school psychologist to work on anger management issues, but it doesn't appear that Drew and Santos were ever in her office."

"Bucky was referred to the school psychologist," Rachael echoed tersely.

"Yep, but Kennick said Bucky skipped out of most of those sessions."

"And they just let him?"

"Kennick said the records show that the school was considering transferring Bucky to an alternative school after the incident with Drew, even though Bucky's parents had already nixed that option earlier in the year. The school's disciplinary task force was planning a meeting to discuss expulsion and making the transfer mandatory when Bucky ran away."

Rachael sat back in her chair. "Did you ask him…Does he think Drew or Santos could've…could've…"

"Could've killed Bucky in a fit of rage?" Will finished for her.

"Yes."

Will shook his head. "Kennick barely remembers Drew, other than that he was quiet, a good student and he had a stuttering problem. He remembers even less about Santos. He did say that Lyle Downing—that's Drew's father—was livid when he came to the school to complain about what happened to Drew. He stormed into Kennick's office the day after it happened and demanded to know what the school planned to do about Bucky. He apparently didn't like Kennick's answer because he called the cops that same afternoon. But a few days later, the Downings dropped their civil complaint. And that was the last Kennick heard about it. A couple weeks later Bucky disappeared."

Rachael closed her eyes. Her head was spinning with images of brute strength preying on weakness. Everything within her wanted to gather into her arms the children Bucky had mistreated. It pained her that those children no longer existed. They were all adults, now. Older than she was. And somehow they had survived.

"What are you thinking?" Will asked.

She opened her eyes and looked at the detective. "I don't know," she answered. "If one of those kids did do something accidentally to Bucky, or even if it was one of those kids' parents who did it and didn't really mean to, I can't say as I blame them. I mean, I know it doesn't make it right, but, Will, I can hardly blame them."

Will leaned back in his chair. "That doesn't surprise me that you would feel that way. That's why you got the letters."

ELEVEN

Rachael awoke Thursday morning restless and moody. It annoyed her that she felt that way on her day off. She normally anticipated the end of the week as a soothing opportunity to cleanse her mind from the ills of society gone wrong. Thursday and Friday—with no court business, and no civil petitions to file—usually mentally prepared her for a stress-free Saturday with Trace and McKenna and a restful Sunday spent absorbing grace and mercy, eating out, and lounging around with the mammoth Sunday edition of the *Star Tribune*.

But her waking thoughts that morning were of April Howard Madden, who once loved cats and talked to butterflies, and who ran home in disgrace and tears the day Bucky grabbed her breasts in broad daylight with the sole intention of humiliating her.

Rachael rolled over in bed, seeking the comfort of Trace's warm body next to her, but as she turned she saw that he was already out of bed. She had forgotten he was driving to Rochester that morning to deliver completed illustrations and meet with the art director of Mayo's publications department. She rose from the bed, grabbed her robe and made her way down the open staircase to the main floor of the loft. As she descended the stairs she could see that McKenna was enjoying The Weather Channel from her walker while stuffing dry Cheerios into her mouth.

"Good morning, Cutie," Rachael said to her daughter as she closed the distance, leaned over and kissed the top of McKenna's head. "Did Daddy get you up?"

"I did," said Trace, Rachael turned. Trace was coming toward her with a mug of coffee. "And I changed her diaper, too. It was a real good one. You would've been impressed with how I managed."

She grinned and took the mug. "I'll make sure to mention that the next time I'm called upon to extol your abilities."

Trace smiled. "Want to come to Rochester with me?" he said. "You and McKenna could do the mall thing while I'm in my meetings, then we could have a late lunch."

Rachael lowered herself to the couch. "I don't think so. I don't feel like going to a mall today. Thanks anyway, Trace."

Trace sat down next to her. "Don't spend the day brooding, Rachael."

She smiled as she took a sip of her coffee. "You know me too well," she said softly as she pulled the mug away from her lips.

"So you won't do it?"

"I promise I will try very hard not to brood," Rachael answered.

"That's my girl." He leaned over her and kissed her forehead. "I've got to get dressed and get on the road."

Trace stood and began to walk toward the stairs. "Hey, you can think of something strange and abnormal to fix for dinner tomorrow night when the guys come over," he called over his shoulder.

"But we volunteered to take care of the food so we could have something that *isn't* regularly featured on the Discovery Channel!" Rachael replied.

"Okay, have it your way. But I won't be able to help you much with the menu." Trace stopped on the second step and turned toward her. "I haven't done my homework yet."

Rachael had put out of her mind Fig's suggestion that he, Trace, Sidney and Brick come up with sketches of how Bucky might've accidentally died at the hands of a desperate classmate or angry parent.

"So, you're really going to sketch something?" she said.

"I don't want to be the only one who doesn't," Trace answered as he continued up the stairs. "You know the others will do it."

"You think?"

Trace stopped again and turned to look down on her. "Definitely. They loved helping you out with Josh's case. I did, too, actually."

"How come?"

Trace looked thoughtful for a moment. "Because we were creating art that actually mattered. You know. In the end, it changed the course of someone's life."

He turned back around and took the rest of the stairs two at a time, leaving Rachael to ponder his answer. For several long minutes she wished she had Trace's artistic ability—and the enabling sense of space, dimension and depth needed to visualize life in motion. But it just as quickly occurred to her that her abilities lay elsewhere, and that they agreeably complemented Trace's creativity. Her blossoming talent—she blushed even as she complimented herself—was intuition. She provided the scene's details, the colors on the palette. The artists would have nothing to work with without her impressions. And she seemed to ply her talent best when she was in the position to observe.

This last thought birthed an idea that was sudden and complete. She immediately formulated a plan for her day. Rachael stood up and strode to the kitchen to make some toast for herself and McKenna.

She wouldn't exactly be breaking her promise to Trace. Brooding was not what she had in mind. Brooding was a passive activity and what she had just decided to do was arguably, if not decidedly, intentional.

A mid-morning sun bathed the St. Paul suburb known as St. Anthony Park in soothing radiance. In the yard of the corner house on Willow Street adjacent to where Rachael parked her car, infant tulips and crocuses bowed in a gentle breeze. A leaf blower buzzed off in the distance, as did construction machinery. Birds flung their songs across the treetops in between the crunch of heavy equipment.

Finding the street where Bucky had lived—and been buried—hadn't been difficult. Nor was finding Carole Bielke's and the Howards' addresses. Carole and her husband Arnold, as well as the Howards, were listed in the phone book. She had found both addresses within minutes of Trace leaving the loft for his trip to Rochester.

She turned her car off and checked to make sure she had both addresses in her pants pocket. The folded piece of notepaper was there, but she still wasn't entirely sure what to do with it. Walking up to the Bielke or Howard house with McKenna in tow and ringing the doorbell didn't seem like a very wise thing to do. She wasn't on duty. Plus, it was never a good idea for a prosecutor to question a witness outside the court-room; that was the police department's responsibility and kept prosecu-tors from having to testify on the stand.

"But I'm not the prosecutor on this case," she said aloud, as if in disagreement with herself.

"Um gah," McKenna replied from the backseat.

"Well, I'm not."

"En dazsh!" McKenna said happily.

But Will would be peeved if she made physical contact with Carole Bielke or the Howards. And Trace wouldn't like it either. It was remotely possible that one of the Howards or Carole Bielke herself was the letter-writer. Plus, she wouldn't be able to identify herself as attached to the case in any way. Her identity as the recipient of the tip was to be kept secret. She wasn't a detective and she wasn't a trial attorney.

Rachael had no bona fide reason for being on Willow Street that morning. But on the fifteen-minute drive from Minneapolis to St. Paul she had affirmed to herself that she was heading to Willow Street simply to visualize what happened there twenty-five years earlier. She wanted to see where Bucky lived, and where his body had been discovered. She wanted to see where Drew and April and Santos had lived. And where they had endured Bucky's abuse. She knew the street wouldn't be the same and that she wouldn't learn a whole lot more than she already knew. But her instincts were needling her. She needed to see it.

She got out of the car and surveyed from a distance the houses on both sides of the street and the construction site that lay at the dead end.

She pulled the stroller out of the backseat, unfolded it and then reached for McKenna.

"Want to go for a walk, Princess?" she said.

"Choo!" McKenna babbled as Rachael lifted her out.

With McKenna buckled in and the car locked, Rachael set out at a leisurely pace. She pulled out the piece of paper bearing the addresses and glanced at house numbers as she passed each home. Rachael noted that the third house on the even-numbered side of the street looked newer than the others. It was definitely a replacement, perhaps only five or six years old. Three doors past the newer house was the Howards' home: sky blue, landscaped and tidy, followed by Carole Bielke's—a Tudor style with ivy snaking its way across the bricks and stucco. On the other side of Carole's house was the last house on the west side of the street. There were nine altogether on the left side of Willow, and nine more on the other side. At the dead end was a sprawling field of broken dirt and felled trees. Earthmovers and a crane were moving slowly on the site, breaking the still sounds of the morning with blasts of power and strength.

Rachael looked across the street from the Bielke house; she knew from Will's consultations that the house directly across from the Bielke home had been the Bucketts'. She saw a tired, faded green rambler in need of fresh paint. A rusting Buick Skylark sat in the driveway and a healthy swath of dandelions bloomed in the patchy lawn. Yellowing and ignored free shopping newspapers lay in varying stages of disintegration on the cement doorstep. She knew that Bucky's family no longer lived there, but she got the impression that not a whole lot had changed for that particular house in the past twenty-five years. It looked like it was still a dwelling for people who'd decided there are no fair breaks in life.

Rachael turned her head slightly to look at the house next door to Bucky's old house. It had been Drew's. The two-story house was painted a soft shade of coral with white trim. Redwood boxes of newly planted impatiens bloomed under the front windows and a clematis vine was just beginning its yearly clamber up a trellis by the front door. The garage door was open, revealing a swept concrete floor and a vacant spot where a car could be parked.

Two doors beyond Drew's house, was a tan and taupe home that had been Santos and Elena's. The curved walkway to the front door was lined with emerging hostas and tiny bursts of purple and white alyssum. A basketball hoop hung over the garage roof and a motorcycle was parked inside the open garage. Rachael turned her body to look at the house three doors down from the Howards' home where Stacy had lived. It was the biggest home on the street with a wrap-around porch and stained, leaded glass above all the downstairs windows. On the opposite side of Stacy's house was the newer home; the one Rachael thought was too modern for the 1940s-era street; even for a remodeled job. Something about the new house bothered her.

She swung her body back around to study the houses. April's. Bucky's. Drew's. Santos's. And Stacy's. She willed any preconceived notions about the children to fade away. She wanted to be open, observant. Discerning.

God, is there anything I should be seeing here? she said inwardly.

She waited and watched but nothing out of the ordinary presented itself, other than the fact that the new house seemed to pick at her mind, like a buzzing insect. She turned and stared at the house.

There was something unsettling about the new house, something that pestered and perplexed her. But she couldn't identify the source of the irritation.

"Lopna," McKenna said from within the stroller a moment later. Rachael came out of her befuddled reverie and looked down at her daughter. McKenna was kicking her legs and looking wide-eyed at the earthmovers.

"You like those, Princess? Want to see them better?" Rachael wheeled McKenna closer to the edge of the construction site and looked out over the expanse of broken earth. She wondered what the lot had looked like before construction began. Will had told her the tree growth had been dense. The lot itself seemed to stretch back quite a way.

"If you're thinking of buying one of those condos, the developer has a sign up over on Birch. That's the access road," said a voice behind her.

Rachael turned. A woman with silvery-gray hair was standing there holding a little dog in one hand and the day's mail in the other.

"Oh. Hello. No, I'm not thinking of buying one, but thanks anyway."

"I wouldn't buy one either. Not to save my life. You can't have pets for one thing. Not even birds. And if you get one of the inside units, you barely have any windows. No yard of course. And only one space in the underground garage."

Rachael blinked, unsure if she was expected to comment.

"But they're selling like hotcakes," the woman continued. "I don't know who's buying them."

Rachael wondered if perhaps she was having an impromptu conversation with Carole Bielke. It was entirely possible. Neither Will nor Trace could fault her if she was. She hadn't sought her out.

"Do you live on this street?" Rachael said.

"Yep, right there. Been in that house for thirty-four years." The woman pointed to the Bielke house.

"Must be hard to see this complex go up," Rachael said noting this with veiled satisfaction. "I hear there used to be woods here before."

"Well, there's not going to be access to the thing from our street, thank heavens. This will still be a dead end. People will have to use Birch, the next street over to get to the front of the building. So there shouldn't be more traffic on our street. And the woods were kind of wild and unkempt. It would have been nice if the owner had turned it into a park instead but you don't get millions of dollars to turn your land into a park."

Rachael decided to throw out a breadcrumb to see if Carole Bielke was in the mood to follow. "This site was in the news. A body was found here," Rachael said. Neither sentence was a question.

"Oh my, yes. I was quoted in the paper when that happened. And on the news. Cops came and talked to me, even. The body they found had been buried there for 25 years. Can you imagine?

"That's a long time."

"You're telling me. The thing is, the body belonged to a horrible kid who lived across the street from me, right there in that green house. He was the meanest, most insolent young man I had ever had the misfortune to know."

"I've heard that about him."

"Well, it's all true. And the paper didn't print even half of what I told them. That Bucky was nothing but trouble. He was mean to all of the kids on this street. He was even mean to me. I know I should feel sorry for him that he ended up dead somehow but I don't."

Rachael made a mental note. *Carol Bielke shares too freely to be the letter-writer.* "Why didn't anyone stop him from being mean to the children on this street?" Rachael asked.

"He wasn't *my* kid," Carole Bielke said defensively.

"And the parents of the kids he was mean to, they didn't do anything either?"

Carole was thoughtful for a moment. "You know, I don't think those parents really knew how mean that Bucky was to their kids. The little girl who lived next door to me, she was alone all the time. I don't think her parents knew what Bucky was like."

"But you did," Rachael said gently.

"Yes, but like I said, he wasn't my kid, and the kids he harassed weren't my kids, either. People don't like it when you stick your nose into their business, you know. But I tell you, there was this one time Bucky was on my side of the street and I saw him push the little girl who lived next door to me—her parents still live there—and he knocked her right to the ground. I marched over to him and I told him if I ever saw him hurt a girl again I was going to call the cops!"

"That was really good of you to intervene like that," Rachael said.

"Yes, well, I even told April's parents about it later that night but they just made it seem like I was being a busybody. So you see? People don't like nosey neighbors. They just don't. I've learned to just mind my own business."

Rachael looked away from Carole Bielke and tried to make her voice and tone nonchalant. "So how do you think Bucky ended up dead in the woods?" she said, as casually as she could.

For the first time since their conversation began, it seemed Carole Bielke didn't have a ready answer. When she didn't answer right away Rachael turned and looked at her.

"I don't know, really. It scares me to think someone whom Bucky had mistreated had anything to do with it, but it sure makes sense."

"You think so?" Rachael said.

"He was a menace like you wouldn't believe."

"You think one of the kids he tormented was responsible?" Rachael said.

"Well, it seems likely in theory but those kids were, well, they weren't strong kids. They were all kind of weak and vulnerable. I just can't picture any one of them doing anything like that. Maybe Bucky had enemies I didn't know about. You know, kids from another part of town who had something against him."

"Mmm," Rachael said, and she turned her head back toward the construction site. She was aware of Carole Bielke's eyes on her.

"Do you live around here? I don't think I've seen you before," the woman said.

Rachael turned back around. "No. I don't live around here. I actually came here today to look at the place where the skeleton was found."

"Really?" Carole's eyes were wide. Rachael was no doubt the only spectator to gawk at the crime scene with her hands on the handle of a baby stroller. "How come?"

Rachael decided on an answer that was frank but would not give too much away. "It interests me," she said.

Carole Bielke readjusted the weight of her little dog in her right arm. "Well, there's not much of any interest here now. They've taken the yellow police tape down and everything. It's back to normal if you ask me."

But Rachael didn't ask her. She didn't need to.

It wasn't normal at all.

Rachael turned and looked over her shoulder to the new house up the street. "That house looks pretty new compared to the others on the street," she said, wondering if Carole Bielke would find the shift in conversation odd. She didn't seem to.

"The original house sat empty for the longest time," Carole answered easily. "Then one day—this was a couple years after Bucky ran away, or so we thought—it caught fire. Lightning most likely. Burned to the ground. There was an empty lot there for years. Then a family came in and bought the land and built a new house. It doesn't really fit with the other houses on the street, but it's better than an empty lot. And ten times better than that eyesore before it burned."

Rachael remembered then what Stacy Kohl had seen from under her porch when April Howard was walking past the uninhabited house. And what Bucky had done there. He had said something to April when he grabbed her breasts. Rachael involuntarily shivered.

"What…what did the house look like?" The question was out of Rachael's mouth before she realized she had asked it. Or why.

"Well, it was nice in its day," Carol replied. "But by the time it burned down it was a dilapidated trash heap. It was white once, with dark green trim and shutters. One-and-a-half stories. It was just like the one across the street and up one, only this one had three half-circle steps leading to the front door. It had an old-fashioned storm cellar, too, on the north side there with angled doors; you know like Dorothy and the Wizard of Oz. The owner hadn't lived in it for years. I don't know why he didn't just raze the thing when he couldn't sell it. The city made him keep the grass mowed, but that's all the upkeep it got. It was a mess."

As Carol talked, Rachael stared at the new house. And as she gazed at it, she was abruptly enveloped by the notion that something had happened at that house. Something inside, not on the sidewalk. Something bad. Something that involved Bucky.

"Are you okay?" Carole Bielke was saying.

Rachael sucked in a breath and turned back around. "What?" she said.

"You look pale all of a sudden. Are you okay?"

Rachael shook the half-vision from her mind. "No. I mean, yes, I'm fine. Nice talking with you."

Rachael spun the stroller around and began walking back in the direction of her car. She had to get away.

"Well, bye then," Carol called after her.

As Rachael neared the new house, her breath came in short wisps. Her heart began to pound. The very ground the house stood on seemed to reach out to grab her ankles and suck her down into the black, suffocating dirt. She quickened her pace.

Rachael was nearly running when she reached her car. She placed McKenna back in her car seat with shaking hands and then raised her head. Down the street Carol Bielke was standing there, watching her.

TWELVE

The loft was quiet when Rachael returned from Willow Street. She was immensely grateful that Trace wouldn't be popping in for lunch; he'd be in Rochester until well into the afternoon. She didn't feel like explaining her morning just yet. She barely understood it herself.

Rachael fixed a lunch of cottage cheese and mashed peaches for McKenna—she had no appetite herself—and then rocked her to sleep, holding her daughter's warm body close to hers long after McKenna's breathing was slow and even.

What had come over Rachael while she walked past the new house that morning completely amazed her. It was not natural. It wasn't something she could explain. And yet it had been real. She hadn't imagined any of it.

And that just didn't sit well with her.

Rachael was getting used to the idea of having a new and keen sense of awareness. She was even starting to enjoy what seemed to her to be a gift from God—an ability to perceive that transcended the obvious.

But what happened to her today was wholly of another caliber. What she felt within when she walked past that house was more than just momentary insight. She had been allowed to partake of raw fear; fear that was not her own, but had belonged to someone else.

One of Bucky's victims, perhaps?

Something happened at the house that was no longer there; the house where no one lived.

Something bad. And Bucky had been a part of it.

And even though the house no longer stood, it had called out to her anyway.

The thought was chilling.

…As was the notion that Bucky had derived such intense pleasure from hurting other children. She stroked McKenna's silky curls, mesmerized by the twin pull of mother-love and the instinct to protect. She would walk through fire to protect McKenna from a monster like Bucky.

But what if she didn't know McKenna was being hurt? What if one day McKenna were to be victimized by someone who threatened her with worse violence if she told someone? What then?

God, she whispered. *Don't let it happen. Don't let what happened to those kids happen to my McKenna. Please. Don't let anyone hurt her like that.*

She rocked her sleeping daughter for a while longer, repeating the prayer as if she were memorizing lines for a play.

Then she stood slowly, laid McKenna down in her crib and went into her bedroom to call Will.

He answered on the third ring.

"It's me. Rachael," she said.

"Hey. So what are you doing on your day off?" he replied casually.

"Will, I went to Willow Street. I didn't go to talk with anyone. I just went to see the street. To see where those kids lived."

Will was silent for only a moment. "But you did talk to someone, didn't you?" he said.

"Well, yes. How did you know?"

"Because you wouldn't have called me if you hadn't. Who was it?"

"Carol Bielke—but she initiated our brief conversation."

"Well, that must have been educational. So. What did she say that I need to know? And what did you say that I need to know?"

"Will, she had no idea who I was. None. And I didn't tell her."

"Wasn't she curious as to what you were doing scrutinizing her street?"

"I told her I was interested in what had happened. I told her I knew a skeleton had been discovered at the construction site and that I wanted to see where it had been found."

Will sighed audibly. "What did she tell you?"

"Nothing that you haven't already told me. I told you, Will, I didn't go there to question anybody."

"So you just wanted me to know you had an encounter with her?"

"Yes. And…and to tell you something else."

She paused.

"Okay," he said.

Rachael could feel a wave of nervousness steal across her body. What she was about to say made no sense. But she simply had to tell Will what she had experienced when she walked by the new house. She knew she couldn't explain it but she also knew what she felt had been real. He needed to know. He needed to ask the right questions. And she needed to convey her unexplainable insight in a way that didn't make her sound crazy.

"Remember when you told me Stacy Kohl once saw Bucky groping April in front of that house no one lived in?" she said tentatively.

"Yes."

"That abandoned house is gone now."

"Yeah. I noticed that."

"Carol Bielke told me it burned down a couple of years after Bucky disappeared."

"Okay."

"Will, I think something bad happened at that house. I can't prove it to you. It's just…it's just one of my hunches. I just thought you should know so that when you interview the others you can ask the right questions."

"The right questions?"

"Will. You know what I'm getting at. I think Bucky hurt one of those kids inside that house. And I'm wondering if maybe the house was intentionally set on fire by one of them because of that."

"Rachael," Will began, but she cut him off.

"You don't even need to believe me, Will. I know it doesn't make any sense. But it can't hurt to just ask April and Drew and Santos and even Santos's sister if Bucky ever lured them into that abandoned house to hurt them. What harm is there in asking? If he didn't, they will quickly say he didn't. But if he did, I guarantee they will pause before answering. And I think you might want to see if the fire was really ruled as caused by lightning."

Will was silent on the other end.

"Okay?" she said.

"All right," Will answered, after another moment of silence. "I'll ask. And I'll look into that fire."

Rachael closed her eyes as a strange sense of relief fell over her. "I'm not crazy, Will," she said, opening her eyes. "I can't explain what comes over me sometimes but I'm not crazy."

"I know you're not crazy, Rachael."

"Thanks."

"Rachael?"

"Yes?"

"Enjoy the rest of your day *off*," he said.

"Okay, okay. Goodbye, Will."

She hung up the phone and headed downstairs to make a cup of herbal tea to chase away the headache that had been brewing since she left Willow Street.

As she filled the kettle with water she began to rehearse what she would tell Trace. He would need to know what happened today. She would rather just let it go but he had to know before she confessed to the other artists on Friday night that she had an odd request.

She wanted them to draw an abandoned house that no longer existed.

The pungent, entwined aromas of roasted garlic, basil, and asiago cheese greeted Sidney, Fig, and Brick as they arrived at Trace and Rachael's loft on Friday evening. An early May sun was just beginning to set, casting panels of gossamered light across the hardwood floors and on McKenna as she scooted in her walker across the smooth surface.

"Kumquat! That smells divine! What are you making?" Fig called out as soon as his feet were over the threshold. He dodged McKenna's walker and headed for the open kitchen.

"Just some bruschetta, Fig," Rachael answered as she drew out a pan of sizzling bread slices from under the broiler. Fig, wearing a Hawaiian shirt and a leather beret on his head, bent to close the oven door for her. He scarcely waited until her hands were free to kiss her on both cheeks. "*Buona sera, Raquel.* I brought my homework!" Fig grinned widely and held up a thin, black folder with white paper corners sticking out of it.

"So you found time to draw something for me?" Rachael said, turning back toward the stove to stir the pasta.

"Trace and I commandeered the Idea Couches this afternoon and worked on some sketches. Well, I worked on mine. Tracer snoozed half the time. He did a couple, though. He was moody today."

Rachael glanced over toward the others. Trace was talking to Sidney and Brick and leaning down to pick up McKenna. "That's probably my fault," she said quietly so only Fig could hear.

"Yeah. He told me about where you went yesterday. And the creepy thing with the house that's not there."

Rachael had been stirring the carbonara sauce but she looked up at Fig when he said this. There was no mocking tone to his voice. None at all.

"You don't seem shocked to hear a non-existent house was trying to tell me something," she said.

Fig smiled. "That's because I know you don't think it was an invisible house talking to you. You think it was God."

Rachael turned back to the stove. "And you don't find that a little odd either?"

"Well, no. Not coming from you. I think God still talks to people. Why do you think I'm doing Joan of Arc on spec? Some days I wish I didn't have someone interested in her."

Rachael turned the heat off the creamy sauce. "Thanks, Fig," she said.

"No problem."

Rachael grabbed the pot of angel hair and carried it to the sink. "Actually, it *is* kind of a problem."

"For you?"

"For Trace," Rachael whispered, as she poured the contents of the pot into a footed colander sitting in the sink.

She and Fig both looked over at her husband. Trace was still chatting with Sidney and Brick and was completely unaware of the conversation in the kitchen. "He just loves you, Kumquat," Fig said softly. "He doesn't like it when stuff happens to you that doesn't also happen to him. It's that whole they-shall-be-one-flesh thing. He told me that today."

Rachael picked up the colander by its handles and shook it. Her eyes were on Trace across the room. "Then I'll have to do a better job of making him feel like he's a part of this," she said.

"Part of what?" Fig said.

"This keeps happening to me, Fig. I keep having these hunches about things. It started when McKenna was born. I had them when we were all trying to figure out what had really happened to Josh, and I've been having more of them since we moved back to Minneapolis. The one I had yesterday was the strongest one yet. Something happened at that house, Fig. It was a long time ago, I know. But it happened."

She grabbed an oversized serving bowl and slid the pasta into it.

"Trace said you want us to draw that house tonight," Fig said, cautiously.

"I do."

"Do you even know what it looks like?"

She reached for the pan of carbonara sauce and began to ladle giant spoonfuls onto the steaming pasta. "Actually, I do."

Rachael convinced Fig to leave the sketches until after dinner had been enjoyed and McKenna put to bed. He was fairly bursting with anticipation when Rachael came back down the stairs after laying McKenna in her crib.

"Let's lay them all out on the countertop like we did with Josh's drawings," he said as he sprang from the couch and grabbed his mini-portfolio.

"I only had time to do one," Sidney confessed. "I had a busy week."

"*You* had a busy week!" Brick exclaimed. "I had an art show at the school. It was crazy. I did my sketch on the john this morning with the only free ten minutes I've had all week."

"Okay, okay, enough about *that*," Fig scolded. "I really only have one decent drawing. Give yours to me."

Fig reached out his hands to Brick and Sidney and took their drawings. He placed them on the granite countertop and put his own and Trace's next to them.

"Interesting," he said as he laid them all out.

"You're cheating," Sid interjected, rising from the couch to stand next to Fig.

"I'm not cheating. I only said they were interesting."

"I don't think anyone should say anything until Rachael looks at them," Brick said, walking over to the counter as well.

"All right, all right. I shall be silent. Come, Kumquat."

Rachael began to walk over to the open kitchen, mentally preparing herself for troubling images of how Bucky might have died.

"Now, we e-mailed each other on Tuesday so that we all wouldn't pick the same cause of death," Fig said as she walked. "We decided we couldn't sketch a bad fall or a severe blow to the head, 'cause, you know, that would've shown up in the bones."

"And they wouldn't let me draw a gunshot wound because the Monday morning quarterbacks here said it would've been too hard for the bullet to miss a bone." Brick sounded a bit annoyed.

"And no rat poison either," Sidney said. Rachael couldn't tell if he was joking. "Hard to get someone to accidentally ingest it."

"We figured it had to be something a shunned teenager or angry, normally-law-abiding-parent could pull off," Trace added.

Rachael closed the distance to the counter.

Sidney's was first.

It was a simple cartoon. A bloated teenager with a swollen neck was lying on the ground gasping for breath. Around him lay Planter's Peanut wrappers and assorted mushrooms. Flying around his head were fat

bumblebees with sinister faces. Another teen—a gawky, skinny boy—
was standing at the swollen boy's side, eyes wide in surprise. He held a
slide rule in one hand as if to strike the gasping teen.

Rachael looked up at Sidney. "Anaphylactic shock?" she said.

"Told you she'd get it," Trace said to Sidney.

Sidney shrugged. "It's perfect. Any of those wimpy kids could have
watched him asphyxiate and not run for help. No marks. No premedi-
tation. He was going to bean him with the slide rule, but then he didn't
have to. It works."

Rachael nodded but in her head she was hearing the words *It wasn't
supposed to happen...* She doubted a fatal reaction to a bee sting or mushrooms claimed Bucky's life. There would be no culpability on the part of
one of the kids. It had to be something else.

She moved onto the next drawing. Brick's. In his typical exaggerated
fashion he had drawn with brown and gray chalk a wildly out-of-propor-
tion Bucky lying with a hunting knife stuck to the hilt in his chest.

"A knife?" she said.

"To the heart. Slicing in between the bones of the rib cage. No trace
of entry. Quick bleed out," Brick answered.

Sid leaned over the drawing. "You know, that's not much of an accident, Brick."

"It is if you meant only to threaten the thug and he lunged at you and
you thrust it at him to protect yourself," Brick replied quickly.

"That might be seen as self-defense," Trace suggested.

"If you're bold enough to confront someone—even a weasel like that
kid—with a knife in your hand and he ends up dead I doubt your first
reaction would be, 'I'll get off with self-defense!' Not hardly," Brick huffed.
"You need to watch CSI more, Trace. And anyway, you guys made me
draw the knife. It's far more likely Bucky was threatened with a gun.
Nobody but gang members and bad actors in B horror movies threaten
people with knives. Like these little victims were gang members. Don't
make me laugh."

"Artists have thin skin," Fig whispered to Rachael. "Sometimes you
can see Brick's entire circulatory system through his flesh!"

Rachael smiled and moved to Fig's drawing. Bucky lay on a field
of grass. A bottle of Dr Pepper lay spilled at his feet. And a creamy-

brown prescription bottle. Fig immediately sidled up to her. "Here's how it could've happened. See, Bucky had threatened one of those kids with some kind of payback for snitching on him. Like maybe he said, 'Friday at four-thirty, you're dead meat!' And so our anguished victim thought up a hasty plan. They went into their parents' medicine cabinet and got the sleeping pills. Then he or she dissolved way more than was safe into a Dr Pepper. They lured Bucky to the woods on pretense of a peace offering. A truce. They figured Bucky would go along with it only to trounce them at the last moment 'cause he likes doing stuff like that. But if he drank the Dr Pepper, he'd be snoozing when four-thirty rolled around and the victim would be somewhere else, safe. But after Bucky drank the Dr Pepper, he collapsed and his eyes rolled back in his head. He stopped breathing. By the time our killer realized they'd put too many pills in the drink, it was too late. They got scared. Decided to bury the body right there. Convincing, uh?"

"Why wouldn't they've just called their parents or run to a neighbor's house at four-thirty? Or hid?" Brick asked. "I mean, if this person was just going to drug Bucky, well, he'd wake up eventually, be really ticked off and then really let them have it."

"It's obvious you were never bullied, Brick," Fig retorted. "You don't just *run* to a neighbor's house."

"No, indeed. You put Sominex in the creep's soda. That makes a lot of sense," said Brick dramatically.

"It's called moment-to-moment survival, Brick," Fig exclaimed. "You don't stop to think about what the bully might do tomorrow. You only think about how to survive today."

"He's actually got a point there," Sid interjected. "By the time you're this desperate, you just want to get through one more day."

"I suppose some kind of drug could explain how someone like April might have done it," Rachael said politely, though she seriously doubted Bucky had been drugged.

"You know, he could've been electrocuted," Fig suggested. "I tried to think how he could've been and well, I couldn't come up with anything. I'm not too imaginative when it comes to appliances."

Rachael moved on to Trace's drawings, a series of three scenes. In the first, a rough-looking teen—Bucky—was putting food in his mouth while another teen, shorter and slender—Drew, perhaps?—stood by him. In the second, Bucky was obviously choking while Drew stood gaping in surprise. In the third, Bucky was lying at Drew's feet. Bucky's eyes were wide with panic and his hands were tight around his throat as if to push the food out of his windpipe with his own meaty fists. Drew stood next to him.

Drew wasn't looking around for help.

He wasn't pounding Bucky on the back to dislodge the food.

He wasn't kneeling down in panic, wondering what he could do to help.

He was just standing there watching.

Rachael studied Trace's sketches for several long minutes, absorbing the images. Testing them, tasting them.

"Of course, Trace wins again." Brick mumbled, throwing up his hands and walking back to the couches.

"Trace always wins," Sidney muttered and he sauntered off to the fridge, opened it and began to study its contents.

"I didn't say he *won*," Rachael replied. "It's just the way the shorter kid is just standing there. Watching."

"He didn't plan to teach Bucky a lesson," Trace said to her. "It just came to him all of a sudden while he watched Bucky gasp for breath. He thought to himself, 'I could just stand here and watch Bucky struggle and maybe say something like, "See, Bucky? This is what's it's like to feel helpless, like you're dying inside."' He had planned to get help at the last minute but he waited too long."

"Why bury the body then? It's not his fault the kid choked," Sid said.

"But he felt like it was. And he wasn't an adult who could think things through. He was a kid who was messed up."

Rachael said nothing, but continued to gaze at the image of the teen standing there, whispering to Bucky as he fought for air, "See, Bucky? This is what's it's like to feel helpless, like you're dying inside."

"You don't have to say Trace won, Kumquat. We can tell you like his best. But that's okay." Fig said. "Besides I like drawing houses. I want to draw the house." Fig pulled out blank pieces of paper from his portfolio and set them on the counter.

"What house?" Sid said looking away from the fridge.

"Rachael wants us to draw a house," Fig said, pulling pencils and pens out of his shirt pocket.

"I just drew her a kid!" Sid yelled. "And she didn't like it."

"I didn't say I didn't like it, Sid," Rachael countered. "I suppose it's possible Bucky was allergic to peanuts."

"Yeah, and he just forgot when one of the skinny kids he liked to torture gave some to him," Brick said derisively.

"The peanuts and mushrooms were the comedic elements," Sid retorted hotly. "I'm a cartoonist! The bee sting, on the other hand, is perfectly plausible, Brick-head."

"Cut it out you guys. This is serious. Rachael needs us to draw a house." Fig said, frowning.

Sid closed the fridge door without taking anything and turned around to face Fig. "Whose house? What's a house got to do with any of this?"

"Well, the thing is, I'm not sure exactly whose house it is. Was," Rachael replied.

"Was?" Brick said from the couches.

"The house doesn't exist anymore. It burned down a long time ago," Trace replied, casting a look of support Rachael's way.

"So why draw it?" Sid's tone was more cynical than curious.

"Because I…. Because something…" Rachael could not finish. She looked to Trace.

"Because like it or not, Rachael can sense things the rest of us can't," Trace said, looking at her before turning to Sid. "Something happened at a house that burned down. It involved these kids. She just wants to be able to visualize the house. It'll help her. It helped her the last time we drew something that we weren't sure was even there. And you're her friends and she shouldn't have to explain everything."

"Well said, Tracer," Fig announced. "No wonder she likes you best. Gather 'round, Picassos. We've got a job to do."

Brick and Sidney walked back to the counter and Fig tossed a few pencils their way.

Across the counter, Rachael mouthed the words "thank you" to her husband.

Trace winked once and picked up a pencil.

THIRTEEN

It was well after midnight when the sketch of the house was complete. In the end Fig drew it alone—with copious advice and input from the others—as Brick's impressionistic flair and Sid's penchant for cartoonizing everything wasn't getting the job done. Trace begged off by saying his forte was the anatomy of the human body, not architecture. Rachael knew he deferred to Fig because Fig enjoyed doing it so much.

Rachael felt like a witness describing a perpetrator to a forensic artist as she fed the particulars to Fig. Some details she knew were true, some she could only imagine. *One and a half-stories. Peeling white paint with faded green trim. Three, half-circle stairs to the front door. Four-paned front room window. One car-garage, door slightly off track. Kitchen window to the right of the front door, boarded. Narrow chimney. Former flowerbeds overgrown with weeds. Cracked pathway to the front door. Forlorn. Empty. Unappealing.*

The more the details came together, the more uneasy Rachael became. Not because Fig wasn't getting it right, but because she was sure he was. Mostly. When he was finished, she knew there was something not quite right about the way she had described the house. But the hour was late, she was tired and she couldn't think what it was.

"I'd set fire to that if I had to live next door to it," Sid announced when Fig laid his sketching tools down. "That's the kind of eyesore that'll drop your property value quicker than action figures sink in a toilet."

That comment drew looks from everyone.

"Braden tossed some soldiers into the commode. They sink."

"So is that what it looked like?" Trace said, changing the subject and turning to his wife.

"I think so. I'm not sure, really. The lady who described it to me said it was similar to a house across the street. I think we've got it. I'm just… I don't know. It's close, I think. Thanks, Fig. And thanks everyone else, too. I mean it. I'm really grateful."

"Anytime, Kumquat," Fig replied. "Now then. Let's watch a movie. A B horror movie where a lousy actor threatens someone with a knife!"

Brick tossed a crumpled piece of art paper at Fig from one of Fig's first tries at the house.

"You guys go ahead. I'm going to bed." Rachael gathered the drawings of Bucky and the house. Trace leaned over and kissed her neck.

"Put those away when you get upstairs, Rach. Don't fall asleep with that on your mind. Okay?" Trace nodded toward the drawings. His voice was tender but authoritative.

"Okay," she whispered. "See ya, fellas," she said to the others.

Sid, Fig and Brick wished her a good night.

Rachael climbed the stairs, peeked in on McKenna and then headed to the master bedroom. She put the drawings on her dresser, fully intending to leave them there until morning.

But when her pajamas were on, her teeth brushed and face washed, and as she sat propped up in bed with a magazine, her eyes kept traveling to the drawings. She slipped out of bed, walked over to the dresser and reached for them. Rachael walked slowly back to the bed as she leafed through the sketches. There were any number of ways to get killed without crushing so much as the littlest bone. But in reality, she knew that the body really needs just three things to stay alive: air, a beating heart and blood. Bucky had been denied one of those things. Accidentally, somehow. How could one of his victims have played a part in depriving Bucky of one of those three things, to such an extent that he or she felt responsible? Culpable? Compelled to bury the body and pretend nothing happened?

She turned to the sketch of the house. It was a fairly good sketch, she thought. Good enough to evoke some troubling feelings within her. But something wasn't quite right. She laid her head back on the pillow and tried to think what it was that niggled at her....

Rachael awoke with a start. Her eyes snapped open. Morning sunlight peeked through the blinds and challenged her laziness.

Her waking thought was that she suddenly knew what was missing from the sketch of the house.

A storm cellar.

Angled doors, facing the sky.

Around the side of the house.

Accessible only from the outside.

Rachael bolted up in bed expecting to see the drawings all round her body. She felt all around the covers. They were not there. She turned to look at Trace next to her; he had one eye open.

"They're on the table by the window," he said groggily.

She looked past him to the cherrywood table under the south windows. A little pile of papers rested there.

"Trace," she said, leaning down to him.

"Mmmm."

"I figured out what's missing in the sketch of the house."

Trace closed the open eye. "I didn't realize anything was missing."

"There is! I just couldn't remember it last night. It's a storm cellar. You know, the old-fashioned kind outside a house with the wooden doors? Like Auntie Em's in *The Wizard of Oz*."

"Okay. So?"

"So it needs to be there. You can draw it in for me, can't you? The drawing's not right without it."

"Rachael. It's Saturday. Can't you let this rest for the weekend? Please?"

Rachael swallowed her initial answer, which was "No, I can't let this rest!" Trace was right. The weekend belonged to her family. And to herself. But the storm cellar was crucial somehow. She didn't know why. "If you draw it in for me at breakfast, I promise I'll put all the drawings away until Monday."

"You promise?"

"So help me God," she said, in mock-courtroom fashion.

Trace reached for her and she cuddled into his arms. "I don't usually do storm cellars," he said, kissing her forehead.

"I don't usually ask you to."

An hour later, after McKenna had eaten a bowl of Cream of Wheat, and after Trace and Rachael had drained a pot of coffee, Trace held his hand out for Fig's drawing of the house. Rachael handed it to him.

"Which side of the house?" he said, pulling a pencil out from behind his earringed right ear.

"Left side. The doors sit at an angle, like maybe thirty degrees. They had been green once. But the paint was chipped and faded."

"Shall I draw a lock on these doors?" Trace said as he began to erase some of the grass Fig had drawn.

A queer shiver ran through Rachael's body.

There had been a lock at one time. But it had rusted and broken off.

"Rachael?"

She shook away the strange, unaccounted for thought. "Um. No. No lock."

Trace didn't seem to notice her mental stutter-step. He penciled in the cement frame, the wood doors, the metal handles.

"Want to hand me that?" He pointed to the dark green pastel Fig had used the previous night to trim the dilapidated house.

Rachael wordlessly handed Trace the colored chalk and watched as the doors took on life and dimension.

Trace set the chalk down. "There."

Rachael reached for the drawing.

Something stirred within her as she looked at what Trace had added. The cellar completed the image somehow. Made it accurate. Made it a place where something of note had happened. She wanted to say, "That's it!" But she knew Trace really didn't want to hear it.

And she wasn't even sure why she felt that way about the drawing. The house no longer existed. And neither did the storm cellar.

Monday found Rachael scurrying to prepare for Tuesday's court appearances. She wanted to check in with Will when she first arrived that morning but it was after two o'clock in the afternoon before she had a chance to call the detective and see if there were new developments in the investigation.

"Rachael, we do have other homicides to work on," he said when she finally got through to him. "If this didn't involve you I would have long since passed it off to the cold case team. No one here is burning any midnight oil when we've got drive-by shootings nearly every week and stabbings in the park and you don't want to hear the rest."

"So does that mean you've learned nothing since I talked to you last week? You haven't talked to anyone?"

"I didn't say that."

"Will!"

"Samantha's chatted with Drew Downing's parents and Santos Valasquez's mother on Friday."

"And?"

"And Dad Downing is still a potential suspect as far as I'm concerned."

"Really? What did he say?"

"Samantha said he is still quite angry over the lack of support he got from the school when it came to Randall Buckett. He said everyone knew Bucky preyed on vulnerable kids. All the teachers knew it. All the administrators knew it."

"Well, did they?"

"Samantha told Mr. Downing there are only a handful of bullying incidences listed in Bucky's records. And Mr. Downing said, and I quote: 'I can close my eyes and not see you but that doesn't mean I don't know you are sitting in my living room at this very moment.' End quote."

"So he thinks the school turned a blind eye to Bucky's abuse?"

"You could say that. He said he knows Bucky was actually caught inflicting physical pain only a half-dozen times but that it was no big secret that Bucky lobbed plenty of verbal and mental abuse with only a wrist-slapping now and then."

"So why did he drop those charges, then?"

"You already guessed why, Rachael. Drew begged him to. Drew didn't want to be in a courtroom testifying against Bucky. Especially not with his stuttering problem. Lyle Downing said it was against his better judgment that he dropped the charges. He did it for Drew's sake only."

"If the bullying had been going on for so long, why did Mr. Downing wait until Drew was attacked at school to do something about it? I mean, the abuse at school was one thing, but some of this happened at home, Will. Drew lived next door to Bucky, for heaven's sake. This can't be all the school's fault."

"No, it's not all the school's fault. Samantha asked him if he ever tried to talk with Bucky's parents. Lyle said nothing he said ever made any difference. And Drew didn't like it when Lyle or his mother intervened for him. Lyle enrolled Drew in karate when he was twelve to give him some confidence in defending himself against Bucky."

"And?"

"And he said Drew hated it. Lyle let him withdraw after a year."

"What did Glennis Downing say this whole time?" Rachael said.

"She was quiet for most of the interview, Sam said. She interjected a comment here or there, but she deferred most of the questions to Lyle. Sam said he clearly had the lion's share of the anger. Which makes him somewhat of a suspect and somewhat not."

"Somewhat because if he were the letter-writer, he would've toned down his anger?"

"Yep. But it's possible he may have killed Bucky and someone else wrote the letter. Someone who knows what he did."

"Like Drew?"

"Or Glennis.

Rachael thought for a moment. What Will was saying made sense. Perhaps she had jumped to the wrong conclusion. Perhaps it was one of the children, now an adult, who wrote the letter, but it hadn't been one of the children that caused Bucky's death.

"Samantha asked about Drew's sisters, but I'm not very inclined to believe they are involved with this," Will continued. "They were seven and five when Bucky disappeared. Lyle and Glennis both said they didn't think their girls were aware of how dangerous the kid next door was. At least the girls never talked about him. They stayed out of his way, like every other kid did who wasn't a target."

"So is Sam planning on talking to Drew, then?"

"Actually I'm clearing my schedule to do that. Hopefully by the end of the week.

"Okay. So Sam talked to Santos's mom, too?"

"Yesterday. Sam said Marisol Valasquez wasn't the angry parent that Lyle Downing was, but that she appeared plenty unnerved by Sam's visit. Could just be that she's the kind of person who gets anxious around cops or it could be that she's afraid Santos is a suspect. She didn't share a whole lot. Santos's dad died a few years back, so it was just her that Sam talked to."

"So does she think the school should've done more, too?" Rachael asked.

"Sam said she got the impression Marisol blames Bucky's mother and stepfather more than the school, that they should've been taken to task for how Bucky liked to get his kicks."

"And who should've taken them to task?"

"Marisol said the police should've hauled Bucky off to a juvenile detention center long before he disappeared. She said that if a Latino boy did what Bucky did, he'd be kicked out of school and removed from his home."

"So why did she drop those charges when she finally called the police?" Rachael asked.

"Because, she said, Bucky's parents were planning to file counter charges. Santos threw the first punch, remember? Santos told her to just let it go. They wouldn't win and it would just make matters worse for him. So she dropped them."

Rachael tapped a pencil on her desk. Motives seemed to be springing up everywhere. "Will, did Samantha ask the Downings and Marisol if they thought their sons were desperate enough to try and threaten Bucky somehow? Or did they seem shaken after Bucky disappeared?"

"Both sets of parents vehemently reminded Samantha that their sons were victims, not perpetrators. And that their sons were noticeably relieved when Bucky ran away. As were they."

"So when are you going to try and meet with Santos?"

"I want to talk with both him and his sister next week sometime. I'm going to try and chat with April Madden, too."

Rachael paused for a moment as the wealth of new information settled in her mind. The more she learned about what Bucky had been like, the more she was convinced that someone had planned a retaliation that went horribly awry. It wasn't a bee sting or choking on a jawbreaker or a spiked Dr Pepper that killed Bucky. Brick's drawing of the knife was starting to edge out past the others as the most plausible and yet she couldn't picture any of the people Will and Sam had interviewed stabbing someone.

"Will, do you have any idea how Bucky died?" she asked.

"Nothing conclusive, Rachael. There's nothing indicative in the pH levels of the surrounding soil, no broken bones, no skull fractures—we just don't know."

"What's your gut feeling?"

"To be honest, most spur-of-the-moment murders are committed with a gun, at least in my experience. And I say 'spur of the moment' because the writer made it clear Bucky wasn't supposed to end up dead. I don't think it was premeditated."

"And do you really think it was a gun? I mean, wouldn't a bullet have hit a bone, at least grazed it?"

"A bullet can miss a bone and still be fatal. Besides, that skeleton has been in the ground for a quarter of a decade. The bones were in good shape, but not perfect. It's not conclusive that he was shot, but it's also not conclusive that he wasn't."

If only thin-skinned Brick could hear this, Rachael thought. She wondered if she should tell him the next time she saw him. She decided to ask Will one more question before letting him get back to work.

"Will, I had Fig draw the house that burned down, at least as it might've looked based on what Carol Bielke told me," she volunteered. "I'd like to bring it over this week sometime. You might want to, you know, familiarize yourself with it. I really think you need to ask Drew, Santos and April if anything happened at that house."

Will was silent for a moment. "You can bring it by, Rachael. I'll look at it. And I assume you're not giving details to Fig that would jeopardize this case?"

"I'm being very careful, Will. It just helps me sort things out if I can visualize them."

"May I remind you that you're under no obligation to sort this out?"

Rachael smiled. "So you've told me."

As she said this, her assistant Kate poked her head into Rachael's office. "Trace is on line two. He says it's important."

"I'll let you go, Will. Trace is on another line," she said.

"Okay. I'll see you later in the week, then."

"Bye." She pressed the flashing button on her desk phone. "Hey Trace. What's up? Is McKenna okay?"

"McKenna's fine," said Trace on the other end of the phone. Rachael sensed that his tone was one of irritation. "Your mother has her out in the stroller. I called because I just got the mail."

Rachael's breath tightened. "Yes?" she said.

"You got another one."

FOURTEEN

The third letter looked exactly like the first two: unsigned, plainly typed and sent from St. Paul's main post office.

Rachael allowed Will to examine the envelope before she ran her fingernail under its partially sealed flap. He had wanted to open it himself, and had actually requested Trace bring the letter down to the station when Rachael immediately called Will back and told him a third letter had arrived. But Rachael told him if he wanted to meet her at her place, then he could be there when she opened it.

"It's addressed to me, Will," she had said.

"It's evidence."

"It's a letter."

He had acquiesced.

Now Will sat across from Rachael in her loft. Trace sat next to Rachael and Eva Harper paced back and forth in the open living room with a refusing-to-nap McKenna in her arms.

Rachael drew out the folded single sheet of paper. She read the typed words aloud:

Dear Mrs. Flynn:

Things are beginning to get complicated. I'm uncertain what I should do. This is all very confusing for me. I need to meet with you. I need to talk to someone who'll understand. Meet me at the Starbucks on Grand Avenue in St. Paul this Wednesday at four o'clock. Pick a table outside. I'll wear a red shirt.

I know what you look like.

Please don't tell anyone. Come alone. I need your help. The police won't understand. Please.

Trace bolted forward in his seat. "No way. No. Way!" he said firmly. "You're not meeting this person."

"Oh my goodness. Oh my goodness," Eva muttered as her pacing speed intensified.

Rachael silently read the letter again. She felt no fear, no exhilaration, no intense emotional charge. Just a sense that she was ready. She looked up at Will sitting across from her. His eyes betrayed nothing. He reached for the note and she handed it to him.

"Rachael, this is not your problem," Trace said, leaning toward her now and seeking her eyes with his own.

"He's right. It's not your problem," Will echoed. Rachael turned toward him and saw that he was looking at the note, not at her.

"Are you saying you don't want me do this?" she said to Will. This was a huge break in the case. Huge. She couldn't believe he would so easily discount it.

"I'm saying it's not your problem," Will replied, looking up at her. He reached his hand out again. It took Rachael a second to realize he was waiting for her to give him the envelope.

"But we could solve this thing in a moment if I met with this person," Rachael said, as she handed it to him.

"It's not your responsibility to solve crimes." Trace's voice was controlled but forceful. "It's his." He tossed this comment Will's direction.

Rachael turned to her husband. "I know it's not my responsibility, Trace. Believe me, I do. But you can't say I haven't been given an opportunity to help solve one. I know I don't have to do this." She turned now toward Will. "But I want to."

Will said nothing. His eyes, though, were communicating approval; she was sure of that.

"Rachael, it's just not safe," her mother chimed in from across the room. "What if this person is a serial killer? Or completely nuts?"

"Mom, please."

"Well! What if he is?"

"Mom, I don't think for a moment this person wants to harm me. I think…"

But Trace cut her off. "You don't know anything about this person, Rachael. He may not be a serial killer, but you don't know what he's really after!"

"I think this person knows that Will and Sam are getting close. I think it's someone in the circle of people they are interviewing or will interview. They're looking for someone to hear their side of what happened. Someone who will understand."

"And *then* what?" Trace said. "They tell you how it really happened and you're supposed to say, 'Oh, you poor thing!' and then you just leave and tell Will nothing? Does this person think you're not going to go to the cops with what they tell you?"

"I think they already know they're going to be found out and they just don't want to wait until Will is at their house with handcuffs. I think they want to confess."

Trace sighed and turned to Will. "What is she supposed to do with this?"

Will paused for a moment before answering. He leaned forward and cleared his throat. "Rachael is under no obligation to anyone to meet with this person. But if she chooses to, she will be under police protection the whole time."

"Will!" Rachael interjected.

"The whole time, Rachael. There's no way I will let you keep that appointment without an undercover cop in the restaurant and you wired. No way."

Trace sat back on the couch, looking somewhat vindicated. But his eyes still danced with anger.

"But don't you think they'll somehow know if the police are involved?" Rachael asked.

"If they recognize my undercover cop and somehow pick up on the fact that you are wired, then this person is no innocent vigilante whose plans somehow got screwed up."

"I want to go with her," Trace announced.

"Trace, there's no point in me going if you're sitting there with me," Rachael said gently. "They won't stay one second if they see that I'm not sitting alone. Besides, you were in that picture with me when the *Star Tribune* did that story after Josh's second confession. They know what you look like, too."

"I am *not* just going to sit at the studio while you do this!" Trace exclaimed.

"You can sit with me across the street, Trace," Will offered. "I can't be seen either. I've already met with some of the people on the list. You and I can watch from the Café Latte across the street. It's nothing but windows on the second floor. We'll be able to see everything."

"But you'll stay back from the windows, right?" Rachael said anxiously.

"Believe me, Rachael, I've done this before," Will stood. "I need to set this up. Please don't mention this to anyone. Eva, that includes you. The less who know about this the better."

Rachael and Trace stood, too. "Thanks for letting me do this, Will," Rachael said.

Will pocketed the letter. "You can always change your mind. Even at the last minute you can change your mind."

"But you do want me to do this, don't you, Will?" she asked, needing to hear his affirmation.

Will glanced at Trace before turning his head back to her. "Yeah. I do."

The door closed behind Will and Rachael turned toward Trace. "It's going to be okay, Trace," she said. "Will won't let anything happen to me."

Trace looked away from her. "That's my job," he said quietly and he grabbed his studio keys and followed Will out the door.

Tuesday's court cases kept Rachael distracted and occupied until after four. At four-thirty Will arrived at her office to go over the procedure for the following day. When Will walked in with a man she'd never met before she began to feel nervous for the first time since reading the note 24 hours earlier. But not in a bad way. Will held a tiny pouch in his right hand.

"Rachael, this is Detective Ted Purlman," Will said. "He's a cold case guy, so this is right up his alley."

Rachael stood and shook the other detective's hand. Ted looked fifty-ish, with a graying goatee and rimless glasses. His handshake was firm, his smile warm and genuine.

"Nice to meet you, Rachael."

"Please sit down," Rachael said, motioning to the two chairs in front of her desk.

"Ted's going to arrive at Starbucks before you," Will began, as he took a seat. "He's bringing props that will make him look like he's a professor from St. Thomas or Hamline grading term papers. It won't seem odd that he stays longer than the average time someone takes to sip a mocha."

"Okay," Rachael said.

"The tables outside that Starbucks are like this," Will said, and he picked up a pen from her desk and grabbed one of her yellow legal pads. He drew a series of rectangular tables. "The manager has been apprised of what's taking place at the coffee shop but no one else has. He's going to work with us to make sure you're able to sit at a table directly behind Ted, like this, so that our letter writer will be forced to sit with his back to Ted. Okay?"

"All right."

"You're going to drive your car from your office to Grand Aveue and park just like you would if you were just going shopping. A plain-clothes cop in an unmarked car is going to be following you to make sure you get there. When you get to Starbucks, Ted will already be in place. Don't approach him. Don't look at him. He's not going to be looking at you. Don't look for the person in the red shirt. Go into the coffee shop and buy whatever it is you would normally buy. Cup of coffee, cappuccino, mocha, whatever. Take it outside and sit at this table behind Ted. Let the person in red come to *you*. Place your purse on the cement by your feet, all right?"

"Okay."

Will opened the pouch and poured out onto her desk a flesh-colored, pea-sized piece of plastic and a tiny jeweled brooch the shape of a dragonfly. Will picked up the flesh-colored object.

"This is your earpiece," Will said, handing it to her. "It fits inside your ear and is practically unnoticeable. Just wear your hair like you normally do. Put it in your ear before you leave the loft, okay? Try very hard not to fiddle with it, Rachael. Just put it in and forget about it. You won't hear anything until you're on Grand. When we know you've parked, we'll make radio contact with you. You will hear my voice. I will be in the restaurant directly across the street. Do you know the Café Latte?"

"Yes. I've eaten there."

"I'll be with you the whole time and I will be able to hear what you hear with this." He picked up the brooch and handed it to her. "This is a transmitter. The signal from this will be picked up by a service van that will be parked across the street. I'll get relayed the signal up in the Café."

"A service van?" Rachael said.

"It will be a dummy vehicle. It will look like a commercial van, but it will be ours."

Rachael fingered the brooch. "So I just wear this on my blouse?"

"That's right," Will replied. "The on/off switch is on its belly. Just flip it before you pin it on. In fact, we're ready to give it a try right now so you can see how it works. Go ahead and flip the switch, pin it on and slip the ear piece inside your ear."

Rachael placed the pea-sized earpiece in her left ear. It felt strange and foreign. Then she turned the brooch over and flipped the tiny black switch. A miniscule red light began to shine. She turned it over and pinned it onto her suit jacket.

"Okay, why don't you ask Samantha if she likes sauerkraut?" Will said.

"What?" Rachael said, grinning.

"Ask Sam if she likes sauerkraut."

"Is she listening?"

"Why don't you find out?"

Rachael smiled and she spoke. "Samantha, do you like sauerkraut?"

In her ear a voice replied. "Only when I'm out of real bug repellant."

"So where are you?" Rachael said.

"In the parking lot. In Will's car," said Samantha's voice in her ear.

"Pretty cool," Rachael said, looking down at the brooch.

"This thing's really sensitive, Rachael, so you don't have to speak up. It's mainly so we can hear what your date says. Okay?"

Rachael cringed at the word 'date.' "All right."

"Okay then. I'm going to switch off and come inside."

"Okay. Thanks, Sam."

The earpiece went dead and Rachael carefully removed it from her ear.

Will handed her the little pouch. Rachael slipped the earpiece inside. She removed the brooch, turned the power off and slipped that inside as well.

"Any questions?" Will said.

Rachael fingered the pouch. "What should I say, Will?"

"I really think you're going do fine in that respect, Rachael. But if there's a lull and it seems like the conversation is going nowhere, I will prompt you with a question. We'll also have a hostage negotiator in the service van. He might pipe in with a few conversation starters, too."

"A negotiator?" Rachael didn't want to say the word "hostage."

"They're good at asking questions."

"So I suppose you'll be taping the whole thing."

"Yes."

"And if he or she confesses to me, you'll arrest them on the spot."

"Rachael."

"Can you at least wait until I've started to walk away? Please don't do it when I'm sitting there across from them. Please?"

"I don't know if…" Will began.

"Please, Will. Unless I give you the go-ahead. Please don't do it with me sitting there if they say they aren't ready to go the police yet. If they do confess, let me try to get them to the point where they're ready. Please don't rush in. Let me try to get them to invite you in. Please?"

Will looked to Ted. Ted shrugged.

"Okay." Will said, turning back to Rachael.

"Thanks," Rachael said, relief flowing through her.

"One more thing, Rachael," said Will, and his voice took on a serious tone. "If at anytime you feel you're in danger—if you see a weapon or are passed a threatening note or if you know that something has gone wrong and you're not clear that we can tell—you are to say the word 'tissue.' Okay?"

Rachael blinked. "Tissue?"

"Yes. You say 'tissue.' When he or she says something like, 'What did you say?' you just respond with, 'I need a tissue.' Then you reach down as if to get a tissue from your purse. And you stay down. Okay?"

Rachael felt her pulse quicken a bit. It really had not occurred to her that she would be in any danger. She didn't believe she was.

"Okay, Rachael?" said Will firmly.

"Yes," she replied. "I understand."

FIFTEEN

The loft was quiet when Rachael arrived home that evening; not a huge surprise. Trace and Fig often stayed at the studio on Tuesdays with McKenna until Rachael got home from the courthouse. She changed out of her Evan Piccone suit and into denim capris and a cotton blouse, and then went into the kitchen to grab a bottle of water before heading over to the studio.

Her hand froze on the refrigerator door, however, as her eyes settled on a drawing taped there. Fig had left her a note to tell her where they were. The note was a drawing of Fig, Trace and McKenna coming out of an upscale hair salon with shaved heads. The trio was smiling broadly and the balloon McKenna held in her hand suggested it was actually a quartet of hairless skulls smiling back at her.

"Oh no!" Rachael breathed.

She had no idea if Fig was being playful or truthful. She never could tell with him.

"Trace, tell me you didn't," she said to the inked sketch of her husband. The water forgotten, Rachael turned from the kitchen and headed for the living room to pace until Trace and Fig returned from wherever they had gone with McKenna.

Fifteen minutes later, the lock turned in the front door and Trace and Fig walked in, both laughing—and both bald. McKenna was in Trace's arms, a pink sunbonnet on her head.

Rachael ran to them and snatched the bonnet off as Fig greeted her with a hearty hello.

McKenna's silky, honey-blonde curls were still there.

"Ha! We got you!" Fig said joyfully, closing the door behind them.

Rachael looked up into Trace's eyes, which seemed bigger now that there was nothing on his forehead and cranium but skin. "You and Fig get a little bored, today?" she said softly, still unable to fully comprehend what he and Fig had done.

"Actually, Fig has wanted to shave his head for a long time," Trace answered quickly. "Haven't you, Fig Newton?"

"Indeed I have, Kumquat," Fig replied, plopping into one of the oversized chairs in the living room. "It's quite freeing, you know. I feel very transparent. Don't you feel transparent, Tracer?"

"Transparent's a good word," Trace said, handing McKenna to Rachael.

"So you just decided to shave your head because Fig wanted to shave his head?" Rachael said, trying not to sound like a lawyer.

"It's my head," Trace replied, and he leaned over and kissed her cheek. He began to walk toward the kitchen. "I vote for kebabs on the hibachi. What do you say, Fig? Think it's too windy on the roof for charcoal?"

"Nah, it's just right," Fig responded. "Just enough breeze to keep the coals wickedly happy. I've some lovely prawns I could defrost. And some Portobello mushrooms. Do you have any green peppers and Bermuda onions?"

Trace turned to Rachael. "Do we, darling? Do we have any green peppers and Bermuda onions?"

Rachael was still standing near the door with McKenna in her arms, still processing the notion that the only hair Trace had on his head were his eyebrows. "Um. Red. We have red peppers."

"Just red," Trace said to Fig, as if Fig hadn't heard.

"Well, green would look better. I'll go see what I've got." Fig stood and walked to the door. "Rachael, it's quite the fashionable thing to do, you know. Trace has a nicely shaped head. Simone said so."

"Simone?" Rachael said, looking at Fig's skull and unable not to gawk at the vastness of it.

"My hairdresser."

"Except now you have no hair to dress," Rachael said coolly.

Fig roared with laughter. "Nice one, Kumquat. I'll be back. Don't get in a big fight while I'm gone, you two. Wait until I get back."

Fig opened the door, sailed out, and shut it behind him.

Rachael turned back toward her husband.

"So. How was your day?" Trace said, opening the pantry door, reaching in and taking out two purple-hued onions.

Rachael walked over to McKenna's high chair and placed her daughter in the seat. "Not nearly as exciting as yours." She turned around, reached for a container of vanilla wafers on the counter by the stove and handed one to McKenna. "Prepared for court all morning, sat in court all afternoon."

Trace leaned against the granite countertop and crossed his arms like he was waiting for more.

Rachael sighed. "And yes I saw Will."

"Got your marching orders?"

"I got my instructions," she answered, opening the fridge and taking out a sipping cup full of apple juice. "Nothing can possibly go wrong tomorrow, Trace."

"So Will says."

Rachael turned from giving the cup to McKenna. "So you talked to Will, too?"

"He called me today. Told me how it's going go down. Told me where and when to meet him. And to get there 20 minutes before you do."

"So I'm sure he told you they've got everything under control, right?"

Trace remained at the countertop with his arms across his chest. "He told me he's not expecting any surprises. That's a little different."

Rachael paused for a moment before saying anything else. "So, really, Trace. What's with the hair?" she said, a couple moments later.

Trace smirked. "It's my disguise. You don't like it?"

She allowed a grin and reached for one of the onions he had taken out of the cupboard. "Your disguise," Rachael echoed.

"You said I could be recognized from that *Strib* photo. Well now I won't be."

Rachael peeled away the onion's papery outer skin. "Sunglasses and one of Fig's crazy hats would have been a little less drastic," she said.

Trace turned toward the counter and grabbed the other onion. "Darn! I didn't think of that!"

Rachael put the onion down and turned to face her husband. "Okay. I get it. You're stressed out about this. I understand that, I really do. But, Trace what do you want me to do? Really. What is it you want me to do?"

Trace put his onion down, too. A moment of strained silence coated the room. When Trace opened his mouth, he didn't turn to her at first. "Look, I shaved my head because it felt really good today to have control over something, Rachael." Then he turned to her. "And because what I want you to do is come home to me at the end of every day. And I don't have control over that."

She hesitated only a moment before erasing the inches of distance between them and wrapping her arms around his torso. "It's going to be all right, Trace. Really it is. I know it."

He leaned his bare head down and nuzzled her toast-brown hair. "You can't know that," he whispered.

"But I do." Rachael pulled away enough to look at his face. "I do know it."

"Rach."

"I do. I'm not afraid, Trace. This person just wants help, I'm sure of it."

"Dah-wonn!" McKenna said from her chair, but Rachael and Trace remained in their embrace.

"I hope you're right," he whispered.

"I *am* right."

"Do you hate it?" Trace said, several seconds later.

Rachael looked up and then reached a hand to touch the smooth skin on Trace's scalp. "I don't hate it," she said. "It's different. And Simone whoever-she-is is right. You do have a nicely-shaped head." She stroked the skin and Trace closed his eyes. "It's very soft, reminds me of something," Rachael murmured.

"Mmmm?" Trace replied, obviously enjoying the massage.

"Ah, yes. It's just like McKenna's little behind," she said playfully.

And Trace tightened his hold on her and tickled her. Rachael shrieked with laughter and McKenna shrieked as well, nearly drowning out the ring of Trace's cell phone. Rachael broke away and Trace fished for his cell phone in his pants pocket.

"What's up, Fig?" he said, answering on the third ring. There was a momentary pause and then Trace looked over at Rachael. "She's fine with it. She's in the bathroom right now shaving her own head. Yep." Another pause. "Well, okay. So be it. See you in five."

"Okay, what?" Rachael said.

Trace lightly tossed his cell phone on the granite countertop. "The package Fig has in his freezer isn't full of prawns."

Rachael waited.

"It's eel."

Rachael tried to stay busy on Wednesday but the morning passed interminably slowly. Will called her at ten to see if she had changed her mind about meeting the letter-writer.

She hadn't.

At eleven, Tony Brimm, her supervisor and one of several managing prosecutors, told her she could take the afternoon off if she needed to prepare for the meeting and Rachael had just shrugged.

"I don't know what to prepare for, really."

"Well go home a little early then, arrange your thoughts, calm your nerves," Tony said. "You want to be relaxed but on guard."

"But I am relaxed," she countered.

Tony started to walk away. "Then work on being on guard," he said. "Go home early. That's an order."

"Okay, okay," Rachael replied, picking up the phone to tell Will she'd be leaving for Grand Avenue from the loft in Minneapolis not the Ramsey County courthouse. He would need to tell the undercover cop who'd be tailing her.

Rachael arrived back in downtown Minneapolis a little after one, parking her car on the street like Will had asked instead of in the underground garage. She skipped the loft altogether and walked to the studio, calling Trace on his cell as she walked so that he could open the door for her.

She was glad to be able to spend some time with Trace and McKenna but the forced time away from her desk wasn't preparing her for what lay ahead. If anything, it was making her jittery.

Trace met her at the fire door that led to the mezzanine and the studio. "I hear you have a few hours to kill," he said lightly.

"This is so unnecessary," she replied, giving him a peck on the cheek. "I don't know what I'm going to do with myself until it's time to go."

"Fig was just about to do the Soduku puzzle in today's paper when you called. He's saved it for you. And half his tofu quiche."

Two hours later, at a few minutes after three, Trace pulled off his paint-smeared smock and threw on a silk camp shirt. He grabbed Fig's leather beret off of one of the Idea Couches and placed it at an angle on his bald head. "How's that?" he said to Rachael.

Rachael looked up from patting McKenna's back while the baby lay on the plush rug resisting a nap. "You look very European. Will's not going to know it's you."

Trace nodded and then walked over to her. He knelt down on the rug. "You've got the little dragonfly? And the little ear thingy?"

"They're both in my purse, Jacques," she answered.

"Very funny. Are you completely sure you want to do this?"

"Totally."

"Give me your hand."

Surprised, Rachael reached out her left hand to Trace, not knowing what to expect. He took it, closed his eyes and began to pray. It took several seconds for Rachael to close her eyes also. Trace never prayed out loud.

"Keep her safe. Make her right. Bring her home. In Jesus' name, amen," he closed the prayer softly and sprang to his feet.

"I'll be watching you," he said as he moved toward the door.

She smiled at him.

"Don't forget to turn the dragonfly on," he said as he opened the door.

"I won't."

He turned and left.

Rachael sat for a few minutes longer stroking McKenna's back but it didn't appear that McKenna had any intention of sleeping. Rachael rose to her feet and walked toward the long, clear curtain in the corner of the room. She pulled it back to reveal Fig working on Joan of Arc with a set of thick headphones plastered to his bare head.

He looked down when he saw her, removing one earphone and leaving the other, creating a comical, alien look that made her want to laugh.

"I've got to get ready to go, Fig. And McKenna won't fall asleep," she said.

Fig yanked the earphones off completely and tossed the pick he was using onto the canvas sheet below him. "No problem! I'm on it."

While Fig lay next to McKenna reciting the alphabet to her in Dutch, Rachael put her hand in her purse and drew out the little dragonfly and earpiece. She placed the flesh-colored pea in her ear and then turned the dragonfly over and flipped the tiny switch. She pinned it to her blouse and hoped that it looked natural.

Her cell phone rang. She knew it would be Will telling her the tail was in place and she was free to start out for Grand Avenue.

"I'm ready," she said as she answered the phone.

"Officer Knowles is in a blue Impala. I don't want you looking for him, I just want you to know who's following you."

"Got it."

"Okay. Keep your phone on until you get to Grand and we make radio contact. Then switch it off so it's not a distraction to our guest."

"Okay, Will."

"All right then. Any questions?"

"Nope. I'm good."

Will paused for a moment. "Thanks for doing this, Rachael."

"You're welcome. And remember we have a deal. Don't rush in. Let me try to invite you in. Okay?"

"I remember our deal," Will said gently.

"Okay, then. See you later, Will."

Rachael switched off the phone and tossed it back into her purse. She turned to Fig. "I'm leaving. Bottle's in the diaper bag if you need it."

Fig smiled at her. "We'll be fine. McKenna and I go way back."

"Thanks for taking care of her, Fig."

"'Tis nothing," Fig replied. "You're very brave, Kumquat. I'm proud of you."

Rachael shook off the compliment. "It's no big deal, Fig. See you later. Call Trace if you need something. I'll be turning my cell off in a little bit."

She opened the studio door, waved and then shut it behind her.

Fig's comment was rather undeserved, she thought. She wasn't brave. A brave woman does something terribly heroic in spite of being afraid.

But Rachael wasn't afraid.

SIXTEEN

Rachael found it difficult not to look for the blue Impala as she walked out onto the street. She feigned interest in the flow of traffic around her as she walked to her car, unlocked it and opened the door. As she maneuvered her body inside, she saw across the street and perhaps 20 yards behind a silvery blue car with a man behind the wheel. He appeared to be looking her way. She turned her head away.

"Okay, God," she whispered as she started her car and entered the easy flow of traffic. "Help me ask the right questions, help me be the person this writer thinks I am. Help me understand."

Rachael eased her way toward St. Paul, barely aware of the route Will had asked her to take to get there. Every few minutes she found herself peeking in her rear view mirror, making sure the Impala was in sight. But her thoughts were mostly of April, Drew, and Santos. She knew they would no longer resemble the school-portrait images swirling in her head but nevertheless these were the images floating across her mind. She was unable to picture Lyle and Ginny Downing, or Marisol Valasquez or Santos's sister Elena. She had not seen their pictures. Instead, three 25-year-old photographs paraded around in her mind as she drove, along with snippets of conversations and observations about the kind of person Bucky had been.

Bucky slammed Drew up against a set of lockers and attempted to shove a pencil down his throat....

Bucky called April "Ape, and he'd make gorilla sounds around her and drag his arms around.... He threatened to kill the neighbor's cat and blame her for it.... He fondled her breasts when he thought no one was looking....

Bucky pummeled Santos Valasquez when Santos attempted to defend his sister's honor. A window was broken. Santos was given a day of in-school suspension....

Twice the police were called and twice the charges were dropped....

When she turned onto Grand Avenue, her pulse began to quicken, but not with alarm. She felt a strange kinship to Bucky's targets. Perhaps it was because her brother Joshua had been a loner growing up, or maybe it was because she spent every working moment at the county interceding for neglected children, or maybe it was because becoming a mother had so revolutionized her sensitivities to the vulnerable. She knew that the letter-writer still suffered, even 25 years later, and she wanted peace for that person.

As she pulled into the municipal parking lot Will had instructed her to use, a tiny stream of static filtered into her left ear and she cocked her head involuntarily.

"Rachael, this is Will. Do you copy?" Will's voice seemed tiny and bereft of its normal baritone richness.

"I hear you, Will," Rachael answered, feeling as though she was speaking to an invisible playmate or a ghost. She looked around the lot. "I don't see my tail, though."

"He's parking elsewhere. Don't worry about it. You've got a good ten minutes to get inside the coffee shop and get something to take outside. Go ahead and start walking over there. Make sure you turn off your cell phone."

"Okay," Rachael said. She parked, got out of the car and then reached inside her purse for her cell phone. She switched the power off and tossed it back inside.

The lot was just a block from Starbucks and Rachael was walking toward it in less than a minute. She saw a blue, windowless van parked across the street. The doors displayed a logo for an electrical repair service.

"I can see you, Rachael," said Will's voice in her ear. "Don't look up but Trace and I are right above you on the opposite side of the street. When you go inside we'll lose visual, but I've got someone inside. He'll make sure you're covered if you're approached from inside. You don't need to answer me. Better if you don't."

Rachael was now in front of the café. The tables were nearly all occupied. Ted Knowles was sitting at one of the tables with a Venti at his elbow, an open laptop in front of him and a pile of papers covering the rest of the tabletop. She kept her eyes down as she walked past him. When she raised her eyes again she saw that someone was sitting at the table where she was supposed to sit.

At the second her mind began immediately to race with questions, Will's voice broke in. "Don't worry about the gal at the table. She's a plant. She'll leave when you come out with your coffee. You just take her table when she gets up. Don't say okay."

Rachael walked past the woman and stepped inside the café. The heavily scented air was thick with noise, talk and brewing coffee. She casually surveyed the eating area and noted that no one was wearing a red shirt. She took a place in line.

"Rachael, our guy inside sees no one in red, so we're thinking you're alone in there," Will's voice said. "So far, so good."

A few moments later, Rachael held a mocha in her hands and was walking back into the late afternoon sunshine. As she neared the little table behind Ted, the woman sitting there suddenly rose, picked up her cup and left. Rachael slid into the vacated seat so that her eyes were on Ted's back.

Everything was in place. She set her cup down and casually looked at her watch. It was a minute after four.

She sat back in her chair and looked about her.

"We're not seeing anyone in a red shirt, Rachael," Will's voice broke in. "They may've decided to wear something else so you won't be on the lookout. Who knows? Just hang tight."

Rachael sipped her coffee and waited. All about her the afternoon appeared to be playing itself out in a completely ordinary way. Coffee-drinkers came and went; the tables around her and emptied and then filled again.

She looked at her watch. Eleven minutes after four.

"This happens sometimes, just stay cool," Will's voice was calm in her ear.

A short, Caucasian man in a gray polo shirt was suddenly standing in front of her. "Is this seat taken?" he said. He was pointing to the available chair at her table.

She hesitated. Was this Lyle Downing? He looked a little young to be the father of a 40-year-old man. It couldn't possibly be Drew. There was absolutely no resemblance.

"Tell him you're meeting someone," Will said in her ear. "If this is our guy, he won't leave."

"I'm actually meeting someone," Rachael said politely, feigning disinterest.

"Oh. Okay."

The man moved away. Rachael sighed.

"It's okay, Rachael." Will.

She continued to sip her drink and the minutes continued to tick away. Ahead of her, Ted continued to type at the laptop and peruse papers. When her cup was drained she looked at her watch again. Four twenty-nine.

"This happens, too, I'm afraid," said Will. "Sometimes they back out, Rachael."

"Can we give it a few more minutes?" she whispered.

"We always do."

But by a quarter to five, no one in a red shirt had appeared. No one else spoke to her. The busy-ness of the café was ordinary and routine.

"I think we've got a no-show," Will said, speaking not only to her but to whoever was listening in the van, and probably Ted as well. "Rachael, it could be that they set you up to see if you came alone, and if they're watching, then the smartest thing you can do is leave alone. I want you to go back to your car, get in and drive home. I'll call you later and we'll talk about what happened today."

"But I want to wait a little longer," Rachael said softly, looking around for a flash of red in the crowd.

"He or she's not coming. Not now, Rachael. And if they're watching, it's not a good idea for you to be talking to yourself. So go ahead back to your car. You can look disappointed if you want, just don't look like you've got company. Trace will follow in about twenty minutes. Then I'll call you at home. We're wrapping it."

Rachael pushed back her chair and rose, biting back another plea to wait a little longer. Will was no doubt right.

The letter writer had changed his or her mind.

And Rachael was pretty certain she was indeed alone. The writer hadn't come to test her trust. He or she hadn't come at all.

"They're not here," she mumbled as she threw her cup away.

"Let's just play it cool all the same," Will said gently.

Rachael walked back to her car at a brisk pace. All the preparation had been for nothing.

The writer hadn't come.

She pressed the unlock button on her remote, opened her car and slid inside.

What made the letter-writer change his mind? Was it fear? Anxiety? A change of heart? She wondered when she would know. If she would ever know.

Rachael turned the key in the ignition and the engine sprang to life. She backed out of the parking lot, and then turned her car toward Minneapolis, toward the sun sitting low and unhurried on the horizon.

***

"It's nothing you did or didn't do, Rachael. This happens. They don't show up. They get cold feet." Will's voice on the other end of the phone was calm but commanding. "We did everything right. *You* did everything right."

"You sure went to a lot of trouble for nothing," Rachael grumbled as she sat on an Idea Couch with McKenna playing at her feet.

"It's never 'for nothing,' Rachael. We look at what happened today as the completion of a well-executed exercise. If we hadn't got stood up it would have been a well-executed take-down, but it wasn't a waste of time."

"Take-down?" She punched the word out. She didn't like it and she wanted Will to know it.

"Sorry. But really Rachael, this was only a minor setback. Sam and I are making progress. I don't think our writer will be anonymous for much longer. I really don't."

Rachael sighed and toyed with the dragonfly wings of the brooch she still wore.

"You think they will write again?" she asked.

"Who knows? But I think in the course of our questioning, they're not going to be able to continue the charade much longer. They have already confessed to so much. If Sam and I haven't interviewed the writer already, we will in the next couple of days and my guess is it's all going to come out. Maybe not the first time we talk together. But as we gather more information and continue to revisit for questioning, they will spill."

"So you'll just keep going back with one more question, one more opportunity to make them feel uncomfortable around you." Rachael said glumly. "Like Colombo."

"Is that a compliment?"

Rachael entertained a tiny grin. "Sure. Who doesn't like Colombo?"

"Rachael, I talked to my chief about an idea that came to me while I was driving back to the station. He thinks it might work. And so do I. So does Sam."

"What kind of idea?"

"Well, it's an idea that involves you."

Rachael sat up on the couch and her hand fell away from the brooch. "Me?"

Out of the corner of her eye, she saw Trace look up from the art table he was standing at.

"I'm fairly certain our letter-writer is within the circle of people we've interviewed or will interview. The most recent letter suggests that our questioning has shaken them up a bit, just like I thought it would. If the letter-writer isn't someone we've already talked to, they've certainly been in contact with the people we have. I'm sure the Downings called their son to tell him I called them, and I'm sure Marisol Valasquez called her kids, too. We've not talked much with April Howard, but she knows we're going to contact her now that her husband is home. That means everyone on my short list is in the loop."

"I'm with you so far," Rachael said.

"Between now and this time next week, I will have talked with everyone else on the list."

"All the victims," Rachael reminded him.

"Yes. Rachael, I'd like you to come with me when I question them."

For a second Rachael thought she certainly must've misheard Will. Prosecutors didn't accompany detectives when they interviewed suspects or witnesses.

"But Will," she began, "how can that work? I mean, what would my role be?"

"You'd be coming as the recipient of the letters and not as a county prosecutor. You'd be introduced as such but that would not be the reason you'd be there."

"And what would be the reason?"

"To give our writer another chance to talk with you. They had wanted to talk to you in person today but they chickened out at the last minute. So we'll bring you to them. Make it easy for them. If they open up to you, fine, if they don't, well, we tried."

Rachael cast a glance toward Trace. He was watching her; a mix of interest and angst crinkling the flesh around his eyes.

"So, you think this will work?" she said to Will, turning back around.

"I think it's as good a strategy as any. The writer already has respect for you. They've already attempted to make personal contact with you. This will either draw them out or chase them back. But either way, when you walk in with me, we're going to get a reaction from the writer. I can't imagine that we won't."

"And what if the writer isn't one of these people?"

"Well, Rachael, you already believe that it is. If you're asking me how *I* feel about it, well, that's obvious. No harm done. Why don't you think about it before you say yes or no? Talk it over with Kojak."

Rachael smiled at Will's comment on Trace's new bald look.

"So when's your first meeting?" she said.

"I'm visiting with Drew Friday afternoon at four, at his home in Chaska. I gave him the option of meeting at the station or his office. He chose his house."

"And I would meet you where?"

"Here. We'll go in my car. Sam's working on cases that are really more urgent than this one so you can ride shotgun."

Rachael already knew she wanted to be there when Will talked to these people. But she also knew she had to discuss the plan with Trace first—and that he probably wouldn't be too thrilled with the idea.

But the new plan was really no worse than the failed meeting at Starbucks. If anything, she'd be safer. She'd be with Will, who never left the station unarmed.

Besides, it would also mean the end would come sooner rather than later. The letters would stop. Life would return to its normal pace.

And Trace could let his hair grow back.

"I'll call you right back," she said.

SEVENTEEN

Will and Rachael pulled up alongside Drew Downing's two-story home situated in a tract of similar houses sporting similar juvenile trees hugging similar stabilizer poles that outdid the trees in diameter. Will handed her the three letters.

"You only get them while we're here. Then I need to ask for them back," Will said. "I want it to appear as though they still belong to you."

"That feels like deception to me," Rachael said, frowning, but taking the letters anyway.

"There's nothing deceptive about it," Will said, opening his car door. "They are addressed to you."

"You know what I mean," she said, opening her door as well.

"And you know what *I* mean. I want a confession." Will stepped out of the car and she followed. "Just put those in your purse. Don't bring them out or mention them until I do, okay?" he added.

"All right."

They walked up the curving, paved walkway to the front door. Rachael noticed a squirt gun and a Nerf ball on the landscaped lawn. A pair of boy-sized tennis shoes sat haphazardly on the cement step that led to the front door and next to a wooden bench stenciled with vines.

"Ready?" Will asked.

Rachael nodded. Will rang the doorbell.

The front door swung open a moment later. A petite, attractive woman with short, black hair stood in the entry. "Yes?" she said.

Will flashed open his badge. "I'm Sgt. Will Pendleton with the St. Paul police. This is my colleague, Rachael Flynn. Is Drew Downing home, please?"

"Oh. Right." The woman opened the door and stepped aside to let them in. "Drew?" she called out as they moved past her. "You want to sit in the living room or something?" she added.

"Sure. Wherever Mr. Downing would like to sit is fine," Will answered.

"Okay, well come in here, then," and the woman motioned them to a living room just off the entry. "I thought you'd be in a uniform or something. And Drew said there'd be just one of you." She directed this last comment toward Rachael.

"Ah, well, I'm a detective, so it's usually plain clothes for me," Will replied as he took a seat on the sofa. He didn't address her other observation.

"Oh," the woman said.

"And you are Mrs. Downing?" Will asked.

"Oh my goodness, yes. I'm Nadine. Sorry. We've just never had the police in the house before."

"No problem." Will's tone was easy and genial.

"I'll just go see where Drew is." Nadine stepped out of the room, and Rachael heard her head up carpeted stairs off the other side of the entry.

Rachael sat down next to Will and looked about the room. A black, upright Kawai piano stood against the wall across from them. Framed photographs of two adolescent boys in soccer uniforms sat on its lacquered top. A white brick fireplace flanked another wall and a massive print of a night sky splintered by lightning hung on the wall above it. The room was sparsely but elegantly furnished. On the tiled end table next to her was a tall Galileo thermometer. Floating orbs of red, blue, green and yellow dozed in the liquid inside.

At that moment, Drew entered the room, followed by Nadine. Despite the beard and moustache, his eyes, mouth and nose were the same as those in the picture Rachael had seen in his yearbook. She would've recognized him even if she hadn't been sitting in his living room. An ID badge for the National Weather Service hung from the right front pocket of his brown khaki shirt. Drew looked from Will to her and back again. Rachael couldn't tell if he was surprised or confused that she was in the room. Will was intently watching Drew's face also.

Will stood and thrust out his right hand. "Mr. Downing, thanks for letting us stop by. I'm Detective Pendleton. We spoke on the phone. This is a colleague of mine, Rachael Flynn."

Drew shook Will's hand and then he turned to Rachael. "How do you do?" His tone was mechanically polite. He was taken aback by her presence, she was sure of that. But she couldn't tell if it was because he recognized her. "Please sit down," he said.

Rachael and Will sat back down on the sofa. Drew sat across from them in a matching chair. Nadine leaned against her husband and sat on one of the chair's heavily padded arms.

"You have a lovely home, Mr. Downing," Will began. "Great neighborhood to raise the kids. Are your boys here, by the way?"

"They're at my parents' house," Drew answered. His mouth hung on the "p" in "parents" for a second before the rest of the word followed.

"I'm sure you and your parents have talked then about the body that was found on your old neighborhood street," Will continued.

"Of course we've t-t-talked," Drew said, on the verge of sounding terse. "I told you that on the phone."

"You did. My mistake. Well, let's just get right to it, shall we? Mr. Downing, we have reason to believe that Ronald Buckett was the victim of foul play. I know that sounds a little ridiculous, doesn't it, that Bucky was a victim, after all that he did."

"It sounds ludicrous," Drew replied evenly.

"Yes, I'd have to agree with you there. He was one mean individual. I've been through his school files and I've talked to your parents, as you already know. I know he made your life difficult."

"He made it hell," Drew said, emotionless.

"I'm with you there. No kid should have to suffer what you did. I wish things had been different for you, that you could've gotten help from the police or your school. Must have been very frustrating."

Drew said nothing for a moment. "You said on the phone that you had some questions you w-w-wanted to ask me."

"I do. I need to ask the obvious ones, Mr. Downing, if you don't mind. Do you remember the day Bucky disappeared?"

Drew licked his lips. "That w-w-w-was 25 years ago, Detective."

"Yes, I know. But I have to ask."

"I r-r-r-remember what it was l-l-l-like after Bucky disappeared."

"Yes?" Will said.

"It was like being l-l-let out of a Nazi concentration camp."

Rachael saw Nadine lower her arm to Drew's shoulder and stroke it gently.

"Yes. I can imagine it was…" Will began but Drew cut him off.

"I seriously d-d-doubt you can imagine it, unless you've lived through it, Detective."

"Actually, I know what it's like to be teased for something as inane as the way you talk or the color of your skin," Will said. His voice took on a slight edge.

"T-t-t-teased is one thing. Tormented is another."

Will sat forward. "You know, Drew—may I call you Drew?—I've been wracking my brain trying to figure this out. Why did it go on year after year after year? Why didn't you tell your parents or the school or the police about all the things Bucky did to you? I mean, he did more than just assault you with a pencil that day in the hallway. That was just the last straw. Why did it go on for so long?"

"You have kids, Detective?" Drew asked.

"I have two teenage sons."

"Did your sons come to you at t-t-t-twelve or thirteen or fourteen and ask you to fight your battles for them? Did you know no one likes a snitch? Did you know teachers don't like to c-c-c-complicate their lives dealing with kids like B-B-Bucky and parents like Bucky's parents? Did you know when you bring charges against someone you have to prove those charges in court? Did you know society doesn't tolerate wimps?"

Again Rachael saw Nadine stroke her husband's shoulder. Her petite features seemed stretched with concern. She wondered how much Drew had told Nadine about Bucky.

"I apologize," Will said. "That was a thoughtless question. I do need to ask you, though, if you know how Bucky ended up dead and buried in that field."

"He ran away," Drew said. "How would I know how he ended up there? Do you think I c-c-c-cared what happened to him? My life *began* when he disappeared. I couldn't have cared l-l-less!"

"Well, everyone thought he ran away," Will corrected him. "But he didn't, of course. He died. We're not sure how. But he did. And someone buried him in the lot across from your old house."

"I didn't care then, and I don't care now."

"I think I may have mentioned to you that we received a tip that his body was buried at that construction site. A tip in the form of a letter."

"I read that in the paper," Drew said tonelessly.

"Well, what you didn't read in the paper—because we didn't tell the media—is that there have been two more letters. Three in all. Someone knows how Bucky died, how he ended up buried in that field."

"Why are you telling me this?" Drew asked.

"Well, to ask you if you're the letter-writer, certainly..."

"I'm not."

"And to ask if you know who it might be. Rachael, can you show Drew the letters?"

Rachael reached down into her purse and drew out the three letters. She reached across the coffee table, extending her hand toward Drew but he made no move to take them. Nadine intervened, took the letters and handed them to her husband.

"Rachael here is an attorney with the Ramsey County prosecutor's office. She's the one who received the letters. Maybe you could look at them and tell me who you think may have written them?"

Drew shook his head. "How in the w-w-w-world would I know that?"

Will shrugged. "Well, for one thing, you lived on a street where other victims lived. I'm sure you know you weren't the only one who Bucky liked to torment."

"Then why don't you just look up the other victims and ask them?"

"Oh, I will. I'd just like your opinion."

Drew fingered the envelopes but didn't open any of them.

"The writer says it was an accident," Will said. "That it was just supposed to teach Bucky a lesson. Do you know who might've wanted to teach Bucky a lesson? Santos maybe? April Howard? Someone else?"

"Just about anybody who knew Bucky fits that description," Drew replied dryly.

"You're probably right there, Drew. So were you and Santos friends?"

"No."

"Really? You lived on the same street, went to the same school, were about the same age."

"Santos was a year older than me. I'm sure you kn-kn-know that. And we had nothing in common."

"You had Bucky in common," Will offered.

Drew blinked. "Cancer patients have something in common too. It doesn't make them best friends." His voice was measured and calm.

"Fair enough. So what do you say, Drew? Can you give those a look-see and tell us what you think?" Will said, motioning with his head toward the letters in Drew's hands.

Drew slowly leaned forward and placed the envelopes on the coffee table. "No one l-l-l-likes a snitch, Detective."

Will closed his eyes and rubbed his temple. "Just like that, eh?" he said to Drew.

"Did you r-r-r-really think I w-w-would want to help you with this? That I'd want to help you t-t-t-track down who killed him?"

"Yeah, I did," Will said, laughing.

Drew smiled for the first time since he joined them in the living room. It was a tepid smile, void of humor. "Sorry to have made you waste your time," he said.

"Oh, I wouldn't say I wasted my time at all, and I know you're not sorry." Will stood. He fished in his shirt pocket for a business card and extended it to Drew. "If you change your mind, I'd appreciate your calling me."

Drew hesitated, and then stood and took the card. Rachael stood also. It appeared they were leaving. She bent over and reached for the letters resting on the table. Drew was looking at the card in his hands. Nadine watched her though, as she placed the letters back in her purse.

"Thanks again for talking with us," Will said pleasantly and he started to walk toward the front door. Rachael took a step to follow him. "Oh. One more thing." Will added and he turned back toward Drew. "Can I ask you where you were on Wednesday at four o'clock?"

"What?" Drew looked genuinely surprised.

"Four o'clock on Wednesday," Will said. "Do you remember where you were?"

"I was at work," Drew answered quickly.

"And is there a co-worker or two that could attest you were there?"

"Any one of a dozen people could tell you I was there!"

"Great. Thanks." He continued toward the front door. "Don't forget. Call me if you think of anything."

Drew appeared to have relaxed after the question regarding his whereabouts on Wednesday. "I seriously doubt you'll be hearing from me, Detective."

Rachael stepped up onto the tiled entryway. "Thank you," she said, painfully aware it was the only thing she had contributed to the entire conversation.

"Goodbye," Nadine said as cordial as one could expect. She opened the door for them and then shut it as they stepped back out into the late afternoon sunshine.

Will walked briskly to the car and Rachael hurried to follow him.

Once inside and as they were pulling away, Will turned to her. "Now there's a guy with motive."

"Do you think...do you think he killed Bucky?" Rachael said.

"I think he certainly could have."

"You think he could've written the letters, too?"

"Oh, no. Drew Downing definitely did not write those letters."

Rachael looked at the envelopes peeking out of her purse. She reached in for them and placed them on the console between her and Will. She didn't think Drew had written them either.

"No, I don't suppose he did," she said.

"But there's something very interesting regardless," Will said.

"What's that?"

"He wouldn't look at them. He wasn't even curious."

EIGHTEEN

A cloak of soggy clouds spread itself over the urban landscape, dousing the Twin Cities in a chilling rain that began before dawn on Saturday. Plans to take McKenna to the Como Zoo were quickly called off and instead the day was passed quietly indoors.

Rachael secretly thanked the heavens for the dismal weather that kept her, Trace, and McKenna inside. She had brought home a boatload of files to slog through in preparation for court on Tuesday, and which she attacked as soon as McKenna was down for a nap and Trace followed suit.

She would only be in the office a few hours on Monday and then she and Will would take off for Elena's home in Cloquet. Santos would be there, too, and she knew Will wasn't too happy about that. The detective had called Friday night, after she had returned from their very intriguing visit with Drew Downing, to let her know that the brother and sister wanted to meet together. Elena had said Santos was visiting her from Wisconsin anyway and it would just be easier.

Will hadn't believed her.

His gut told him Santos Valasquez decided to come to see his sister because she was going to be questioned by the police regarding the discovery of Bucky's remains. And Rachael thought Will was probably right. Santos wanted them to be questioned together.

"So what will you do?" Rachael had asked.

"Coax them into an agreeable state by talking with them together. Then I will ask to speak to each one separately for a few minutes."

"Will they do it?"

"Well, if they don't, that speaks volumes, doesn't it?

"And so what will I do?"

Will didn't hesitate. "The same thing you did at Drew's."

"I didn't do anything at Drew's! I just sat there!"

"You did exactly what I wanted you to do—you made yourself completely available to the letter-writer. Nothing happened because the letter-writer wasn't there."

"All right," she had said. "But Will, this time, can you bring the sketch of the house? Please? You didn't even ask Drew about it."

"I'll bring the sketch, but maybe it would be better if you asked about it, Rachael," Will said. "It would give you a chance to say something, invite a little dialogue. Besides, you're the one who has the hunch about the house, not me."

As Saturday afternoon wore on, Rachael found it hard to concentrate on the files she was studying. Each petition kept bringing her back to Drew, Santos, and April. Each one involved a hurting child who needed intervention, someone to step in front of him or her, hold up a hand and say, "No more!"

By Monday, the rain had moved east and a reluctant sun began to dry out the puddles. Will swung by the courthouse at eleven to pick Rachael up for the two-hour drive to Cloquet.

On impulse, Rachael had grabbed the artists' drawings before she left that morning. When she and Will were twenty minutes into the drive, she brought them out of her briefcase, knowing he would ask about them.

He did.

"What are those?" he said.

"Fig, Trace and the others played around with different ways Bucky could've died," she replied. "It was mostly just for fun, but one of them may be close to the truth."

"Those friends of Trace's have too much time on their hands."

"Well, how do you think he died?" Rachael said.

"We don't know, Rachael. Nothing is conclusive. There's no way *to* know."

"Yeah, I know you don't know for sure. But what do you think?"

Will shrugged. "What do *you* think?"

"I think it has to be something that made the letter-writer feel responsible; responsible enough that they feel they could've stopped it or prevented it somehow. Otherwise they wouldn't have buried the body. They would've just let Bucky be found dead. That's why Sid's drawing doesn't work."

"Sid's?" Will said, eying the road but stealing a glance at Sid's cartoon.

"Anaphylactic shock. You can't really plan that. You can't plan to teach someone a lesson that way. There'd be no reason to cover up the death."

Will smirked. "Are they all this way?"

"No," Rachael said, in mock annoyance. "Brick wanted to draw Bucky getting shot, which you told me earlier you thought was fairly possible since most crimes of passion involve a gun. But the others talked him out of it because I told them there were no bullet holes in any of the bones. They didn't think someone could shoot a person and miss a bone."

"Hmmm," Will said.

"You're mocking me," Rachael said.

"No, I'm not. This is very interesting," Will replied. "What else have you got?"

Rachael paused for a minute, unsure if Will was serious or not. "Fig thought maybe he got electrocuted."

"And how did our vigilante arrange that?"

Rachael frowned. "He couldn't figure that out. But I've been thinking, Will. About the abandoned house. Something happened in that house. What if Bucky died inside it?"

"The house wasn't occupied, but it wasn't exactly abandoned, either.

It did belong to somebody," Will said. "When it burned all the outside doors were still locked. I did check on it like you asked. The cause is listed as lightning."

Rachael was about to suggest that someone could've entered the house through a window when she had a sudden mental picture of weathered, wooden doors, angled at the ground.

"The storm cellar," she said, more to herself than to Will, but he heard her.

"The storm cellar?" he echoed.

"Will, there was a storm cellar, the old-fashioned kind with an outside entrance. I'll bet you anything those doors weren't locked. And I'll bet you anything, whatever happened, happened in that cellar!"

"Like what? What happened there?"

"Like maybe Bucky got shot there. Maybe he choked to death there. Maybe he got stabbed there. Or was poisoned there."

"Why move the body, then, and risk the chance of being seen?"

"Because…because there was no lock. It would've smelled. It would've attracted attention. The person responsible wanted everyone to think Bucky was gone because he ran away, not because he was dead! I bet if his body had been left in the cellar, it would've been found within weeks, if not days."

"Maybe," Will replied. "But that eliminates April Madden for sure. There's no way she could've hauled his body out of a cellar. And I'm having a hard enough time believing she got his body out to the woods anyway. If April did it, Bucky died right where he was buried. In fact, I'm having a hard time believing any of those kids could've hauled a body, unseen, into the woods to bury it. Lyle Downing could have, but not one of the kids. To be honest, I don't think Bucky died at that house. I think he died in the woods."

Rachael said nothing as she stared ahead at the road in front of them. Will was the voice of reason. Hers was the voice of speculation.

But it was more than that. She had felt something when she stood where the house had been. What she felt had been real.

Something happened in that house. In that cellar.

After a quick run through a Cloquet fast-food restaurant, Will and Rachael made their way to Elena's house, using a map Will had produced on the Internet. The Brighton home was nestled in a secluded neighborhood of stately, older homes. The house bearing Elena's address was a three-story Victorian with gingerbread on its peaks and gables and a circular tower with leaded glass.

A silver Porsche was parked inside the open three-car garage, which at one time had surely been a carriage house. In the driveway was a dust-covered pickup truck with Wisconsin plates and an Eau Claire landscaping logo on the driver's side. The truck's bed was filled with garden implements.

"I'd say Mr. Brighton has money," Will said as he parked his car behind the Porsche and next to the pickup.

The two got out of the car and walked up the flagstone walkway to the covered porch. Will rang the bell.

The door was opened a second or two later by a tall, sturdy man with handsome features and a healthy tan.

"Good afternoon, I'm Sgt. Will Pendleton of the St. Paul police and this is my colleague, Ms. Rachael Flynn. I believe Mrs. Brighton is expecting us."

The door opened wide and the man smiled politely. "I'm Vince, Elena's husband. Come on in. Elena and Santos are in the dining room. Right this way."

"Thank you very much," Will said.

The inside of the Brighton home reminded Rachael of a magazine spread. The floors and woodwork glistened and fresh flowers in expensive vases seemed to be everywhere. Well-oiled antiques lined the walls. The hallway Vince led them down was tiled in white and black marble squares and the twin scents of lavender and lemon permeated the air.

Vince turned into an arched doorway and entered a room lined with eight, ten-feet-high, paned windows. The walls were a dusky red. A long, dark-hued table commanded the center. A woman and man sat at one end. Each of them held a tall glass of lemonade.

When Rachael entered the room, the two heads turned toward her. It was difficult to see if Santos and Elena were surprised to see her; sunlight was the only illumination in the room and the dark walls seemed to absorb it hungrily. Sister and brother both stood in one, swift motion. Santos's build had not changed from his yearbook photo. He was much shorter than his brother-in-law, and barely taller than his sister. His black hair was gelled away from his face and a pencil-thin moustache lay straight across his upper lip. Elena's white silk blouse and understated silver jewelry gave her a look of calm refinement. At her neck a silver cross with a tiny diamond at its center glistened on a delicate chain. Her long hair fell across one shoulder but her smile was weak and forced, Rachael thought. Santos's face was expressionless.

"Hello, I'm Sgt. Will Pendleton." Will walked briskly toward them, closing the distance, no doubt wanting to gauge their reaction. "This is my colleague, Ms. Rachael Flynn. Thanks for seeing us today."

"I'm Elena, this is my brother Santos," the woman said. "Please have a seat."

Rachael took a chair across from the brother and sister. Will sat down next to her.

"Can I get you anything? Lemonade? Water?" Vince said.

"No, thank you. That's very kind of you," Will replied. "We'll try to make this quick for you. I know this must be an inconvenience for you. Vince, you probably had to get off work early to be here."

Vince smiled easily. "Well, I know the boss pretty well."

Elena smiled. "He *is* the boss," she said. "My husband owns an electronics firm, Sgt. Pendleton."

Will laughed. "Good one! Very good. Say, Santos, this is great timing, you being in Minnesota right now. I wasn't looking forward to two long drives in one week. I'm so glad this worked out for both of us."

"Yes," Santos said, but nothing else.

"You've come a long way and I don't know that we will be of much help to you," Elena said gently. As Rachael's eyes adjusted to the light in the room, she could see that the woman was extraordinarily beautiful.

"Sometimes it's the people who think they have the least to offer that end up helping the police the most," Will replied amiably. Rachael thought she saw Elena bristle in her chair the tiniest bit.

"You have a lovely home here," Will said, as if his last remark was a comment on the weather. "Your girls are in school today?"

"Yes, of course," Elena said.

"Do you have kids, Santos?" Will turned his head toward Elena's brother.

"I have two boys and a girl," Santos answered, with little inflection.

"Kids are great, aren't they? I've got three myself. Can't imagine life without them."

Rachael resisted the urge to turn and look at Will. He was either trying to put Santos and his sister at ease or fluster them completely. Maybe he was thinking either would be fine.

"So what's this all about? This body you found?" Vince said, pulling out a chair to sit next to Will.

"Oh, yes. The body. Well, as I told your wife's mother, and as I'm sure she told your wife—and Santos, too, for that matter—the remains we found belong to Randall Buckett. He was known as Bucky when he was alive. He lived on the same street as Elena and Santos when they were kids. He ran away 25 years ago, or so everyone thought. He has actually been dead all this time."

Will stopped and Rachael noted his eyes were resting on the two people in front of him.

"So how did he die?" Vince went on.

Will turned then to Vince. "Unfortunately after 25 years underground, the human skeleton doesn't give up many clues, I'm afraid."

"Oh. Well, how can Santos and Elena help you? They were just kids 25 years ago," Vince continued.

"Indeed they were. That's precisely why they might be able to help us. Bucky lived four doors down from your wife and your brother-in-law. They both knew him. When we suspect someone's been a victim of foul play, we always talk to the people who knew them."

Rachael saw Santos flinch slightly when Will called Bucky a victim. Will had certainly hoped to get a rise out of Santos. But Santos remained silent.

Will turned toward Santos and his sister. "So, really, what I need to ask you both is what you remember about the days leading up to and right after Bucky disappeared. If you saw anything strange, saw any strange people in the neighborhood, that kind of thing."

"That was such a long time ago," Elena said.

"Yes, but we know that Bucky was a bully. We know that he harassed the children who lived on his street. For a lot of kids, it's the traumatic memories that stay with them." Will said this to Elena, but then he turned to Santos. "I'd like to ask you each privately what you remember. I know Bucky mistreated you, Santos. I'd like to talk to you in private about that."

"There's nothing to talk about. He mistreated a lot of people," Santos said quickly.

"To be sure," Will said, nodding his head. "But—how can I say this— you, having obviously been able to move past it, will surely be able to help us figure out how to understand a person who couldn't. We have reason to believe it was one of his victims that buried him in that lot. And I'd like to ask you about the incident when you and Bucky broke the window at school, Santos. About what you and Bucky were fighting about." Will tipped his head slightly toward Elena.

Santos's eyes widened slightly. "Can we go into your study, Vince?" he said.

"Sure. Of course," Vince said, standing up quickly.

"We won't be long," Will said cordially to Elena as he stood. Santos stood as well and the three men walked toward the arched opening. Will turned back toward Rachael and glanced down at her purse. She nodded her head slightly in understanding.

"Vince, if you don't mind, I'll take that lemonade now, if that's all right," Will said cheerfully as he left the room.

"No problem."

The men's voices disappeared down the hall.

Rachael turned to look at Elena. The woman seemed about to stand, maybe to leave the room also. Rachael leaned forward, startling the woman somewhat.

"Um, Elena, Will called me his colleague, but what I really am is an assistant prosecutor with Ramsey County. Would you mind looking at something while the others are gone? It's important."

"What?" Elena said.

"I have something I'd like you to look at. Three things actually…"

And Rachael bent down and reached for the letters in her purse.

NINETEEN

The room was eerily quiet. A quiet ticking sound told Rachael there was a clock somewhere in the dining room, and it produced the only sound in the room as she placed the three letters on the table in front of her. Across the table, Elena was watching her wordlessly.

"I was sent these letters," Rachael said softly, breaking the silence. "Someone who thought I would understand what they have been through sent them to me. They're about Bucky. And how he died."

Rachael stopped and studied Elena's face, but there was nothing to study. There was no shock, no curiosity, no amazement written across the woman's face. Whatever Elena was feeling, she was hiding it. Rachael couldn't believe that the letters provoked no emotion at all. Not even interest.

"They're not signed," Rachael continued. "But this person very much wants to be understood. He or she wants me to know Bucky's death was an accident."

Elena looked up from the letters lying on the table. "Why are you telling me this?" Her voice was whisper-soft, and laced with hints of hesitation.

"Because I want to understand. I want to help this person. I really do," Rachael replied, leaning forward in her chair.

Elena shrugged. "I don't see how I can help you with that."

The woman's tone was aloof and almost impolite, and it didn't suit her. Rachael was certain Elena was hiding something. Her attitude reminded her of Drew, who had refused to even look at the letters. Rachael decided at that moment she would make it hard for Elena to do the same. She picked up the first envelope, took out the letter and pushed it toward Elena.

"Maybe you can tell me who you think wrote this," Rachael said.

Elena seemed to take her time leaning forward and reading the letter. Rachael watched as the woman's eyes moved across the words. She appeared to be actually reading them, suggesting that maybe she was reading them for the first time.

She could also be giving the appearance of reading them for the first time.

Elena pushed the letter back toward Rachael. "I'm sorry. It means nothing to me."

Rachael opened the second letter and pushed it to Elena. "How about this one?"

This time, Elena leaned forward quickly and read the letter. *It's getting easier for her to pretend,* Rachael thought.

Elena shook her head. "I just don't know. I was pretty young when all this happened."

"You were thirteen," Rachael said.

"It was 25 years ago," the woman said, sitting back in her chair.

"But you saw what Bucky did to Santos, didn't you? And you saw what he did to Drew Downing. And April. And maybe he was even abusive to you. Was he, Elena? Did Bucky hurt you?"

"Bucky hurt everybody. He was a walking nightmare," Elena said, her eyes seemed to darken in anger.

"Yes, he was. He never should have been able to do the things he did. Someone should have stopped him. The adults should've stepped in. It shouldn't have been up to you kids to have to find a way to make him stop."

"Look, I don't know what you're talking about. I can't help you." Elena pushed the second letter back toward Rachael with enough force that it fluttered to the floor at Rachael's feet.

Rachael bent down to get the letter. She carefully folded it and placed it back in the envelope. She did the same with the first letter, hoping the silence was speaking to the woman across from her.

"Accidents happen, Elena," Rachael said, laying the envelopes atop each other. "Sometimes things just get out of control and the unthinkable happens. You were just a kid when all this happened. All of you were. And all of you had been left unprotected by the people who were supposed to guard you. I really do understand that."

Elena's eyes seemed to take on a shimmer. "I can't help you," she said again. Each word was slightly punctuated.

Rachael heard Vince's voice down the hall. He had no doubt given Will his lemonade and would soon rejoin her and his wife. She had only seconds. A glimmer of silver caught her eye and Rachael's eyes went to the cross pendant around Elena's neck. There was no way to know if the necklace was just jewelry or if the cross really meant something to the woman. Rachael decided at that instant to assume it did.

"Elena, will you swear to me before God that you didn't write these letters?" she said softly, but urgently.

"I told you I can't help you." Elena's voice was crackled with held-in emotion.

"Swear to me before God you didn't write these letters!"

Elena flicked away one lone tear that she had been unable to keep back. "I swear before God I didn't write those letters," she said. She raised her eyes to look at Rachael as she said it.

Rachael knew at once that Elena was telling the truth. But she was also instantly aware of something else.

"But you know who did, don't you?" Rachael said.

The woman across from her said nothing and a second later, Vince came back into the room.

"Change your mind about that lemonade?" he said to Rachael.

Rachael turned to face him. "No, thank you."

"How about you, Elena? Want some more?" Vince said, apparently unable to sense he had walked in on a tense moment.

"I can get it," his wife said. And before he could say anything else, Elena grabbed her glass and was on her feet. She left the room, and Vince watched her go.

"Well, this has all been very interesting," Vince said as he slid back into the chair he left minutes before. "You know, this is the first I've heard of this guy, Rocky or whatever his name is."

"Bucky, actually."

"Yeah. Santos and Elena have never mentioned him before. And it's been 25 years! I don't remember what the heck I did 25 years ago, or what I saw."

"No, you probably wouldn't unless it had a profound impact on you," Rachael said, nonchalantly putting the letters back in her purse.

A few minutes of awkward silence fell between them. Then Will appeared at the archway. Santos was right behind him.

"Where'd Elena run off to?" Will said casually.

Vince stood. "She's just in the kitchen. Here, I'll show you." Vince left with Will, leaving an obviously uncomfortable Santos with Rachael. The man stayed in the archway, neither in the room nor out of it.

Rachael stood and walked over to him. Santos leaned back against the wall and crossed his arms.

"So, you have a landscaping business?" she said, attempting small talk.

"Yes."

"Must be nice to be outdoors so much."

A nod.

"So what do Minnesota landscapers do in the winter?"

"I work in a factory in the winter."

"Oh."

Rachael decided to plunge ahead. "Mr. Valasquez, did Sgt. Pendleton mention to you that we received a tip that the body was located at the construction site? That the tip was an anonymous letter that was sent to me?"

"Yes."

"I've actually received three letters. In each one the writer says Bucky's death was an accident. Did Sgt. Pendleton tell you that?"

"Yes."

"Do you know who might've sent them?

"No."

"Would you like to take a look at them? I have them here."

"They're not my letters. They're yours."

"Yes, but I'd like to show them to you. I'd really like to know what you think."

Santos blinked several times, as if in deep thought, as if choosing his words carefully. "What I think," he said, slowly at first, "is that you cops are only concerned with catching someone who you think killed some white boy. You don't know anything. You never did."

"Mr. Valasquez, I'm not a cop," Rachael replied.

"Then why are you here?"

"I want to help the person who wrote me these letters!"

Santos's eyes flashed with anger. "You want to help the police arrest the person who wrote those letters! I'm not stupid!"

Rachael was stunned into silence. No appropriate words of response came to her. Santos wasn't right, but he wasn't wrong either. It was indeed Will's job to find out how Bucky died and who played a part in it. Someone was responsible for his death. Someone believed what happened to Bucky was incriminating and they buried his body because of that.

It was very likely when the truth came out, an arrest would be made. Charges would be filed.

She said nothing.

And neither did Santos.

She returned to the table, sat back down and waited.

Ten minutes later, Will, Elena and Vince appeared in the hallway and Rachael rose to meet them. Vince had his arm around his wife and Elena appeared to have been shaken by her interview. Santos shot her a look of concern. She attempted what looked to Rachael like an "I'm-all-right" smile.

"Here's my card, if you think of anything or just want to talk," Will said, handing his card to Elena. He turned to Santos and handed him one as well. "We really appreciate your time. Thanks for the lemonade. Rachael?"

As they made their way to the front door, Rachael leaned in close to Will. "The sketch of the house?" she whispered.

"Oh, sure," Will said. And he stopped, pulled out from his notebook the drawing of the house. "Do either of you recognize this house?" Will held up the drawing so that Elena and Santos could see it.

Their faces registered nothing.

"It probably doesn't look exactly right, but it's supposed to be the house across the street from where you grew up."

"The one that burned?" Rachael noted with surprise that Elena's voice was devoid of sentiment. The house meant nothing to her. She looked at Santos's face. His too, was blank.

"Yes, that's the one."

"It looked similar to that, I guess," Elena said, looking at the sketch. She wore a look of confusion now.

"No one lived there when we lived on that street," Santos said. He, too, seemed perplexed.

"As far you know, did anything strange or bad happen there?" Will said.

Something passed over Elena's eyes just then. It was so slight, Rachael almost missed it. Elena turned her head away from the sketch and the look vanished.

"It caught on fire and burned to the ground," Santos said, his voice on the edge of sarcasm. "That's not usually good."

"This would be before it caught fire. Nothing?" Will said.

Silence.

"Okay. Thanks," Will slipped the sketch back into his notebook and turned toward the door.

"Goodbye," Rachael said, following him. Elena tipped her head and then looked away. Santos did nothing. Vince held up his hand and offered a lukewarm smile.

Moments later Will and Rachael were backing out of the Brightons' driveway.

Rachael sat back in her seat and sighed quietly. She knew Will would want to fill the long drive home with talk about what she learned in the moments she was alone with Santos and Elena, as well as their ho-hum responses to the sketch of the house. And he'd certainly tell her what he learned in his interview with them.

Part of her wanted to know what he found out.

And another part, the larger part, just wanted to curl up against the window, shut out the world and sleep her way back to St. Paul.

"So," Will began. "Still think something bad happened at that house?"

"Yes." Despite her weariness, Rachael didn't hesitate. "I do. Elena had a look on her face when you asked. It didn't last long, but it was there."

"What kind of look?"

Rachael fought for the right words. "I don't know. A *knowing* look. Like yes, something bad did happen there."

"I didn't see it."

"But I did."

"Anything on the letters?" Will said, apparently ready to change the subject.

"Elena swears she didn't write them," Rachael answered. "And I believe her, Will. But I think she knows who did. Or she suspects someone. She knows more than she's telling me. Santos wouldn't even look at the letters. He thinks the only thing we care about is finding a killer and making an arrest."

"I asked Santos straight out if he knows how Bucky died and he said no," Will interjected. "I asked him if he was there when Bucky died and he said the same thing, no."

"Do you think he's telling the truth?" Rachael asked.

"Haven't the foggiest. When I asked him if he knows who did kill Bucky, he said if he did, he would never tell me. Even if he's innocent, he's not going to help us out."

"I don't blame him," Rachael mumbled.

"No, I don't suppose you do."

"Did he tell you anything else?"

"He described some of the abuse Bucky was adept at dishing out. Most of it you know already. Lots of shoving, racial slurs, hitting, socking, slamming. And he told me about what led to the fight in school when that window got broken. Bucky had made some pretty raunchy remarks to Santos about what he would do to Elena if he had her alone. If Bucky had said that to me about my sister, I probably would've slammed his head into a window, too."

"Does Elena know what that fight was about?"

Will shook his head. "She knows Santos went after Bucky because of comments Bucky made about her, but Santos doesn't think she knows how horrible those comments were."

"Did Elena tell you anything that you didn't know already?"

"Not really," Will said. "But I'll tell you this. She's not very good at pretending she doesn't remember things. I think you're right about her. She has ideas about who killed Bucky. She suspects someone. She may even know."

TWENTY

Rachael was awake before dawn on Tuesday, though not by choice. Her sleep had been restless and her dreams vague and troubling. She couldn't clearly remember the dreams upon waking but she was certain she didn't want to. Bucky was in them somehow. Menacing, relentless and unstoppable. When her eyes snapped open at a quarter to five, she sensed she had been fleeing from someone or something in the seconds before she awoke. She didn't want to lie in bed and consider which one it had been—or fall back asleep and resume the flight.

The loft was quiet and dark as she slipped on some sweats and her running shoes. Trace didn't like her to run alone on the darkened downtown streets and she wouldn't have wanted to that morning anyway. She would instead run up and down the six flights of stairs in her building until she was breathless and her waking thoughts flung far away.

Rachael left the loft and headed to where the stairs began—to the door that led to the parking garage—swinging her arms to loosen them from the inertia of sleep. She wanted to be on her game today. She had four hearings coming up that afternoon—none of which she was expecting to be a breeze. And the minute she was finished in court, Will wanted to leave for Coon Rapids to meet with April Howard Madden. It was going to be a long day.

As she began to ascend the first flight in an easy jog, she mentally ordered the afternoon's agenda, picturing each child whose care and safety seem to lie in the balance of the court's scales. Parents would be angry today. Especially the ones who really believed they had done nothing wrong.

Her mind flew to the father who had purposely burned his child's hand on a gas stove to supposedly teach him about the danger of fire and the need to obey. The child was recovering from first-degree burns in a temporary foster home and the father would be in court today demanding his son be given back to him.

"I only wanted to teach him a lesson," the father had said in his statement to the police. "He wouldn't listen to me about playing with my lighter." Human services had been called to the hospital when the father and his wife brought their weeping son to the emergency room.

The words "to teach him a lesson" swirled about in her head as she pounded the concrete stairs and her thoughts quickly traveled without permission to Bucky. Then to Drew. Santos. Elena. April. Their parents.

Someone had wanted to teach Bucky a lesson. The lesson had backfired. And Bucky had died.

The death had been an accident. But the police were not called.
Because the police wouldn't understand.
They never did.

Rachael tried to get her mind back on what awaited her at the courthouse but the collection of dilemmas had fused in her head. Images of the mistreated children in her files were getting mixed up with images of four children who had long since grown up.

Fifteen minutes later, with her chest heaving and her mind spinning, Rachael returned winded to the loft.

It was still dark. Still quiet. The day hadn't even truly begun yet.

Will was waiting for her outside the courtroom later that afternoon.

"Not to rush you but it's already past four," he said as she emerged from the double doors.

They began to walk briskly toward the attorneys' offices so she could secure her case files.

"I know, I know," Rachael said, as she hurried. "Everything just took longer today. One of the parents didn't even show and then another wanted to settle, but all on her terms. It took forever."

Ten minutes later they were in Will's car and nudging their way into St. Paul's rush hour commute.

"Do you have the sketch of the house?" Rachael asked Will as they headed north to Coon Rapids, half an hour away. It irked her that she had forgotten about the drawing when they were at Drew's and that she and Will were nearly ready to leave before the sketch was shown to Elena and Santos. She didn't want to wait until the last minute with April.

"It's right there in my notebook. Backseat. You can bring it in with the letters if you want."

Rachael looked behind Will and saw a sheet of paper with crinkled edges peeking out of Will's folio. She reached back, withdrew it and placed it on her lap. She ran her fingers lightly over the ink and chalk, turning the very tips of her fingers greenish gray. A fluttering sensation gripped her and quickly gathered weight. It seemed to settle to her stomach with sudden heaviness.

God, what are you trying to tell me about this house? she prayed. *This is not just my imagination. It can't be. What is it?*

Will's voice intruded on her plea for understanding.

"This may be a very short visit," he said. "April called me this morning and asked if I could come another time. Said she wasn't feeling well. Then her husband called right back and said she's just nervous and to go ahead and come so we can just get this matter over with. Exact words."

"So what are you thinking?" Rachael asked.

"I'm thinking April knows something, of course."

"Can they *all* know something?" Rachael said impatiently. Every time they turned around it seemed the case went a new direction.

"Actually, I have a theory," Will said. "I'm thinking the person who wrote the letters is not the person who orchestrated Bucky's death. But that person knows who did. And he or she is protecting that person."

"Well, how did the writer protect that person by tipping us?"

"We weren't really tipped, Rachael. An actual tip tells us something we wouldn't have found out on our own. Bucky was going to be uncovered by that construction company, note or no note. Even the writer knew that. They said so in the first letter. So the writer wasn't letting us know there was a body. They were letting us know it was an accident that there was one. They figured we'd be able to ID the body with a little help from DNA technology and the crime lab. And when we did, we'd start looking up people who knew the victim. We'd discover Bucky was a bully and that he tormented the children on his street. I think the writer figured we'd be able to track down those former victims. Which is exactly what happened."

"But I don't see how those letters protect whoever was responsible," Rachael said.

"They don't really. But they do paint that person in a different light. The letters tip the scales a little more in the guilty party's favor. It introduces the idea of an accident rather than a homicide. I think the writer knows an accidental death is not usually our first assumption when we uncover a body."

"So I suppose you've been pairing people in your head?" Rachael said. "Like who might've written the letters in defense of someone else?"

"Of course."

"Well, tell me what you think!"

Will smiled. "You're the girl with the hunches. You tell me."

Rachael sat back in her seat and pondered the possibilities.

"Ginny Downing could've written them to cover for Drew," she mused aloud.

"Or for her husband," Will said.

"Marisol could've written them to cover for Santos," Rachael continued.

"Or Elena could've written them to cover for Santos."

Rachael ignored Will's suggestion that Elena wrote the letters. She firmly believed Elena hadn't. But it would make sense that Elena knew who did kill Bucky if the writer was her mother.

"April could've written them in defense of someone," Rachael said instead. "But who would she feel compelled to protect?"

"Who indeed?" Will said.

"So how will you find out?

"I'm going to have to ask the right questions, draw her out somehow. If she'll let me. She seemed rather mousy on the phone."

"Mousy?"

"Timid, untrusting. Afraid."

"Probably because she is," Rachael said, placing the sketch in her brief-case next to the letters. "And who can blame her."

The Madden house was set back from the road in a fairly rural neigh-borhood near city limits. The tarred driveway was long and S-shaped and led to a yellow two-story house with white shutters and trim. Freshly planted pansies and petunias fluttered in raised, bricked flowerbeds. Hummingbird feeders hung on the porch supports and a silver tabby cat lazed in the May sun near the doormat. Will rang the doorbell.

The door swung open and behind it stood a man of average height and ample build. His hair was thinning, but it was the only thing on his body that was.

"Yes?" he said. His tone was neither welcoming nor shunning.

"Mr. Madden?" Will said.

"Yes."

"Sgt. Will Pendleton, St. Paul police department. And this is my colleague, Rachael Flynn. We talked on the phone this morning?"

"Come in," the man said. He opened the door and Will and Rachael stepped inside. The house was cool and quiet and the first floor seemed to be completely decorated in multiple shades of blue and white. Jay Madden motioned them to a living room just off the front door, but which was open to a family room, kitchen and staircase. "You can sit in here. I'll get my wife."

Will took a seat on one of two matching padded chairs. "Such a friendly guy," he mumbled.

Rachael sat next to him in the other chair. She looked about the room. A basket of knitting sat by the couch. Books lined one wall in a shelving unit that stretched from floor to ceiling. A cat bed occupied one corner of the room and an entertainment center dominated another. A vase of fake gardenias and fanned-out *Midwest Living* magazines lay on the glass-topped coffee table in front of them.

They waited for several more minutes before they heard footsteps on the carpeted stairs leading into the living room. Rachael looked up. The woman entering the room had the tender eyes of young April Howard, as well as the plump cheeks and shy expression. She seemed to have dressed to match her house. April's powder blue pantsuit stretched across her roundish body and puckered a bit at the thick waistline.

Jay was right behind her. He spoke first. "This is my wife, April. April, this is Sgt. Will Pendleton. And this is…I can't remember who you are."

April was staring at Rachael as Jay fumbled for her name. April's eyes on her both unnerved and energized Rachael.

"Rachael Flynn," Rachael said. "How do you do, Mrs. Madden?" Rachael stuck out her right hand and April dropped her eyes. She held out her hand and Rachael took it. It was limp and clammy.

"You can call me April," the woman said. Her voice was soft, gentle.

"Thank you so much for meeting with us," Will said. "We really do appreciate it and we'll try and make this quick. Why don't we all sit down?"

Will and Rachael retook their seats and the Maddens sat on a cadet-blue sofa across from them.

"So, your parents tell me you work in a library," Will began. "They say you know just about everything there is to know about children's books."

"Well, I don't know if I know everything, but I do work in the library here. Just in the mornings." April's tone was tentative but polite.

Rachael recognized Will's opening question as an effort to win April Madden's trust. She wanted to win it also. She sensed she must have it.

"My mother works in a library, too," Rachael offered.

April looked at her and then looked down. "I work in the children's section."

"So does my mom."

April's full cheeks had taken on a rosy hue, as if she was embarrassed to be talking with Rachael. Will looked at Rachael. He had noticed it, too.

"Do you mind if we just get on with whatever brought you out here?" Jay Madden said.

"Sure," Will said. "We just need to ask your wife some questions about the disappearance of a teenager named Ronald Buckett."

April's cheeks got redder.

"Do you remember the day Bucky disappeared, April?" Will continued.

"Not really," April said quietly.

"This was the kid who disappeared, like, twenty years ago, right?" said Jay, a bit acerbically.

"Twenty-five, actually," Will replied. "Long time ago."

"I'll say. Do you really think April's going to be able to tell you anything? She was just a child."

"Yes. Yes, she was. But this boy, his nickname was Bucky, was the neighborhood bully. He was the kind of person who left an impression. Most people we've been talking to remember him. Not in a good way, unfortunately."

"You've been talking to other people?" April said, not much above a whisper.

Will turned to her. "Yes. We've been able to find some of the other people who lived on that street when you did." His voice matched hers. Pleasant.

Very smart, Will, Rachael thought.

"Do you want to know who?" he added.

April licked her lips and shrugged. "I don't really care. I probably don't remember them. They probably don't remember me."

"Oh, I don't think they've forgotten you. Let's see, do you remember Carole Bielke?"

April's face brightened. "She still lives there. She watches my parents' house when they're away. She was always very nice to me."

"So of course she remembers you!" Will said genially. "And there's Stacy Kohl."

"I remember her," April said, nodding.

"And Drew Downing remembers you. You remember him?"

April's cheeks instantly flushed red. "He lived across the street. He was older than me."

"Do you remember Santos and his sister, Elena?"

"They…they lived across the street, too," April said, looking down at her lap.

"Did you ever play with Elena?"

April raised her eyes. "What?"

"Did you ever play with Elena? She was about your age, wasn't she?"

"She…she was a year older than me. And she…she liked sports and was pretty. She…she had lots of friends."

"So, she never confided in you. Talked to you about things?"

"No," April said, shaking her head, but looking at her lap.

"Were there any other kids on your street? Anyone else who might've known Bucky?"

April shook her head.

"Must've been hard having three boys across the street and only the one girl."

April looked up. "Bucky was the only…the only mean one. The others weren't."

"What were Drew and Santos like?"

"I don't know. They…they were just regular boys." Her eyes fell back to her lap.

"Did you ever see Bucky tease Drew or Santos?"

April sighed. "Yes."

"Did it happen a lot?"

April laughed, but not one of mirth. "All the time."

"Why didn't anyone do anything about it?" Will said.

"What could anyone do?" April replied.

"Well, couldn't the teachers or their parents put a stop to it?"

April looked away, toward the window, as if to look back into the past. "They didn't always see what Bucky did," she said. "And sometimes if you told on him, it just got worse. And the worse it got, the more other kids didn't want to be around you."

Will leaned forward. "Bucky teased you, too."

April turned her head, back toward the room, but dropped her eyes to her lap. "Yes," she whispered.

"Can you tell me what he did?"

April's eyes gleamed and her cheeks turned crimson. Rachael turned to Will and shook her head slightly. But Will wasn't looking at her. His eyes were on April.

"I'd really rather not," April said.

"It would help the investigation if…" Will began but April quietly interrupted him.

"No," she said.

Will opened his mouth but Jay spoke up before Will could say anything. "She said she doesn't want to talk about it, Sergeant. I personally don't see how any of this pertains to your investigation, anyway. My wife has no idea how that body ended up where it did. If you ask me, it sounds like that kid had plenty of enemies and deserved what he got."

Will turned to Jay. "Well, Bucky had the same constitutional rights that you've got, Mr. Madden. Doesn't seem fair, I suppose. What he deserved was to be charged with his crimes and found guilty in a court of law. And I can tell you right now, if he had been, he wouldn't have been executed. So I can hardly agree with you that he deserved what he got."

Rachael felt the interview disintegrating around them. Will hadn't won April's trust. And she was sure she hadn't either. She spoke before Jay could come back with a rebuttal.

"April, you don't have to tell us what Bucky did. It's okay," she said. "We know whatever it was, it wasn't right and you shouldn't have had to endure it."

Jay murmured something under his breath.

"The thing is," Rachael continued. "It was an accident that Bucky died. We know it wasn't supposed to happen. It was just an accident. The person who was there when it happened got scared. They probably wanted to call the police but they were afraid they wouldn't be believed. So they buried the body."

April's eyes stayed glassy.

"Someone wrote to me, April. I'm an attorney with the Ramsey County prosecutor's office. The writer told me it was an accident." Rachael reached in to her briefcase and placed her hand around the letters. She felt the sketch and grabbed it, too. She placed the drawing in her lap and set the letters on the table by the vase of gardenias. "I have three letters from someone who knows what happened to Bucky. This person feels alone and afraid, but they wrote to me because they thought I would understand. And I want to tell them that I do. I do understand."

April had dropped her eyes to stare at the letters. But she said nothing.

"Do you know who wrote these letters to me?" Rachael said.

April slowly shook her head.

"Can you think who might have?"

"She already said she doesn't know!" Jay said hotly.

But April's eyes had moved from the letters to the drawing on Rachael's lap. Her head was cocked slightly as she took in the sketch from its upside-down angle. The glassiness in her eyes was dissipating; being replaced with something else, something Rachael couldn't define. Rachael turned the drawing around in her lap and watched as April's eyes followed the image righting itself.

"That house burned down," April said, her voice was vacant and toneless.

"Yes," Rachael said, watching her. "It sat empty for a long time before it caught fire."

April blinked slowly. "Are we done?" she said, languidly. "I don't feel well. I want to lay down."

"I think we can be done for today," Will said, as he stood.

"We're done. Period." Jay grumbled, standing as well. Rachael picked up the letters and the sketch and placed them back in her briefcase. April made no move to stand.

"I'd like to give you my card, April," Will said, extending his business card to April. She didn't reach out her hand to take it. Jay took it instead. "Call me if you think of anything."

As Will walked to the front door ahead of Jay, Rachael grabbed one of her own cards, and a pen. She sat back down and hurriedly wrote her home phone number on the back, praying she was doing the right thing. She stood and handed it to April with the handwritten number facing the woman.

"And here's mine," she said to April, fixing her eyes on April's eyes. The woman reached out and took the card.

"Thank you for talking to us, April," Rachael said, searching the woman's face for a clue as what she was thinking, but April only nodded, stood, and walked away, turning to climb the carpeted stairs that led to the rest of the blue and white house.

TWENTY-ONE

Rachael waited until she and Will had turned off the Maddens' driveway and onto the main road before she broke the silence in the car.

"Are you waiting for me to say something?"

Will didn't look at her as he negotiated a lane change. "I'd like to know what you think."

Rachael frowned. "I honestly don't know what to think. I feel like we're being lied to. By everybody. But there's no question in my mind that house figures into all of this, Will. Did you see the look on April's face when she saw that drawing?"

"I saw it."

"And?"

"And you may very well be right. But at the moment it's a morbid hunch you've got and nothing else. I can't log a gut feeling into evidence."

Rachael didn't argue with him. "I wish I had more time with her. I think maybe if you and her husband hadn't been there, she may have been more willing to talk with me."

"I actually have to agree with you there, but I seriously doubt she would've agreed to that. She didn't want to meet me without her husband there, remember?"

"Yes, but that's because you're a cop."

"Well, to your average taxpayer, you're practically the same thing, Rachael. You work for the county prosecutor."

"Yes, but the letter-writer sees me as different than that. If April wrote the letters, then she probably really does want to talk with me, Will. But not with you there."

"Perhaps I could arrange another interview at her house and have someone call me while we're there. I could take the call, give you a few minutes."

"I don't think that would work," Rachael replied. "I'd need more than just a few minutes. So would she. And I really don't think she'd open up with her husband right there. And with you still right there in the house."

"Well, you're not going to be dispatched to talk to her alone, Rachael. The chief won't allow it and neither will I."

"You were perfectly willing to let me meet with the writer last week."

"That was different and you know it." Will's voice was parental. "You were participating in a covert operation under police surveillance. My sending you off to question a suspect or a witness alone is out of the question. It's not your responsibility to interview suspects. We've been over this before."

Rachael sat back in her seat. "I just feel like me coming with you on these visits has had the complete opposite effect of what we'd hoped. Instead of it encouraging the writer to confide in me, I feel like it's driven them back underground. Maybe I shouldn't have come at all."

Will turned to face her. "I wouldn't say that. I really didn't expect any couch confessions, Rachael. I never suggested to you that I did. If you remember, I told you that your coming would either draw the writer out or chase them back but that either way we'd get a reaction. That's what has happened. After meeting with Drew and Santos, I'm quite certain they didn't write those letters. But I can't say the same about April or Elena. I think we're close, actually. Closer than we were before you came. I'm thinking the writer is a woman and she's covering for someone. Someone she loves or pities. That means it could be any of them. April, Elena, Marisol, or Ginny."

"So you're thinking Drew, Santos, or Lyle Downing killed Bucky."

"Don't you?" Will said without a second's hesitation.

The fact was, Will was right. She did think it was one of the men.

"So now what?" she said, without answering him out loud.

"I'd like to revisit Marisol Valasquez and Ginny Downing. And I'd like you to come with me."

"And what if the same thing happens?"

"I'll be surprised if it doesn't, Rachael. You being there will most likely make our writer uncomfortable. I'm expecting to get a cool or scant reaction to those letters."

"And what does that accomplish?"

"If either Ginny or Marisol is the writer, it will alert them that we're close." Will's tone was confident. "Decent people like this writer can't live indefinitely with something like this hanging over them, especially when it involves someone they love. That's why you've gotten three letters. What had been nicely buried for a quarter century has now been exposed and the whole thing is driving them crazy. Our visits have made it worse. And I still believe it's very important to them that we understand that the guilty party—that person they love—is not really guilty. That person just got unlucky one day, as was typical for them back then, and then they got scared and buried a body when they should have called the police. The letter-writer knows what happened that day. And they've kept it a secret all this time out of devotion. But now the walls are coming down and they don't want the person they love to get crushed under them."

"And if Marisol and Ginny don't offer up any information, then what?"

"We wait a little bit, find out a little more from other sources and then go back. And you continue to check your mail every day."

Rachael sighed.

"I almost wish…" she began, but then she let her voice fall away.

"You almost wish you hadn't gotten the letters?" Will finished for her.

"No. It's…never mind." She didn't want to tell him she almost wished she'd never shown him the letters in the first place.

The loft was empty and quiet when Rachael returned to Minneapolis that evening. Trace was no doubt still at the studio with Fig and McKenna.

She tossed her briefcase onto the couch, kicked off her shoes and walked across the smooth wood floor to the kitchen. She picked up the phone with one hand and opened the fridge for a Diet Coke with the other. As she walked back to the couch, she punched in the speed dial for Trace's cell phone. Rachael let her body drop onto the sofa cushions as the phone rang.

"Hey," Trace answered on the other end. "You home?"

"Just got here. You and McKenna going to be long?"

"I'm getting ready to wrap things up. But Fig and Jillian have McKenna out in the stroller at the moment."

"Was she giving you guys trouble this afternoon?" Rachael said.

"She was just bored and Fig said he had hit a creative snag with Joan. He needed a few minutes away from her to get his groove back. Or so he said. I'll come as soon as they get back. So. How'd it go today?"

"All right I guess. I don't know. Will thinks everything's moving along just like it should but I'm feeling like it just gets more complicated every day."

"What happened today?"

"Well, nothing really. I mean, April denied writing the letters and she says she doesn't remember much about the day Bucky disappeared. But then she refused to describe the ways Bucky teased her and nearly went into a trance when I showed her the picture of the house. Will noticed it, too. It wasn't just me this time."

"But?" Trace said.

"But she wouldn't say anything about it. She just said she wasn't feeling well and asked if we could be finished so that she could go lie down. And Will said yes."

"Really?"

"I think it's a ploy Will uses with witnesses like April Madden. I think he told her we could be finished because he actually wants her to lose sleep over all this. He wants everyone we've talked to to dwell on it, fret about it. And then maybe write me another letter. Or be so torn by the whole thing that the next time he calls on them they will simply give up and tell him the truth. He thinks the writer is one of the women and that they are protecting the person responsible for Bucky's death."

"Protecting?"

"Vouching for their overall innocence, really. Out of love or pity."

"And so April would be protecting whom?"

Rachael sat back on the couch, realizing that she already knew April probably didn't know Lyle Downing well enough to feel the need to protect him. But April had seen what Drew and Santos had to endure month after month, year after year. April knew their pain. Pity probably didn't truly describe what she felt for them. It was more like profound empathy.

"Drew or Santos, I think," she said.

"So now what?"

"Tomorrow Will is going to revisit the two mothers, Drew's and Santos's. He wants me to come with him. If April or Elena didn't write the letters, then he thinks it could've been one of the moms."

"And if it's not one of them?"

"Then the letter-writer had no reason to contact me because we don't have any other leads," Rachael said. "The writer contacted me not to say that there was a body and that it was Bucky's, but to let me know that it was an accident that he died. The writer thought we'd figure out pretty quick who was responsible. And that we'd naturally assume it was no accident."

"Because…?"

"Because people call for an ambulance when there's been an accident, they don't bury the body."

"I think I hear Fig and Jills on the stairwell," Trace said, after a pause. "We'll be home soon."

"Okay, see you in a bit."

Rachael clicked off the phone and placed it on the coffee table in front of her. She grabbed her Coke and took a long drink. As she set the can back on the table, she noticed the drawing of the house poking out of her briefcase next to her. She had forgotten to give it back to Will.

And the letters, too.

She reached inside the briefcase and pulled out the drawing and the three envelopes. For a moment, she considered jogging down to the studio and using Trace's copier to copy the letters. But it just as quickly occurred to her that it wasn't the letters themselves that were that important. It was the words. Rachael took out a legal pad and a pencil, opened the letters and laid them on the table. She copied down each sentence, giving each one its own line on the paper:

A body is going to be found at the River Terrace construction site.

He deserved what he got, but it was still an accident.

You understand about accidents; I've read the papers.

You need to know it wasn't supposed to happen.

After all this time, everything's happening too fast.

I don't know what to do now.

You had to tell the police, I guess. But I don't think they will understand.

They never understood.

I don't know what to do.

I shouldn't have told anyone.

I thought you would understand.

Someone needs to understand it was an accident.

It was only supposed to teach him a lesson.

Things are beginning to get complicated.

I'm uncertain what I should do.

This is all very confusing for me.

I need to meet with you.

I need to talk to someone who'll understand.

Meet me at the Starbucks on Grand Avenue in St. Paul this Wednesday at four o'clock.

Pick a table outside. I'll wear a red shirt.

I know what you look like.

Please don't tell anyone. Come alone.

I need your help. The police won't understand.

Please.

Rachael set the pencil down and sat back on the couch, studying the words. An odd sense of dread fell over her, an awareness that from the moment she opened the first letter she had been given a glimpse of a 25-year-old wound that still bled. Her eyes moved across the words and phrases that appeared more than once: *It was an accident. I don't know what to do. Please.*

She slowly folded the letters and put them back into her briefcase, along with the legal pad inscribed with the echoes of their contents. Trace and McKenna would be home soon and she didn't want to feel those words swirling about in her head any more today. Rachael glanced at the drawing of the house and grudgingly put it back in the briefcase, too. She doubted Will would ask about it when he'd call to see if she had the letters, which she knew he would. Will didn't know what to make of her internal misgivings about a house that no longer existed or how it figured in with the letters.

And the fact was, neither did she.

Will swung by the courthouse a little after 3:00 on Wednesday and Rachael was waiting for him. He had already called her earlier that morning to make sure she had the letters.

She did.

"We'll try Ginny Downing first," he said as they drove out of the courthouse parking lot. "She doesn't know we're coming. I couldn't risk Lyle knowing if he's the one being protected. If she's not home, we'll try Marisol."

"Does Marisol know we're coming?"

"Nope. I'm pretty sure if I'd given her a head's up we'd get there and find a pickup truck with Wisconsin plates in her driveway. But I'm counting on her being home. She cleans banks in the evenings so the afternoon is her home time."

"And what do you want me to do?

"Just what you've been doing. Look for an opportunity to bring out the letters and to make eye and voice contact."

"All right."

Several moments of silence filled the car.

"Will?"

"Yeah?"

"I almost didn't bring the drawing of the house."

"Oh. Almost?"

"I have it."

"Okay."

"I know you don't think much of it, but I just can't move past the idea that it means something."

"Then don't."

TWENTY-TWO

The drive to the suburb of Woodbury and the Downings' house took less than 20 minutes. Rachael perused Samantha's notes from the initial visit with Ginny Downing as they drove: Ginny had not said much when Sam talked to her and Lyle.

The notes were mostly filled with bulleted statements from Mr. Downing itemizing his disappointment with the school, law enforcement and the human race in general during those years his son was one of Bucky's targets.

"It's like Ginny wasn't even in the room when Sam was there," Rachael said aloud.

"No kidding," Will said. "We may learn quite a bit from her today."

"Or nothing at all," Rachael put the notes back inside Will's case file.

"I always learn something when I question somebody," Will said as he turned off a busy boulevard onto a quiet, residential street. "Even if they say hardly anything. Silence is a response. Okay, Sam says it's on the right side, cream-colored stucco. Twisted junipers in the front."

"I see it," Rachael said, as the Downing house came into view.

Will pulled up along the curb. "Bingo," he said softly as he motioned with his head toward the open garage. A red sedan was parked inside.

"What if that's Lyle's car?" Rachael asked.

"That's not Lyle's car. He still works full-time at General Mills. That's her car. She's home."

Will and Rachael got out of the car and headed up the front walkway. The front door was open and a screened storm door allowed a little white and black dog to hear their approach and begin a frenzied yelping.

"Tom-Tom!" A woman's voice sang above the yips and yaps. "Quiet!"

The woman appeared at the door and scooped up the little dog, which now began to snarl its annoyance. The woman was sixtyish, stylish, with flour on her hands and wrists. "Yes? Can I help you?"

"Mrs. Downing?" Will said kindly.

"Yes."

Will reached into his breast pocket and withdrew his badge. "I'm Sgt. Will Pendleton of the St. Paul Police and this is my colleague, Rachael Flynn. May we talk to you for a few moments? It won't take long."

"What's this about?" Ginny Downing's forehead immediately crinkled with obvious hesitation.

"We just need to ask you a few more questions about the disappearance of Ronald Buckett and the discovery of his remains," Will said.

"But we already talked to the police. We already told a policewoman we don't know anything about any of that." The little dog yipped a commentary on the seeming audacity of such a question. Mrs. Downing told Tom-Tom to please hush.

"Actually, there've been some new developments since Sgt. Stowe was last here, Mrs. Downing."

"Really?"

"Yes."

"In that case, you should wait until my husband can be here. I don't think I should answer any questions without him here."

"Understandable," Will said, nodding his head. "But the last time you were questioned together, you didn't get to say a whole lot, Mrs. Downing, and your opinion really matters to me. I'd really like to hear what you have to say."

"I don't know..." Ginny said. In her arms, Tom-Tom growled and bared tiny stained teeth.

"The thing is, Mrs, Downing," Will said, "we need to get a mother's perspective on what happened to the kids on your old street; the ones Bucky used to bully."

"Well, you should just go back and talk to Drew about all that. I know you were at his house. He told me."

"Yes, we were at his house. And that's why we're here. To hear from *you*. To hear your side on all this."

"Why do you want to hear what I think?" Ginny's face wore a mask of suspicion and doubt.

"Because to be perfectly honest with you, Mrs. Downing, someone knows how Bucky died. It could very well be one of the kids he abused. Could have been your son."

Ginny Downing visibly stiffened. "That's impossible. Drew would never hurt anyone."

"Well, see, those are the kinds of things I need to hear," Will said genially. "May we?"

Ginny hesitated for a moment and then opened the door. "I'll just put Tom-Tom in the laundry room. Please have a seat in the living room. Just to your left there."

Ginny Downing held the door with one hand as Rachael and Will stepped inside and controlled a wriggling demon in the other. As soon as Rachael and Will were standing on the carpeted entry, Ginny took off down to the right with Tom-Tom barking all the way.

Rachael and Will turned into the living room—a large, crown-molded expanse of ivory with accents of mauve and seafoam on the walls, curtains and throw pillows. A family portrait hung above a flagstone fireplace, taken when Drew was most likely a senior in high school, judging from his youthful look but visible facial hair. His smile was genuine, confident. He was standing in between his two sisters, both obviously several years younger. Lyle and Ginny sat in front of their children, smiling broadly. Everyone was wearing autumn-colored sweaters and khaki pants. It was a lovely portrait.

"Please, have a seat," Ginny's voice startled her. Rachael turned and saw that Ginny had returned from locking up Tom-Tom. She followed Will to the sofa. Ginny took an armchair across from them.

The woman said nothing. Her face had taken on a slightly rough edge to it, like she was prepared to do battle.

"Mrs. Downing, when Sgt. Stowe was here before, you and your husband said neither one of you remember seeing anything odd or out of place the day Bucky disappeared," Will said. "Is that correct?"

"As near as I can remember, yes. That happened 25 years ago."

"Do you remember if Drew seemed different or distant when Bucky disappeared?"

"Sgt. Pendelton, if you're suggesting what I think you are, you're seriously headed in the wrong direction. My son had nothing to do with whatever it was that happened to that Buckett boy."

"He might've seen something, though. He might have seen who was responsible for what happened to Bucky."

"I don't think so."

"Why not?"

"Because he would've said something. Drew was a good boy; a straight-A student and he never gave us an ounce of trouble. He was the complete opposite of Ronald Buckett. Complete."

"What can you tell me about Bucky, Mrs. Downing?"

Ginny inhaled, exhaled and tipped her chin. "I can tell you that Ronald Buckett got his kicks by tormenting other children," she said. "We parents didn't see it all, but we saw enough and we were powerless to stop it. Nothing we tried worked. We tried talking to Bucky. We tried talking to his parents. And every time we did, Drew begged us not to step in. It took years for Drew to get over what he suffered at the hands of that monster. And actually, I don't know that he ever truly got over being ridiculed for his speech impediment and the fact that he was smart. He told me once not long ago that he wakes up every day amazed that he has a beautiful wife who loves him and two sons who are liked by everyone. He still lives with fears that he's not good enough, that his lovely Nadine will leave him someday; that he somehow deserved to be treated the way Bucky treated him. But yes, my son seemed different after Bucky disappeared. He seemed relieved. As you would be if you had been him. And you should know that in spite of all that Bucky did to him, Drew is still one of the gentlest souls you will ever meet."

"I'm sure he is, Mrs. Downing," Will said. "No one is suggesting Drew wasn't a victim here. We're just trying to piece together a puzzle. Someone who had been hurt by Bucky and who had finally reached the breaking point tried to teach him a lesson. We think something went wrong and Bucky ended up dead."

"How do you know all that?" Ginny asked, her voice both tense and curious.

Will turned to Rachael.

"Because of these letters, Mrs. Downing," Rachael said, and she reached into her briefcase and pulled out the three envelopes. She opened the first one and laid it on the table between the couch and the armchair. "I'm an attorney with the county prosecutor's office. This first one was sent to me at my office before the body was found."

Ginny reached forward and picked up the letter with a trembling hand. Rachael and Will watched as her eyes moved across the page. When she was done, her eyes were glassy with fear and moisture. "Show me the others," she whispered.

Rachael opened the other two letters and handed them to Drew's mother as she said, "I went to the coffee shop like the writer asked in the third letter, but he or she never showed up."

Ginny took the letters and read them. Her chest was heaving slightly when she was done. "Do you…do you honestly think Drew wrote these?" she said, her voice tinged with disbelief.

"No," Will murmured, leaning forward in his chair. "We thought maybe you did."

Ginny looked down at the papers in her hand and then looked firmly at Rachael. "I didn't! I swear I didn't." She turned her head to look at Will. "Why would I write these? You think I killed Bucky? You honestly think I killed Bucky?" Her voice cracked on the word "killed."

"No, no we don't," Will answered quickly. "We don't think you did. We don't know who did. That's what we're trying to figure out."

"Well, then why do you think I would write these?" Ginny's voice sunk to annoyance.

"To defend your husband. Or your son," Will said plainly.

"*What?*" she whispered, eyes wide with alarm.

"To assure the police that what happened to Bucky was a horrible accident. That it wasn't planned. That it looks like a homicide, but it wasn't. It wasn't supposed to happen."

"But how could you even think that Lyle could kill someone! Or Drew? He was just fourteen! How could you think that either one of them would want to kill Bucky!"

"That's just it, Mrs. Downing," Rachael said, leaning forward. "Whoever killed Bucky *didn't* want to. It just happened. It was an accident."

Tears were freely falling down Ginny's face, splashing onto the letters in her hand. "You're wrong, you're wrong. I would know if it had been one of them. I would know! You're wrong. You're dead wrong!"

"Okay, okay," Will soothed. "We just had to ask. You understand, Mrs. Downing, don't you? We had to ask."

Ginny handed the tear-stained letters back to Rachael. "Does Drew know you thought it was him? Does he know?" Rachael could hear mother-love in Ginny's terse words.

"We never thought it was him, Mrs. Downing," Will answered. "We simply needed to rule him out."

"Well, I sure hope you have now. Because to think for even a moment that Drew would hurt anyone is preposterous. You should've asked me first and I could've told you Drew couldn't have had anything to do with what happened to that boy."

Will stood and Rachael followed. "I'm very sorry to have upset you, Mrs. Downing," Will said. "It truly wasn't my intention. We just needed to make sure you didn't write those letters."

Ginny stood as well. "I assure you I didn't."

"Any idea who did, Mrs. Downing?" Will said. "Can you think of anyone else who might've wanted to teach Bucky a lesson?"

Ginny wiped the last stray tear off her cheek. "Bucky was hateful to just about everybody. You'd have to ask everybody he came into contact with. Including his mother and step-father."

"Did he have any friends, Mrs. Downing? Did you ever see Bucky hanging out with anyone who wanted to be around him?" Will asked.

"He hung around his sister's friends, at least he did when they weren't in jail. They were older and could drive. Sometimes he'd take off with them and not come home for a day or two."

"Why do you think he did that?"

Ginny sighed. "Probably to get away."

"Get away?"

"From his stepfather. He yelled a lot. Hit him, too, I think. His mother did too. I don't know. I almost called the police a couple times. But they always seemed to stop yelling and fighting just as I picked up the phone."

"Must have been hard living next to a family like that," Will said.

"It broke my heart," Ginny replied, her words tangled with emotion. Fresh tears had sprung in her eyes. "I hated what Bucky did to Drew. But I hated what his parents did to him, too. I was glad when Bucky ran away, and I was even gladder when his parents divorced a couple years later and they moved out. We practically had a party on the street."

"I can understand that," Will said. "Say, one more thing. Rachael, the drawing?"

Surprised, Rachael reached into her briefcase and pulled out the drawing of the house.

"Does that house look familiar to you?" Will said.

Ginny peered at the sketch. "I don't think so."

"It's kind of a rough sketch of the house across the street, the one that burned down."

"Oh. Yes. I guess it did look like that."

Rachael watched Ginny's face with interest. There was no sudden change, no recognition. Nothing.

"Do you know if anything odd or unusual happened at that house?"

"Odd? What do you mean?"

"Did the neighborhood kids ever play around it or inside it?"

Ginny looked surprised. "Well, no. I certainly don't think so. It was locked. It had all its windows."

"What about the cellar?" Rachael said. "Were the cellar doors locked?"

"The cellar? I…I don't know. The owner paid someone to mow but the grass around the cellar doors was quite tall. I don't think the mower blades could reach it. You couldn't really see the cellar doors from the street. You would have had to walk up to them and look."

"So Drew never talked about being at the house or seeing anything happen at the house?"

"No. Of course not. Why are you asking all these questions about that house?" Ginny said.

"Just trying to cover all the bases. Thanks very much. We really appreciate it."

Will turned to walk out of the room.

He had his hand on the handle of the screen door when Ginny laid her hand on his arm. "You believe me about Drew and those letters, don't you?"

"Yes, of course, Mrs. Downing. Thanks again."

"Goodbye, Mrs. Downing," Rachael said.

The door opened and closed and Rachael and Will made their way to Will's car. Ginny Downing stood at the door and watched them drive away.

"So do you really believe her?" Rachael said when the house was behind them.

"I believe that she didn't write those letters and that she's certain Drew and Lyle are innocent."

"Do *you* believe they're innocent?"

"If my theory holds true that someone who cares for the guilty party wrote the letters then these two look more innocent than guilty. Would April or Elena write letters to protect Drew or Lyle? I don't know. But yeah, I believe that Ginny didn't. It will be interesting to gauge Marisol's command of the English language when we visit with her. Sam said she seemed fluent, but she wasn't considering if Marisol was the letter-writer when she talked with her. We may know right away whether or not she wrote them."

"Where does Marisol live?"

"White Bear Lake. We'll be there in no time. Are the letters still in one piece?"

Rachael reached into her briefcase and pulled out the letters. She hadn't refolded them or put them back in their envelopes. The second and third letters were spotted with stray tears.

"A few damp spots," she said, waving them a bit to dry them off.

Several minutes of silence passed as he drove and she placed the letters back inside the envelopes.

"Will?" Rachael said.

"Yep?"

"Thanks for showing Ginny the picture of the house."

"Sorry you didn't get the reaction you wanted."

"But you showed it to her. I appreciate that."

"You're welcome."

"Did you do it for me or for the investigation?"

Will paused for a moment before answering.

"Both, I guess. I'm a fan of hunches."

Rachael sighed. "Sometimes I think I just imagined what I felt that day in St. Anthony Park and sometimes I know beyond a doubt I didn't."

Will shrugged. "It's all going to come to light sooner or later. Then you'll know for sure."

Rachael relaxed in her seat. She hoped Will was right. But in the meantime she very much wanted to talk it over with someone who understood about divine intrusions that didn't bow to reason.

She wanted to talk it over with Josh.

It was only Wednesday.

Saturday's visiting hours seemed a long way off.

TWENTY-THREE

Finding Marisol Valasquez's duplex was easy but no one answered the doorbell when Will pressed it twenty minutes after leaving Ginny Downing's home.

"What do we do now?" Rachael said as she stood next to him.

"We see how long we can handle waiting. I'm for giving her half an hour. You okay with that?"

"I guess so."

The two returned to Will's car and got back inside.

Will leaned back in his seat. "I wish I had a peach Snapple," he murmured.

"Diet Coke with lime," Rachael said.

"Honey-roasted peanuts."

Rachael grinned. "Tortilla chips and pico de gallo."

"Corn dogs and hot mustard."

"Lox and bagels."

"I don't even know what that is and it's making me hungry," Will said.

Rachael's grin widened. "It's one of the few things Fig and I both love.

Smoked salmon and cream cheese on a bagel. With capers, if we have them."

"Ah, Fig. Now there's an interesting fellow."

Rachael laughed. "You can say that again."

A moment of silence hung in the car before Rachael spoke again. "Did I tell you he had been bullied in junior high? There was a kid after him who was just like Bucky; a kid who thoroughly enjoyed making other people feel bad about themselves."

Will's eyes were on a couple teens shooting hoops in a driveway several houses away. "I don't think it's that they enjoy it. They feed on it. I've been doing a little reading and also talking with our profiler. A textbook bully needs to make other people look bad in order to look good himself. That's how he does the math. It's like knocking someone off their feet just so you can look taller."

"Like it really matters how tall you are," Rachael murmured.

"It matters if you've been told it matters," Will said turning to look at her. "Told often enough and long enough that you believe it."

Rachael exhaled heavily. "But I don't want to feel pity for Bucky. I think of how he treated people and I don't want to."

"Well if it makes you feel any better, I don't feel pity for Bucky either. He was, however, deprived of his rights. Even pathetic scumbags like Bucky have the right to life, liberty and the pursuit of happiness."

"I know, but Drew and Santos and Elena and April—they were just kids when all this happened. Plus, Bucky was traumatizing them; that had to affect how they handled things. And it happened such a long time ago."

Will looked back toward the teens shooting hoops. "You know Minnesota law as well or better than I do, Rachael. There's no statute of limitation for murder. But no judge, prosecutor or jury is going to discount the fact that these people were juveniles and that they were indeed being significantly abused by a peer."

"And that it was an accident," Rachael said.

Will didn't answer right away. "So we've been told," he said, several seconds later.

Rachael hadn't stopped to consider it was anything but an accident. "You don't think it was?"

"I'm just saying I've taken a lot of statements from remorseful people who said they never meant to pull the trigger, that it was just an accident. There's an obvious difference between watching a person asphyxiate from anaphylactic shock and pumping a bullet into their chest."

Rachael was pondering a response when Will suddenly said, "There she is."

Rachael turned her head toward the duplex and saw that a bronze two-door sedan had pulled into the driveway. A petite woman with coffee-and-cream skin and silvery gray hair was getting out of it.

"Let's go," Will said. He got out of the car and Rachael followed.

Will walked briskly across the street and caught up with Marisol as she was putting her key into her front door. He already had his badge out.

"Mrs. Valasquez? Sgt. Will Pendleton, St. Paul police. This is my colleague, Rachael Flynn. May we have a word with you?"

Marisol looked from Will to Rachael and then back again. "What about?" Her words were pronounced with an unmistakable and lilting Latino accent.

"We've had some new developments in the Ronald Buckett case."

"But I have already talked to the police. I told the woman police I do not know anything."

"Yes, I know," Will said, "but we just have a few additional questions."

"But I already told you all I know. I do not know how that boy ended up in that field."

"Our visit today actually relates to some letters that were sent to Ms. Flynn here. May we come in?"

"Letters? What letters? I do not know what you are talking about." Rachael thought Marisol's face bore the look of someone surprised yet annoyed.

"Would you like to go inside so we can talk about it?" Will suggested.

"No, I would not."

"All right." Will turned to Rachael. "Ms. Flynn, will you show Mrs. Valasquez the letters that were sent to you?"

Rachael reached into her briefcase and pulled out the envelopes. She set the briefcase down by her feet and then opened the first letter. "I'm an assistant county prosecutor with Ramsey County, Mrs. Valasquez," she said. "Someone alerted me that the body would be found at that construction site. They told me Bucky's death was an accident. I've received three letters in all. All of them mention that what happened was an accident. This is the first one."

Rachael extended her hand. Marisol's face was now wrapped in worry. She hesitated before taking the letter. When she was done reading, she looked up and wordlessly handed the letter back.

"Will you look at the others?" Rachael said.

Marisol nodded and Rachael handed her the envelopes.

The woman opened and read the second letter without commenting and then the third. Her face was now impossible to read.

"Why are you showing these to me?" Marisol said, thrusting the letters back to Rachael.

"Because I want to know if you wrote them, Marisol," Rachael said, deliberately using the woman's first name.

"If you met that person for coffee then obviously you know I did not write them," Marisol snapped.

"The person never showed up. I didn't meet with anyone."

"Well, I didn't write them." Marisol turned the handle on her front door as if to flee inside her house.

"Do you know who did?" Will said.

"No."

"Could it have been Elena, perhaps?"

"No!" Marisol said, turning back to face them. "It indeed could not!"

"Why not?"

"She would have no reason to write letters like that!"

"She would if Santos had accidentally killed Bucky and Elena knew it."

Marisol dropped her hand and turned fully to face Will and Rachael. "I told the woman police and I am telling you now. My children were victims. Do you understand me? They were innocent children abused by someone no one bothered to discipline or stop. You dare to suggest my children had anything to do with this? I honestly do not know how you sleep at night, accusing innocent children of killing people and letting hoodlums run the streets doing whatever they please! I have told you all I know. Now get off my property."

Marisol turned back to her door, opened it and was inside slamming the door shut a second later.

Will and Rachael looked at each other.

"I suppose that went exactly as you thought it would?" Rachael said quietly as she picked up her briefcase and turned to walk toward the car.

"You never know how someone's going to react to an accusation of murder, even an accidental one," Will answered. "But I'm not unhappy with the way it went, if that's what you mean."

"Does that mean you're happy?" Rachael opened her door and slid inside.

Will went around to the other side, opened his door and got in. He started the car. "It means I learned a few things. That's always good." He put on the turn signal and pulled away from the curb. "I'm sure you picked up on a few things, too."

"I don't think she wrote those letters," Rachael said.

"I'm certain she didn't."

"Really?"

"Oh, yeah."

"Because of the way she reacted when she read them?"

"No, because of the way she spoke when she wasn't reading them."

Rachael didn't know where Will was going. "She seemed pretty fluent to me. Her English was quite polished, except for calling Sam a 'woman police.' But that's pretty negligible."

"Indeed. Her English was a little too polished. She didn't write those letters. I bet you a hundred bucks she didn't."

"I don't bet. But how do you know?"

"Get the letters out. Count how many contractions there are."

Rachael pulled out the legal pad instead. She read the lines she had copied from the letters.

"What's that?" Will asked, nodding toward the page of sentences.

"It's the text of my letters. They were mine, you know."

"Okay, okay. How many do you count?"

"Ten. I'm guessing you're going to tell me Marisol didn't use very many."

"Rachael, she didn't use any. Not one. She didn't write those letters. The sentence structure of those letters doesn't match the way she speaks."

Rachael put the legal pad back in her briefcase. "I'm more and more convinced it was April who wrote them."

"Or Elena," Will said. "And I've a pretty good idea why Marisol got so hostile toward the end there."

Rachael had a pretty good idea, too.

"She thinks Elena wrote the letters, doesn't she?" Rachael said.

"Yeah, I think she does."

"Do you think she did?"

Will shrugged. "She could have. It's a scenario that makes sense."

"Except Elena swore to me before God that she didn't write the letters, Will."

Will cast a glance Rachael's way. "You don't think people are lying to us right and left in this case?"

"I don't know, Will. I believe her."

"So maybe she's a good liar."

Rachael was silent for a moment as the possibilities tumbled about in her head.

Santos killed Bucky and Elena wrote the letters.

Drew killed Bucky and April wrote the letters.

Santos killed Bucky and April wrote the letters.

Elena killed Bucky and April wrote the letters.

Was it possible? She turned her head toward Will.

"Will, do you remember April saying when she was a child she didn't get together much with Elena because Elena was a year older, was pretty and into sports?"

"I do."

"Do you think it's possible that Elena could've accidentally killed Bucky and that April wrote the letters?"

"It's possible. Not probable. But definitely possible."

Will had already thought of it. That the girls had somehow planned to exact a little revenge and something went horribly wrong.

That would explain their twin responses to the house, although April's had been more pronounced than Elena's.

And if their act of vengeance took place at the abandoned house—most likely in the storm cellar—that would explain the unexplainable and unearthly sensitivity Rachael had toward it.

One girl couldn't have handled Bucky's body alone. But two girls, especially one who was athletic, could have.

She had to find a way to talk to April Madden. There had been no more letters. She didn't think now there would be. And Will had been adamant that she would not be sent over to April's house to speak to her alone.

But it suddenly occurred to her that she didn't have to go to April's house to speak to her alone.

Rachael knew where she could meet with April without Jay or Will present.

And tomorrow was her day off.

A perfect day for her and McKenna to visit the library in Coon Rapids.

TWENTY-FOUR

Rachael awoke early on Thursday, before McKenna had even begun to stir. She eased herself out of bed, tiptoed out of the bedroom and made her way quietly downstairs.

Minutes later, with a mug of coffee in hand, Rachael walked into the living room and toward its long, beckoning panes of glass. Watching the sun ignite row by row the windows of the neighboring skyscrapers always put her in a mood to reflect on the hand of God at work in the world. She liked beginning her day that way. Rachael turned an armchair toward the expanse of windows and sank into the chair's cushions to watch the day begin. The transformation from violet dawn to ginger sunrise was subtle, but powerful. Silent, yet pervasive. Whatever the sun fingered became golden and energized, like the touch of Midas in reverse.

She murmured three prayers to God as the day greeted the world of concrete, glass and steel. *Let April confide in me. Don't let me blow it. Help me convince Trace it's okay for me to do this.*

As she sipped the last swallow of coffee, she added a fourth: *Show me what to do about that house.*

Rachael rose from the couch to refill her coffee cup, aware that the sensation that something terrible had happened at that abandoned house was beginning to dissipate. Which to her meant one of two things: Her intuition had been wrong and she should just let it go. Or she needed to go back to the site and see if Almighty God really did have something to say to her about that house.

It would be easy enough to stop in St. Anthony Park on her way to Coon Rapids and determine which one it was.

She poured the coffee.

It was that easy to refill the cup.

It could be that easy to refill her mind, if that's what needed to happen.

God, if you really are speaking to me about that house, then have at it. I want to know what it means.

She was instantly aware that actually knowing what happened at the house, assuming something horrific did, would likely be hard to absorb.

But not knowing, and yet somehow perceiving that something did, was worse.

"What if Will calls?" Trace was saying as he placed McKenna's stroller into Rachael's car.

"He won't. It's my day off," Rachael replied, watching him close the trunk. She had McKenna in her arms.

"Who says he never calls you on your day off?"

"But he's in wait mode right now with this case. He's waiting for another letter or for one of them to break mentally and call him. He won't call."

Trace sighed. "Why don't you leave McKenna with Fig. I won't be at my meeting for very long. And I can make him promise that he doesn't feed her any chocolate-covered grasshoppers."

Rachael smiled. "Yes, but if he has chocolate-covered aphids, he'll think that's okay."

"Rachael."

"You don't have to worry about us, Trace. I really want April to see that I'm not Will. I'm not a cop. I'm just an ordinary wife and mother. I'm the person she thinks I am. Someone who understands."

"So do you?" Trace sounded doubtful.

Rachael readjusted McKenna's weight in her arms. "Yes, I do."

Trace leaned over and kissed McKenna's forehead and then Rachael's. "Call me if you're going to be late."

Rachael reached up to run her hand across his head. A tiny army of golden hairs had sprouted all across his scalp, calmly reminding her that few things stay unchanged for very long.

"I promise," she said.

She turned and placed McKenna in her car seat and then got in the car. The echoes of the car door shutting sailed around the parking garage, followed by the roar of the engine rumbling to life. Trace waved once as she backed out of her parking space and headed up the ramp to the outside world.

A bank of mid-May clouds had rolled in after the majestic sunrise and stray droplets of rain skittered across her windshield as she drove to St. Anthony Park. Fifteen minutes later she was turning onto Willow Street. Steel frames of the condominium complex reached for the sky ahead of her, splitting the street into two halves—sedate and diminutive at one end of the street and vigorous and imposing at the other. A swarm of workers peppered the landscape of the emerging building; the rest of the street was quiet. She drove past the first couple of houses and parked at the curb in front of the former Valasquez home. Across from her, on the other side of the street, sat the new house resting on old soil.

Rachael sat in her car for a few moments just looking at the new house. Then she reached for the drawing on the seat beside her and held it up, imagining the house in the drawing standing in place of the new house. An almost imperceptible stirring within her made her flinch in her seat.

"O dohn!" McKenna said from the back seat.

"Okay, sweetie. We'll get out for a few minutes," Rachael said absently, her eyes never leaving the grass where the older house once stood.

Rachael got out of the car and contemplated whether or not to get McKenna's stroller.

This shouldn't take long.

If it was at all like last time, it should only take seconds.

She opened the door to the backseat, unbuckled McKenna and lifted her daughter into her arms. Rachael closed the door and walked slowly across the street with McKenna in the crook of her left arm and the sketch in her right.

"A ba jah," McKenna said, reaching for the drawing with a pudgy arm.

"No, baby," Rachael said softly, moving the sketch away from McKenna's grasp, but her eyes stayed level with the lot ahead of her.

Her steps slowed and she stepped onto the sidewalk, directly in front of the house now. She took in the trees around the house, the older ones— the ones that had surely stood there when the older house had. And she studied the very ground itself, which had always been there. As she stood on the sidewalk, the beat of her heart slowly switched to a pounding cadence and a chilly wash of dread fell over her. The sensation was unmistakable.

She glanced at the drawing in her hand and she recoiled as if she had been stung.

God, what happened here? she breathed.

Her eyes were drawn to the cellar doors that Trace had drawn, and which had a lock on them once upon a time, but not when Bucky lived on this street. She was sure of that.

There.

She didn't hear a voice. She actually didn't hear anything.

Sensing the word "there" just then was like waking from a dream with the echoes of the dream's dialogue still in her head.

There.

In the cellar.

Rachael raised her eyes to look at the patch of grass where the storm cellar probably had been and had long since been filled in.

She turned and began walking back toward her car, surprisingly unafraid.

It wasn't just a hunch.

She had been let in on a shadow of a secret.

And it was real.

Rachael turned onto Crooked Lake Boulevard in Coon Rapids at twenty minutes after ten. A light rain had begun to fall and she wished she had dressed McKenna more warmly.

She found the library with little trouble. The ample parking lot wasn't full; only half a dozen or so other cars were there. Hopefully that meant April wouldn't be too busy. Rachael got out of the car and sprinted for the trunk. She grabbed the folded stroller, slammed the lid down and then ran to get McKenna out of the backseat.

A few seconds later she dashed through the rain to the library's covered entrance; a wide-eyed McKenna in one hand and yanked stroller in the other. "Here we go," she said softly as she unfolded the stroller and placed McKenna in it. They went inside.

Rachael was immediately reminded of walking into the St. Cloud library and seeing her mother behind a desk, or kneeling at the stacks, or helping a child choose between P.D. Eastman and Dr. Seuss. She walked past two retired people reading newspapers, two young adults in the computer lab, and three other mothers with their hands on strollers or wrapped around the smaller hands of toddlers and preschoolers. She headed toward the back, where she knew the children's section would be.

Where she hoped April would be.

Rachael found April in a gauzy dress of lemon yellow standing in front of a shelf of juvenile fiction, with a cart full of books at her side. She was putting the books away, but Rachael got the impression that it was just her hands at work; the rest of April seemed far away. The woman looked pale and unrested.

"April?" Rachael said, in as soft a voice as she could produce.

April turned her head and she seemed to sway at the cart for a moment as she took in Rachael's face.

"What…what are you doing here?" April whispered. Her face had gone completely white.

"I just wanted to talk to you alone, April. I knew you couldn't share what you needed to the other evening with Sgt. Pendleton and your husband there. Of course you couldn't."

April said nothing for several seconds.

"There is nothing else I need to tell you." April finally said. Nervousness made her blink like wind was rushing across her face. "Or anyone."

"April, you can't keep this up forever. Look at you. You're trembling. You wrote to me so that I could help you. And I want to. I do understand."

"I didn't write to you," April said, looking beyond Rachael, obviously wondering if anyone was watching them. Or if Rachael was alone.

"Really?" Rachael whispered. "Have you been approached by the person who did kill Bucky? Are they mad at you because you wrote those letters? Is that why you didn't show up at the coffee shop? Did they tell you not to?"

April shook her head, which was still facing away from Rachael. "You don't know what you're talking about!" Her almost-muted voice was strained with emotion.

"Well, then tell me, April! Tell me how I've got it wrong!"

April put her hand on the spine of a book in the cart and closed her eyes. "I have *nothing* to tell you."

Everything within Rachael told her April had plenty to tell her. "April, I can see how terribly this is affecting you. It's written all over your face."

April breathed in deep as if to steel herself. "I'm fine. You're mistaken."

Rachael was losing the edge with April. She decided to play her last card.

"April, what happened in that cellar?"

April pivoted her head, slowly. Her eyes were wide, empty pools.

"How…what cellar?" April replied, blinking nervously again.

"You were going to ask me how I know something terrible happened in that storm cellar, weren't you? You stopped yourself. What does it matter how I know? I know! I know something awful happened there."

April's eyes glimmered, the blinking continued at a frenzied pace and the pallor of her face slowly gave way to scarlet.

"Tell me what happened there, April," Rachael said gently. "Let me help you."

"Em tot," McKenna said, and April looked down at the child in the stroller, noticing McKenna, it seemed, for the first time.

"April?" Rachael said.

"There is nothing to tell," April said tonelessly, her eyes never leaving McKenna's face. "And I don't need your help."

For a few moments Rachael stood and watched as April stared at her daughter. Then she remembered Will telling her about the interview with April's parents and how Mr. and Mrs. Howard said that April longed to have children and yet was childless.

"Her name is McKenna," Rachael said gently.

April didn't look up. "That's an unusual name," she said.

"It was my husband's mother's maiden name."

April sighed. "She must like that."

Rachael hesitated before responding. "She's deceased."

April looked up at her. Her face now appeared devoid of emotion. "I have to get back to work."

She turned back to her cart and withdrew a book.

"Do you still have my card, April?" Rachael said, leaning in for one last plea for cooperation. "Do you have a way of getting ahold of me?"

April didn't look at her. "I won't need to." Her voice was flat and colorless. She placed the book in the stacks and turned to get another one from the cart.

Rachael waited only a moment longer. It seemed the conversation was over.

"Sorry to have bothered you at work, April. Goodbye," Rachael said, turning the stroller around to leave.

April said nothing.

As Rachael walked away she tried to tell herself that Will would say her encounter with April hadn't been a waste of time. She had learned something.

April was lying to her. She was sure of that.

But she didn't know what were the lies and what was the truth.

She walked past the stacks of other books, cataloging in her mind what she believed was true:

April wrote the letters or knows who did.

April knows who killed Bucky.

April knows what happened in that cellar.

As she approached the library entrance, her gaze fell upon the computers at the check-out desk. A librarian was scanning a patron's library card and looking at a computer screen.

Rachael had a card just like that one.

She didn't know why she hadn't thought of it before.

It would be very easy for a library employee to pull up an address of a cardholder from another metro library.

Rachael's home address was in the metro library system's computers.

April Madden was a library employee.

She quickened her steps to get outside. She wanted to call Will.

The drizzle had stopped and a weak sun was peeking through broken clouds. Rachael hurried to get McKenna into her car seat and the stroller stowed in the trunk.

When she was pulling away from the parking lot, she pressed the speed dial for Will.

He answered on the third ring.

"Pendleton."

"Will, it's Rachael. I need to tell you something."

But he interrupted her. "I need to tell you something, too." His voice sounded urgent.

"What is it?" she said.

"I just got a call from downstairs. Marisol Valasquez is here at the station. She just told the desk sergeant she knows who killed Bucky."

"Who? Who did she say did it?" Rachael said, incredulous.

"Eduardo Valasquez. Her deceased husband."

TWENTY-FIVE

Rachael had heard every word. Had mentally processed them and even imagined Marisol saying each one. But still she asked Will to repeat what he said.

"Marisol said it was her dead husband who killed Bucky," Will replied.

"Why? How?"

"I don't know yet. I just got the call that she's here. I'm heading downstairs to talk to her as we speak."

"And the letters?"

"I'm guessing she's going to tell us that she wrote them."

"Even though yesterday she vehemently denied writing them."

"Kinda makes you wish everyone had noses like Pinocchio so we would know when people are lying and when they're not."

Rachael's mind shot into overdrive. She looked at her watch. She could be at the station in less than twenty minutes. She'd need to find someone to watch McKenna for her....

"Will," she said. "Let me come and watch from behind the glass when you question her, please?"

"Well, I guess you could. Where are you calling me from? How long will it take for you to get here?"

"I'm leaving Coon Rapids right now. I can be there in fifteen minutes."

"Coon Rapids?"

"Yes, Will. Coon Rapids."

There was silence on the other end for a moment.

"What brought you to Coon Rapids?"

Here goes.

"McKenna and I went to the library here."

Another moment of silence.

"Is that why you called me?" Will didn't seem overly perturbed. But not too pleased either.

"Yes. There was no danger in my coming here. I just wanted to give April a chance to speak to me without cops or her husband around."

"And did she?"

"Kind of and kind of not."

"What did she say?"

Rachael wasn't sure how to explain that April had said nothing that really mattered; it was her body language that spoke volumes.

"She denied writing the letters and knowing anything more than she told us already, but Will, she was practically sweating blood," Rachael said. "That's how nervous and uncomfortable she was. And when I mentioned the house again, she nearly spilled it all, I think. She started a sentence with 'how' but then quickly switched gears and claimed ignorance. I think she was going to ask me how I knew something bad happened there. I think the killer has been in contact with her. Maybe she was told not to meet me and to say nothing else to anyone. She seemed sick with fear and dread."

"Well, I seriously doubt Eduardo spoke to her from the grave and told her not to meet you for coffee. Marisol might have."

"Do you really think Eduardo did it?"

"No. No, I don't. But if Santos did, I can see where Marisol would tank her dead husband's reputation to save her son," Will said. "And to spoil her own reputation by claiming to write those letters when they were really written by Elena."

"Will, can you wait for me?" Rachael pleaded.

"I'll give you fifteen minutes, but then I'm going to have to start whether you're here or not. I'll have Sam watch for you."

"Thanks, Will."

"Okay. See you."

Rachael pressed the button to end the call and then quickly pressed the number for Kate, her assistant at the courthouse.

"Kate Markham, Ramsey County Attorney's Office," said a voice on the other end, seconds later.

"Kate, it's Rachael. I have a big favor to ask. Do you mind taking your lunch a little early?"

"Well, no. I guess not. What's up?"

"I just need you to take your lunch hour a little early, that's all."

"Okay."

"And share it with someone."

Kate laughed. "With who? You?"

"McKenna," Rachael answered.

As soon as McKenna was in Kate's arms and happily distracted, Rachael made her way out of the county attorney's offices and sprinted across the adjoining parking lot to the police station. She paced as she waited for her turn to walk through the metal detector and was relieved when she saw Samantha waiting for her on the other side.

"This way," Sam said, as she led Rachael through a series of corridors. Sam stopped in front of a door, opened it and led Rachael into a small room with no furniture inside. On one wall was a thick pane of tinted glass. On the other side, in an adjoining room, Will and a uniformed policeman sat with Marisol Valasquez. A tape recorder was on the table in front of them.

"They've just started," Sam said, reaching over to flip a switch that would relay the audio from the other room. "You've not missed much. Just the personal data and Will making sure she understands her rights."

A mounted speaker behind her crackled to life.

"And you understand that you are not obligated to tell me anything without your attorney present?" Will was saying.

"Yes," Marisol answered. She was wearing black slacks, a red silk blouse and no jewelry except a wedding band.

"And you're waiving that right?"

"Yes, I am."

"Okay, Mrs. Valasquez, you told Officer Reynolds here that your deceased husband, Eduardo Valasquez, killed Ronald Buckett."

"Accidentally, yes."

"You saw this happen?"

"Yes. I was there."

"Was anyone else there?"

"No. Just me."

"And how long has your husband been deceased?"

"Five years."

"Okay," Will said, leaning back in his chair. "Why don't you tell me how it happened?"

Marisol cleared her throat, pausing for a moment to seemingly gather her thoughts.

"It was such a long time ago," she said softly. "I may not remember it exactly as it was."

"Just tell us what you remember." Will's tone was gentle, but commanding.

Marisol cleared her throat again. "That Buckett boy had been harassing our children for months and years and no one was doing anything about it," she said. "Eduardo and I could not stand by any more and let that boy harm our children. The school was doing nothing. The parents were doing nothing. The police were doing nothing."

Marisol paused then; perhaps to see if Will would challenge her last point. When he said nothing, she continued.

"So we decided we had to find a way to stop it ourselves. We came up with a plan to teach him a lesson. I approached Bucky when he was outside and told him my husband and I wanted to make a deal with him, that we would pay him to leave our children alone. I told him if he was interested, to meet Eduardo in the woods across from our houses and he would give him the money. I told Bucky we did not want anyone seeing Eduardo paying him, especially Santos and Elena.

"Bucky went into the woods and I followed him. Eduardo was there waiting for us. When we reached him, Eduardo put his hand in his pocket. Bucky thought he was reaching for his wallet. But Eduardo pulled out a gun instead."

"A gun." Will said. He looked dubious. "What kind of gun?"

"I do not know what kind of gun it was," Marisol said, frowning. "The kind with bullets in it!"

"Go on."

"Eduardo told Bucky there would be no more bullying. That we would not stand by anymore and let him destroy our children. Eduardo said he was not afraid to use the gun. Bucky laughed at him and Eduardo got angry. Eduardo, he said, 'Do you think I am kidding? You are more stupid than people say you are.' And when Eduardo said that, Bucky rushed at him and they struggled and they fell to the ground. The gun went off. At first I thought it was Eduardo that got shot. I saw blood on his hands. But then I saw that it was Bucky. Blood was coming out of his belly and he started yelling, 'You shot me, you shot me.'

"Eduardo could not believe it. His face was like in shock. And I said, 'Eduardo, we must get help.' But Eduardo, he just stayed there on his knees looking at the blood. And then the blood stopped coming out and Bucky stopped talking. His eyes went back in his head. And I knew he was dead."

Marisol stopped and closed her eyes. Will waited a moment.

"So then what happened?" he said.

"We knew no one would believe it had been an accident. No one would believe it. It was Eduardo's gun and everyone knew how hateful Bucky was to us. And we had two children at home who needed us. We buried the body because we were afraid. Bucky had run off before. We hoped people would believe he had run off again. This time for good. And they did."

"And no one heard the shot?"

Marisol lifted her shoulders. "I do not know what other people heard. No one called the police to say they heard a shot."

"And you never told your children what happened?"

"Eduardo and I never spoke of that day again."

"Do your children know now?" Will asked.

"I called them yesterday and told them."

"And how did they take that news?"

Marisol eyed the detective. "They were upset, of course."

"Do you still have the gun?"

Marisol shook her head. "I do not know what Eduardo did with it. I never saw it again."

"So those letters that Ms. Flynn got in the mail. Do you know who wrote those?"

"I wrote them."

"Why did you write them, Mrs. Valasquez?"

Marisol rubbed her fingers as if they ached. "Because I was afraid you would think it had been murder. It wasn't. It was an accident."

"Why did you send them to Ms. Flynn? Why didn't you just send them to the police?"

"Because she understands about accidents. Her brother killed someone when he did not mean to. Surely you know this."

"How did you think writing to her would help you, if I may ask?"

"Because someone needed to understand! It was an accident!"

"You didn't show up at Starbucks last week. Why not?" Will's tone was kind, but there was an edge to it.

"I got scared. I decided I had been wrong to write to her. She would not have been able to help me even if she wanted to."

"Why is that?"

"Because she is not in charge of this case. *You* are. And you do not understand."

"Mrs. Valasquez, what did you think would happen when we found the body?"

Marisol lifted her chin. "I thought you would figure out it was Bucky and then you'd start asking questions. You would find the people who knew Bucky."

"And who had been victimized by him?"

"Yes."

"Did you think we would suspect Santos or Elena perhaps?"

"I...I do not know."

"What did you use to write these letters?"

"A computer."

"Yours?"

"I do not have one. I used one at the library."

"Where did you mail them from?"

"St. Paul."

Will cocked his head. "You drove all the way to St. Paul to mail the letters?"

"I did not want you to know where they came from."

"Yesterday you told me you didn't write them."

"Yesterday you came to my house unannounced. I was not ready to tell you everything. Today I came to you on my own."

Will leaned forward and rubbed his forehead. "You know, Mrs. Valasquez, the English in the letters doesn't sound like the English coming out of your mouth."

"I have lived here in the United States for forty-one years! I am fluent in English."

"Nevertheless, I can see differences. You don't use contractions, Mrs. Valasquez. You say 'would not' where the letter-writer says 'wouldn't.' You say 'I do not,' where the letter-writer says 'I don't.' That's a pretty significant difference."

Marisol didn't comment. Her gaze was firm.

"Don't you think so, Mrs. Valasquez?" Will said.

"I think the police worry far too much about little things like letters in a word instead of ridding the streets of criminals." Marisol lifted her chin. "I wrote the letters."

"Okay, Mrs. Valasquez, we appreciate your coming forward. We need to verify your statement of course. So we'll be in touch."

"Verify my statement?"

"Make sure it matches up with other things we know or have discovered."

Marisol blinked. "Then I am free to go?"

"Yes. Officer Reynolds here will see you out. Thanks again for coming in."

Marisol stood, and for a moment it seemed like she was about to say something else. Then she turned on her heel and left the room.

Will turned off the tape recorder and turned toward the two-way glass. He motioned with his hand for Rachael and Sam to come into the room.

A minute later, Rachael and Sam had joined him.

"Well?" Rachael said, anxious to hear what Will thought.

"I think she's lying," he said.

"About everything?"

"Probably."

"She's covering for Santos and Elena, then?" Rachael said.

"I think so. But she's done her homework. Marisol's a smart one. She put a gun in the story that doesn't exist anymore, a wound to the belly that would bleed out very quickly, she even noted the postmark on your letters and remembered it. She probably looked your name up on the Internet to find out why Elena would write to you."

"Or she just called Elena and asked her. Maybe she begged her kids to let her do this for them since they all knew we were getting close," Sam said.

"I'm going to have to go back and talk to them both." Will sounded frustrated.

"I still think it was April who wrote the letters, Will," Rachael said. "She could've gotten my address off the library system's computers. She's a library employee."

"Yes, but Elena could've followed you home from work, saw which building you lived in, and then popped into the foyer and noted which suite number was yours."

Rachael said nothing as they left the interview room. She, like Will, was sure Marisol wasn't telling the truth. Partly because Marisol's story didn't involve the storm cellar, but she didn't think Will wanted to hear that particular detail at the moment.

And partly because she knew firsthand that devotion can most assuredly drive someone to confess to something they didn't do.

TWENTY-SIX

Rachael spent most of Friday morning doing laundry, cleaning out the fridge, and playing with McKenna. But her concentration was riddled with thoughts of April, Marisol, Santos, Elena, and Drew. And when she wasn't wrestling to keep their images out of her head, she unwillingly pictured a storm cellar with weeds all around it and a broken lock on its doors.

Trace had told her before he left for the studio to just relax and enjoy her day off. But she couldn't. Her brain, it seemed, had other plans.

After lunch, Rachael put McKenna down for a nap and headed to the phone to call Will.

He answered after two rings. "Will, it's Rachael. Have you heard anything? Have you talked to Elena or Santos?"

"Rachael, it hasn't even been 24 hours yet."

"I know but I'm going crazy here."

Will laughed, then said, "I tried talking with Elena by phone this morning. Her husband said she was too distraught to talk to me right now. I've left a message with Santos to call me and so far he hasn't. And I'm not driving to Wisconsin if I don't know where he is or what he's doing. That's all I'm going to do about it today, Rachael. Unfortunately, I do have some other bad guys to catch."

"Sorry, Will. I'm just a little obsessed by this. It's ruining my day."

"Well, knock it off. It's Friday. And tomorrow's Saturday."

After she hung up the phone Rachael stood in the kitchen for several minutes, just staring at the floor. McKenna would sleep for two hours at least. That meant she had 120 minutes of quiet, uninterrupted loft-time stretching before her. Two hours to nurse the obsession.

As she moved away from the kitchen she found herself grateful that the evening was looking surprisingly promising. She didn't normally anticipate Trace's friends coming over on Friday nights but she felt oddly thankful knowing they would fill the evening hours. Sid and Brick would come over a little after seven. Fig would arrive next, with Jillian, a tureen of gazpacho and his own, highly innovative version of Pictionary.

But there were many hours to fill before the artists would come and she could forget about the storm cellar, the woods, the wounded people. Just forget about it all.

Unless…

Unless Trace and the others could help her out a little. Maybe help her envision what might have happened in that cellar. If they could embellish their original drawings, or draw new ones…

If she could just visualize what really happened there, somehow picture it, she could probably break through to April and they could end this.

Rachael headed up to her bedroom to put on her running shoes. She would run up and down her own stairs—a hundred times if she had to—to exert her body and brain to numbness. Then when McKenna awoke, she'd head to the studio to tell Fig and Trace to have plenty of art paper on hand for when the gazpacho was gone.

"So what exactly are we doing?" Sid said. He pushed his half-eaten Bananas Foster away and grabbed his original drawing of Bucky succumbing to an allergic reaction. The gazpacho had long since been eaten and McKenna was asleep in her crib upstairs. The artists were sitting on stools around the granite island countertop. Jillian was hovering over Fig. Rachael sipped coffee and leaned against the fridge, ready to defend her newest idea.

"We're putting our original drawings in a cellar, Sid. It's not that difficult," Fig scolded.

"We did this already," Sid grumbled, selecting an art pencil from a Mason jar in the center of the counter.

"No we didn't," Fig countered. "We had the kid dying in all kinds of places and in all kinds of ways. Rachael only wants mishaps that could happen in a cellar."

"A lot of things could happen in a cellar."

"Yes, and you've given us no parameters," Brick said solemnly. "Do you know what it means to give an artist a pencil and paper and no parameters?"

"It means I will have lots of visual images to think over," Rachael said.

"I don't see how this is going to help," Sid said, shaking his head. "You don't know how the kid died. I'm pretty sure it wasn't my way. I don't see how playing Clue with our drawings is going to help you figure out how it happened unless you're expecting a choir of angels to sing over the one that's right."

"But she is!" Fig exclaimed.

"Fig," Rachael said, pulling her body away from the fridge.

"You are," Fig said, turning to her.

"It's not exactly like that," she said.

"Look, let's just do this for Rachael, eh, guys?" Trace interjected. "And Sid, it still could've happened your way. And I don't mean anaphylactic shock. He could've choked or been strangled."

"Sure. People accidentally strangle other people all the time," Sid muttered.

"Something else could've strangled him," Fig said.

"I'm redrawing mine with a bullet wound like I wanted to in the first place," Brick said, reaching for his drawing and settling back onto his stool.

"Okay, then, off we go!" Fig said happily. "Rachael, you can go over to Trace and murmur things in his ear or whatever. Just don't look over my shoulder. It makes me nervous and gives me gas."

"Please, Rachael, go," Sid said.

Rachael turned to the coffee pot and refilled her cup. "I'll go watch the History Channel for a while. Holler when you guys are done."

"I'll join you," Jillian offered.

Forty-five minutes and another pot of coffee later, Trace called Rachael back over to the open kitchen.

"These are crazy," he said as she came near. He was shaking his sparsely covered head.

"It's okay," she said. "The whole idea is a little crazy, I'm sure. But I think it might help me."

The drawings were laid out on the dining table, edge to edge. From a distance Rachael could see that it would be easy to determine whose were whose. Sid's was caricatures, Brick's was wildly impressionistic, Fig's was inventive and Trace's featured beautifully detailed faces.

But they were pictures of death.

She started with Sid's. He had redrawn his sketch completely. Bucky was now hanging from a crudely constructed noose wrapped around a floor joist above his lolling head. Sid had drawn the eye-popping Bucky wearing a cowboy hat, chaps and an empty six-shooter holster around his waist.

"Nice Stetson there, Sid," Trace commented, as everyone gaped at what Sid had drawn.

"Sorry, Rach. I couldn't resist. I'm a cartoonist. But he could've been hanged, you know, if the kids didn't know what they were doing when they threatened him. With his body weight, it would've been hard to cut him down to save him."

"Yeah, especially if they had all ridden away already on their palominos," Brick said.

"Nice one, Brickle," Sid said, making a sour face.

The others were already moving away from Sid's drawing but Rachael's eyes lingered there. She wasn't sure why, especially since the cowboy hat added a sick layer of comedy that made the entire drawing seem out of place. But she was aware that she moved away from Sid's drawing slower than anyone else.

Brick had rubbed out the knife from his original drawing and left the gaping wound. A revolver had been added, lying at an angle near Bucky's bleeding body. The shooter was kneeling at the body, hands over his or her eyes. The gender was impossible to tell. Brick said he did that on purpose because anyone can squeeze a trigger.

"My idea actually works better in the cellar," he added. "The sound of the gun going off wouldn't have traveled far underground. And kids are notoriously unlucky around loaded firearms. A kid with a loaded gun, even if he has no plans to use it, is as dangerous as a sixteen-year-old boy with a new license and his dad's Camaro."

"How do you know so much about kids?" Sid said.

"Because I'm around them all day, of course!"

As she looked at Brick's drawing, Rachael couldn't help but picture Santos pulling the trigger. If Marisol was lying about Eduardo, perhaps she was lying about where Bucky died. Maybe Santos did pull the trigger. But maybe he pulled it from within the cellar. And Santos wouldn't have had much of a struggle getting Bucky's body out of the cellar. It would've been difficult, but he could've done it….

She moved on to Fig's drawing. He had redone his sketch, too. The poisoned Dr Pepper was gone. Instead, Bucky was now standing in a puddle of water in a damp cellar. Loose electrical wires hanging from a decrepit ceiling were just inches from falling into it. Another teen, Santos or Drew, was standing a few feet away, on dry ground, holding a two-by-four in a menacing way. The look on the second teen's face was one of desperation.

"See, the normally good kid is telling Bucky he can't take it anymore," Fig said. "He's got the board and he's waving it around and he's pretty near crazy with frustration. He's going to let Bucky really have it. But he doesn't know that Bucky is a second away from being toasted. See the wires. Zap!"

"Electrocuted," Jillian whispered, as she looked over Fig's shoulder.

"That could happen in a cellar," Fig said.

"Assuming the owner of the house was still paying his utility bill." Sid sounded unconvinced.

"Well, why wouldn't he?" Fig countered. "He'd have to heat the thing a little in the winter or the pipes would freeze and flood the house."

"Assuming he was still paying his water bill," Sid said.

Fig turned back to Rachael. "It could happen that way in a cellar."

Rachael touched Fig's shoulder, but directed her eyes to the last drawing. Trace's.

All he had done was added a few lines to his original drawing: He had sketched cellar walls around a choking teen and the one who watched.

"You're getting lazy in your old age, Trace," Sid said, laughing.

Trace shrugged his shoulders. "I just liked what I had before. Besides. I don't think it's the weapon or the device that's the most important thing here. I think it's what these kids were thinking. I think maybe it all came together very fast, and fell apart the same way."

The room was silent. Rachael stared at Trace, but it was the echo of his words that held her—and the figures in his drawing.

"Okay, that's it. I'm not playing anymore," Sid announced suddenly, breaking the stillness. "Trace always wins."

"Me, too." Brick said, tossing his pencil down. "I want egg rolls. Who wants to come with me?"

"Jills and I will come," Fig said happily. "I know this great place!"

There were a few minutes of bustling activity as Brick, Fig and Jillian left. And then the loft was quiet again. Trace disappeared into the bathroom and Rachael turned back to the drawings. She was intuitively drawn to two: Trace's and Sid's.

And she did not know why.

She pulled Sid's and Trace's away from the others and leaned over them, resting her chin in her hand. Both beckoned to her in a way that unnerved her.

"So, what, you like mine now?" Sid said, making no attempt to hide the slightly sarcastic edge to voice.

"Yes, Sid, as a matter of fact, I do."

"Liar."

"What do you care? You don't like this game anyway." Rachael said, picking up the drawings and placing them one atop each other.

"That's right, I don't!"

Rachael moved away from the stools and walked over to her briefcase on a table by the loft's entrance. She placed the drawings inside.

"You really like mine?" Sid said again in a softer tone. His brow was creased with skepticism.

"Yes. I do."

"How come?"

She stood at the table looking down at her briefcase, knowing she would spend part of the weekend just staring at the two new drawings, as well as the older one of the house. She hadn't a clue why. She didn't know how to explain what she didn't understand herself.

"I don't know."

"That's a dumb reason to like something."

"Thanks, Sid."

"It is."

"You're right."

"You should figure out why you like it."

Rachael knew her visit to Joshua at the prison tomorrow had to be a step in that direction. If God was at the heart of what was happening to her, it would certainly make sense to Joshua, and he in turn could then explain it to her. She was sure of that.

And if she could finally make sense of her strange yet seemingly divine hunches, she might be able to make sense of everything else in the case.

"I intend to."

TWENTY-SEVEN

Joshua's physical appearance hadn't changed in the weeks since Rachael had seen him last; the crayon orange of his prison jumpsuit was the same, his pulled-back pony tail still had the same little comma-shaped curl at its end, and he still looked too thin for his height. But Rachael detected subtle differences in her brother's demeanor as they greeted each other in the prison's visiting commons.

"How've you been, Josh?" she said as she took a seat across from him. "You look...great. Can I say that?" Rachael laughed.

Joshua leaned back in his chair. "It's the food here. Excellent cuisine."

"You're still too thin, so I doubt it's the food," she said, studying her brother. "You look...relaxed. Almost content."

Joshua shrugged.

A realization fell across Rachael as she stared at Josh. She knew this look of his.

"You've found people in here who need you," she said softly.

The corners of Josh's mouth turned up slightly and he looked away. He never did like talking about the hurting people whose lives crossed

his. "You don't have to look very far in this world to find people who need
a friend," he said, as he brought his gaze back to hers. Something in the
way he said it seemed to communicate that that was all he was going to
say about the people now within his circle of compassion. "So how have
you been?" he asked, confirming his change of subject.

Rachael had spent the hour-long drive to the prison rehearsing ways
to explain to Joshua all that had transpired since their last visit—in as
uncomplicated a way as possible. But there was nothing simple about
what had consumed her life for the past month and a half.

Fifteen minutes later, after Rachael had told Josh about the letters, the
investigation so far, her visits with Will and her own visit to April, and
the meeting at Starbucks that never took place, she reached into a bag she
had placed at her feet and withdrew the drawing of the house.

"This is the empty house next door to Stacy Kohl's," she said, handing the drawing to Joshua. "Stacy saw Bucky grope April in front of this
house when Bucky thought no one was looking. It burned down a few
years after Bucky disappeared."

"So where did you find this picture?" Josh said, not looking up from
the sketch.

"I didn't. Fig and Trace drew it."

"So you had a photograph, then?"

Rachael shook her head. "No. I met the woman who was quoted in
the newspaper and on the news when the body was discovered. She still
lives on that street. I didn't seek her out, Josh. She came up to me. I had
gone to see where the body had been found, where those kids had all
lived. She told me what the house looked like."

"She must have a pretty good memory."

"Actually Josh, there's something very strange about this house. When
Fig started drawing it and when Trace finished it, I could sense what
needed to go where. It was like I knew how it looked."

Josh looked up at her.

"Josh," she continued. "When I walked past the lot where that house
once stood, this feeling that something terrible happened inside it swept
over me like a huge wave, even though there's a new house there. I know
it doesn't make any sense. But when I look at this drawing and when I

stand at the sidewalk looking at where that house once stood, I know it figures in to what happened to Bucky. I *know* it."

"So you've been back to look at it?"

"Yes. I was there on Thursday. The feeling was just as strong. Josh, I prayed to God to help me understand what it meant. And when I did, I heard something, but not with my ears. It was like God was telling me it happened in the cellar."

"What happened in the cellar?"

"I don't know! But something did. Something terrible."

"You think Bucky was killed there, instead of in the woods?"

Rachael sighed. "I don't know. Maybe. This is what's driving me crazy. It's like I have intuitions about things, but nothing that I can base on fact, nothing concrete. And it's not just about this house. This kind of thing has been happening more and more since McKenna was born, and since you...Josh, that's how I knew there was a fifth person in the room with you when Vong Thao died. That's how I knew that woman in the parking lot wasn't going to use that gun, not on me. They're like hunches, but more than that. Different. Will Pendleton doesn't know what to make of them. Trace is afraid of them...."

"And what about you?" Josh's face revealed nothing of what he was thinking.

"I...I don't know what to think. I'm frustrated, I can tell you that. I want to understand it."

"Understand what?"

Rachael paused for a split-second. "Well, I want to understand what all this means. How am I supposed to handle being able to perceive things that no one else can when I don't understand them?"

Josh leaned forward. His manner was casual, unhurried. "You handle it like you handle everything else that is bigger than you are."

Her brother's relaxed tone stunned her. "I don't get what you're saying."

"You let go."

Rachael was stymied into silence. Letting go made no sense at all. At all. "Let go?" she echoed.

"You think it's God who has given you this ability?"

"Well, yes."

"Then you don't have to understand how it works. Probably better if you don't."

Rachael sat back in her chair. The one person she thought could help her get a grip on this was telling her to loosen her hold completely.

"Rachael, you're trying to get inside this thing," Josh continued. "I can see that. I'm not even surprised. That's how you are. It's what makes you a good lawyer. But you can't get inside this. If it's from God, it's meant to get inside of you. If he's gifting you somehow, you don't need to worry about making the gift work. It will play itself out in you, in spite of you."

Rachael let his counsel settle in and around her. Despite the surprise that Josh wasn't going to explain anything, his words had a calming effect.

"So what am I supposed to do?" she said.

"I think you're doing just fine, aside from trying to dissect this."

"But I'm not doing anything!"

"That's not true. You're being attentive to what appears to be a message from God; neither ignoring it or allowing anyone else to ignore it."

"Yes, but it's not accomplishing anything."

"How do you know?"

Rachael opened her mouth and then shut it. Josh was right. She had no idea what was racing at that very moment through the minds of the people whom she had shown the drawing of the house to—especially April and Elena. There was no way to know for sure that broadcasting her prescient thoughts about the house was accomplishing nothing.

"So I just keep doing what I'm doing no matter how lost and confused I feel?" she said.

"Rach, you feel lost and confused because you can't explain what's happening. And it's not like you to get caught up in stuff you can't wrap your brain around. And yes, I'd say you just keep doing what you're doing. Stay open, stay attentive, stay available. If God is behind all this, he's also in front of it. You don't need to worry about having all the answers."

Josh handed the picture back and Rachael took it. "It's my nature to want to have the answers," she said.

"And I'm sure that's why God has trusted you with such a powerful gift. You won't waste it. Or disregard it."

Rachael looked at the picture in her hands, at the storm cellar that seemed to summon her. "Why do you think this is happening to me, Josh? I didn't ask for it."

"I wouldn't worry too much about that, either, Rach. Could be this is the answer to Nana's prayer for you. Remember how she prayed over us when we were little, asking God to do great things through us?"

Rachael remembered. Eva's mother had been wildly devoted to God, passionate to the extreme. Rachael had long thought that her deceased grandmother's prayers were the reason Josh's devotion to God was so intense. She had not considered what her grandmother's prayers for her had accomplished.

"Or it could be that this just happens to be the plan God had for you. I've no doubt you are in a position to use this gift for good. You've already used it to help me."

Rachael raised her head to look at her brother, but said nothing. She had always thought of Josh as the one God had gifted. Not her. Josh had said something similar many months ago, before his sentencing. That God had his hand on her in a unique way. The thought was still perplexing.

An intercom buzzed at that moment signaling that visitation hours were over.

Joshua stood and Rachael followed suit.

"I thought I was coming here to get all the answers," she said as she gathered her things.

Josh smiled. "People who have all the answers are highly overrated."

"Then I guess I should stop trying to be someone like that?"

Josh's smile softened. "Most definitely, Rachael. People who have all the answers don't need other people. And they never have opportunities to trust what they don't understand."

The rest of the weekend passed far more peacefully than she had expected. Rachael found her herself able to set the drawings aside, to mentally move past the puzzle of how Bucky died, and to simply enjoy being with Trace and McKenna.

Monday's preparations for the next day's court sessions kept her on

task the entire day and she found that she didn't have time to call Will
and ask if he had spoken yet with Elena or Santos. She left the courthouse
on Monday without having spoken to Will at all.

Trace must have noticed she had reached a level of calm acceptance.
After work on Monday, and as they washed dishes that Rachael didn't like
putting in the dishwasher, he turned to Rachael and told her she seemed
more relaxed than he had seen her in weeks.

"So what gives?" he said. "What exactly did Joshua say to you? You've
not been the same since you saw him."

Rachael dried a goblet and placed it in the cupboard. "He told me
to let go."

"Let go?"

"He could tell that I desperately wanted to come up with all the
answers. Not just about this case, but also about all these hunches I've
been having. I wanted to be able to explain it all. Own it all. And the thing
is, it's too big. I'm not meant to. So he told me to stop trying to control
what's not mine to command. Whatever God is telling me, I will hear
better if I stop running around and asking a million questions. I just need
to shut up and listen."

Trace handed her a plate. "Josh said all that?"

Rachael smiled. "More or less."

"So just like that you let go? It's that easy?"

"No." Rachael set the dried plate on the counter. "But holding on was
harder."

They were silent for a few moments as Trace washed a paring knife
and she dried it.

"I want you to know I'm okay with it," Trace finally said. "With you
being, like Fig would say, one of those psychic cops that sees ghosts."

Rachael laughed. "It's not that way at all."

Trace handed her a serving spoon. "I know it's not…But you're kind
of in on something that I'm not. That really irked me at first. But I really
am learning to be okay with it. You have to be who were meant to be.
We all do."

Rachael placed the serving spoon in a drawer. "I didn't ask for it,"
she said.

"No. But you're good at it. I mean, it's creepy, but you're good at it. You really do seem to get insights the rest of us don't."

She turned to him. "Thanks."

Trace reached into the soapy water and pulled the plug. "Just don't go looking for them, Rachael. Okay? Don't go looking for trouble. I might have to get a nose ring the next time I'm floored by this stuff."

Rachael grinned. "I promise I won't go looking for trouble," she said. "I won't go looking at all."

Tuesday's court schedule kept Rachael busy until after four. A message from Will was waiting for her when she got back to her desk late Tuesday afternoon.

She called him back, mentally telling herself to keep her distance.

"Will, it's Rachael. What's up?"

"I just wanted you to know I talked to Santos earlier today. I flat out asked him if his mother was covering for him, if he in fact was the one who killed Bucky. He told me it's just like a cop to want to catch a live Latino man to send to prison for murder instead of a dead one. He also told me he didn't kill Bucky. But he would have liked to."

"What will you do now?"

"I'm still trying to get Elena to talk to me. She can't claim distress forever. Sam's done a background check on Eduardo. There's nothin' there. What I'd really like is for Marisol to take a lie detector test but she won't agree to it."

"So?"

"So I'll wait until Elena will talk with me. Perhaps you want to come?"

"Sure, Will."

"So. No more letters?"

"No."

"You're not holding out on me, are you?"

"I promise, Will. I haven't gotten any more letters."

"All right. Catch you later."

Rachael hung up the phone.

For the next hour, she busied herself with post-court work and monitoring her other cases. Her mind drifted a time or two to Elena and the others. But she quickly reminded herself that she was already doing all she could. The rest was up to God and the influence of the human conscience.

She left the courthouse a little after five, stopping to get milk and rice cereal on the way home. The commute was hectic as usual, and she pulled in to the underground garage at twenty minutes to six.

The loft was quiet when she unlocked the front door. As she put the milk away, she saw that Fig had left her a note on the fridge, a sketch of where he and Trace and McKenna were. The three of them were pictured at a bookstore. McKenna held a copy of "One Day in the Life of Ivan Denisovich" in her chubby hands. Next to McKenna's hastily drawn image was one of Fig and Trace holding "Curious George Rides a Bike" between them.

"Back soon!' was scrawled across the bottom.

Rachael grabbed a Diet Coke and was studying the contents of the fridge and contemplating supper when the intercom by the front door buzzed. She closed the fridge.

Trace must've forgotten his key. He was probably downstairs in the lobby hoping she was home from work.

She walked over to the intercom and pressed the button to speak. "Yes?" she said.

A momentary pause.

"Mrs. Flynn?"

A woman's voice.

"Yes?"

"I'm sorry to bother you, but I…"

The voice fell away.

"Who is this, please," Rachael said.

Another pause and then the voice returned. Soft and tinged with apprehension.

"It's April Madden."

TWENTY-EIGHT

April accepted the cup of tea with shaking hands. Rachael sat down next to her on the couch and held her own cup. And waited.

After a moment April spoke. "I followed you home. I wanted to come in and talk to you at the courthouse today because I knew that was probably the right thing to do, but I couldn't do it."

"It's okay, April. I really do want to help you. That's why I wrote my home phone on the back of my card. I knew coming to me would be hard for you."

"You've no idea how hard," April whispered.

Again Rachael sensed that she should wait and let April direct the conversation.

"Where, um, where did you get the picture of that house?" April said, and Rachael could see that the very mention of the house made April shudder.

"A friend of mine drew most if it. My husband Trace drew the cellar doors."

April flinched slightly. "But it burned down," she said.

"Carol Bielke told me what it looked like."

"Why did she do that?"

"I asked her. I asked her what it looked like." Rachael paused before continuing. "Look, I know this is going to sound weird, but I went to your old street, April. I saw where Bucky's body was buried. And when I walked past the place where that house used to be, I was overcome with the sense that something terrible happened at that house. Later I stood where that house used to be and I asked God to show me. I don't know what happened, April. But I know *something* happened in the storm cellar."

April's hands began to tremble. Rachael leaned toward her, gently took the hot cup of tea from her and set it on the coffee table. April closed her eyes.

"Did something bad happen there, April?"

Tears began to slide down April's cheeks.

"Did something bad happen to Bucky there?"

April's eyes opened. They were shiny with moisture and pain. And disgust. "Is that what you think? You think something bad happened to Bucky there?" The look on April's face was one of utter betrayal.

Rachael inhaled as she realized she had come to the wrong conclusion.

April shook her head. "I shouldn't be surprised. That's always how it was," she said angrily. "No one ever understood. No one."

Rachael blinked. She had been wrong. Wrong! "April, please tell me."

April said nothing for several seconds. Fear that April would simply get up and leave gripped Rachael. "Please, April?" Rachael said.

"You think something bad happened to Bucky in that cellar."

Rachael said nothing.

"Nothing bad happened to Bucky there," April snapped. "Bucky made bad things happen! Don't you get it? He did bad things. He was the one who did bad things! In that cellar. To me!"

April's voice fell away and she began to weep. Rachael moved to her and wrapped her arms around the woman, holding her as she cried.

"I'm sorry, I'm sorry," Rachael said, over and over. "Please forgive me. Please, April."

For several minutes the two women sat that way on Rachael's couch.

One sobbed and one tried to console. Then April seemed to be spent of tears and her sobs turned to heaves of sadness. Rachael broke away from her.

"I'll get you a tissue," Rachael said. And she hurried to grab a box of Kleenex, silently berating herself all the way to the kitchen and back again. "Here," she said to April.

April dabbed at her eyes. Her tears had subsided but her face was still riven with sadness. Rachael handed her the cup of tea. April took a sip. And then another.

"Please tell me what happened," Rachael said.

"What for?" April said, her voice seemed bereft of strength.

"So I will understand."

April sighed. "I've never told anyone about this. Not even Jay."

Rachael waited.

"I wouldn't tell you now except I can't live with it anymore. And you won't understand anything else unless I tell you."

"I'm listening, April. Tell me what happened."

April inhaled heavily and then exhaled. "Bucky knew I liked cats. He knew I was especially fond of Mrs. Bielke's cat. My parents wouldn't let me have one, so I used to spend a lot of time playing with Mrs. Bielke's cat in her yard and in mine. And wherever else the cat wandered. Her name was Lucy."

April paused. Rachael sensed those had been pleasant memories to recall. And now the gears would shift.

"Bucky liked to chase Lucy with sticks and throw stones at her and he'd tell me horrible things he wanted to do to Lucy. He used to tell me he was going to crush her skull with a bat and then tell Mrs. Bielke I had sat on her. Because I've always been overweight and…"

April paused as a wave of fresh anguish gripped her. A moment later she continued.

"One day after school Bucky told me he had thrown Lucy down the storm cellar of that old house. He knew I was afraid of the cellar. I forget how he knew, but he did. My parents weren't home from work yet and I could see that Mrs. Bielke wasn't home either. Her car wasn't in her garage. At first I thought Bucky was just teasing me, but we were right by that old house and I could hear Lucy meowing like she was in pain. He had really thrown her down there.

"I didn't even think about what Bucky had in mind. I didn't stop to think that he might follow me down. All I was thinking is that Lucy was in that horrible place and was probably hurt."

April brought a hand up to her face. Her eyes were growing glassy again and her face was flushing crimson. Rachael felt her own eyes prickle with tears.

"I hated going inside. I was so afraid of spiders and dark places, but I kept hearing Lucy yowling and I just wanted to get her out of there. I opened the doors and I started to climb down the stairs. They were rickety and full of splinters. I called Lucy's name and she yowled louder. It was dark and damp inside, hard to see. The only light was from the one open cellar door. I had to walk through webs and I felt things crawling on my arms and I was so afraid. When I got to the bottom, I could see that Bucky had tied Lucy by her neck to an old post. I reached down to untie her and the cellar door above me slammed shut. I looked back up the stairs and Bucky was coming toward me. He...he had a flashlight in his hand. He had planned this. He had a flashlight in his hand...."

April's voice melted away for a second and it seemed as though she was reliving the ordeal in her head as she told it.

"He came toward me and said it was time for me and him to become good friends. He put the flashlight down on a stair and then he reached for me. I pulled away and he grabbed my arms. I started to scream and he put his hand on my mouth and said if I yelled he'd kill Lucy right there in front of me. He said if I told anyone about what he was doing he'd kill Lucy. I slapped at him and he slapped me back and he pulled at my shirt and put his hands on my...on my..."

April hung her head. Her breaths came in short gasps. "I was only twelve. I was only twelve, but I had breasts. I didn't even know what they were for. But I knew what he was doing was wrong. I wanted to throw up. I felt the bile in my throat. The more I struggled the more he hurt me. He pushed me to the ground and I was crying, 'Help me, help me!' But I couldn't yell it because I didn't want him to kill Lucy. He moved his hand up my leg and...and then he had his hand on the waist of my jeans. I was so afraid. So afraid.

"And then, the cellar door flew open and there was light and I looked and I saw Drew standing way above me. He said to Bucky, without even stuttering, 'Let her go.' Just like that he said it. Bucky said something back to Drew, I hardly remember what it was. But Drew said it again. Strong and sure as anything. 'Let her go.'

"Bucky took his hands off me and started to stomp up the stairs. I scrambled to my feet and untied Lucy. Then I heard Bucky say something to Drew about minding his own business. And Drew said, 'You so much as look at her again and I swear I'm calling the cops.' But he was stuttering by then. He could barely get the sentence out. I heard Bucky say something else, curse words. Then I heard the sound of someone being hit and then another. I heard gasps. And I knew Bucky was beating Drew up.

"I couldn't see what was happening. I only heard the sound of fists. Bucky called Drew a couple of names. Words I wasn't allowed to say. And then it got quiet. And I thought Bucky had chased Drew away. I heard footsteps on the stairs and I was so afraid it was Bucky coming back to hurt me. But it was Drew. His lip was bleeding and he had a cut above his eye.

"'Come on, April. He's gone,' he said. And I just stood there as Lucy ran up the stairs. Drew looked away from me. 'You can come out. He's gone,' he said, and I wondered why he looked away. Then I realized my blouse was open and everything was undone. I began to cry. But I fixed my blouse. And when I was done I just stood there. Drew took a peek at me and saw that I taken care of things. 'It's all over, come on,' he said. He reached his hand down and helped me up the stairs.

"When we were back outside again he closed the cellar door and turned to me. He asked me if Bucky had ever hurt me like that before. And I told him one time he grabbed me but it was outside and that I had gotten away. He asked me if I told my parents and I said no. He said I should never keep something like that from my parents and that I should tell them. I told him I couldn't tell my parents. I was only twelve.

"I said to him, 'Your lip is bleeding,' and he just shook his head. And then I said, 'He won't ever stop, will he?' And Drew looked very sad, as sad as I had ever seen him. He said, 'Don't walk past this house anymore, April. And don't listen to anything Bucky says.' And I said, 'What about

Lucy?' And he just told me not to worry about Lucy. Then he walked back across the street, touching his lip. And I walked home."

April stopped. Retelling what had happened to her seemed to have sapped her of energy. She sat across from Rachael as if in a trance.

Rachael brushed away tears from her own face, gripped with anguish for what April and Drew had endured. "You wrote the letters to me, didn't you, April?"

April nodded wordlessly.

"To protect Drew because he saved you."

April raised her head slowly and then shook it side to side. "Drew didn't kill Bucky." Her words were lifeless.

Rachael couldn't seem to process the words. "What?" she said.

April's shoulders sagged. "Drew didn't kill Bucky. It was me. It was all of us. But it was mostly me."

TWENTY-NINE

There wasn't a sound in the loft except the faraway hum of the traffic far below. Rachael barely noticed the silence. In her head, April's words were thundering. *It was all of us. It was all of us.*

April's eyes were on her lap, on her folded hands. Entwined in her fingers was a damp tissue. She didn't raise her eyes to Rachael's. The only movement in her body was the slight rising and falling of her chest.

"What do you mean, it was all of you?" Rachael said, attempting to sound calm, knowing she failed.

April kept her eyes down. "I mean all of us."

"Marisol and Eduardo too?"

April looked up then. "No. Neither one of them. Marisol just did what she thought she had to to protect us. To protect Elena mostly."

"Not Santos?" Rachael said.

"Santos…Santos didn't…he…" April struggled for words. "Marisol didn't know anything until just a few days ago. When you and Sgt. Pendleton came to her house the other day, she didn't know anything. But she knew you were looking for whoever killed Bucky. She could tell you thought maybe it was Santos. She called Elena when you left. That's when Elena told her what really happened. Marisol decided she would tell the police that it was Eduardo who had killed Bucky so that the cops would leave her kids and me and Drew alone. She called me and told me she wanted to do this for us. She called me the day before you came to see me at the library."

Rachael's head was churning. "April, what happened to Bucky?"

April twisted the tissue in her hands. "I'm only telling you because I don't want Marisol to have to do this. I wanted to protect Drew and Elena and Santos, but I've made it worse, not better. But I also want you to know I'm really the one who killed Bucky. You have to understand that."

"Tell me what happened, April."

April took a deep breath. "Elena saw Drew fighting with Bucky that day outside the storm cellar. She was upstairs in her bedroom across the street and she saw it all through the window. She saw Bucky knock Drew down, saw Drew helping me out of the cellar. She knew something bad had happened. Elena waited until I got home and then she walked over to my house and rang my doorbell. When I answered it she told me we had to do something about Bucky because no one else was. She said Bucky had tried to grab her too and had told her one of these days he was going to catch her when she wasn't on her guard and he'd have his way with her. I didn't know what that meant then, I just knew how I felt when Bucky had his hands on me and I didn't want that to happen ever again. Elena told me she had a plan. She told me she had a can of pepper spray. And she wanted to teach Bucky a lesson with that and with one of Santos's baseball bats.

"She told me the two of us could do it, teach him a lesson. Make him never touch us again. She said all I had to do was wait until Bucky was outside his house one afternoon after school. Then I was to call her on the phone and tell her it was time. She told me I needed to go outside and pretend like I didn't see Bucky and that I was to skip into the woods like I was looking for butterflies. She was sure Bucky would follow me. She would be watching. She would follow Bucky without him knowing it. Then when we had him alone, she would spray him with the pepper spray and hit him…hit him where it mattered. She said all I had to do was lure him into the woods."

April stopped to take a breath.

"So a couple days later Bucky was in his driveway fixing his bike. It was after school. I called Elena and told her what he was doing. She said to give her five minutes and then to wander outside and not look at him. Just wander off into the woods like I didn't have a care in the world. My heart was pounding in my chest, but I did it.

"As soon as I was inside the trees I could hear him coming. And I thought, 'What will happen to me if Elena doesn't come?' I went in far because Elena told me to and I was praying the whole time, because I could hear footsteps behind me. When they got very close, I turned around. Bucky had this horrible grin on his face. He said, 'Your little boyfriend isn't here to save you, is he?' and he walked right up to me like I was something he owned. I was so scared. I didn't see Elena. I didn't know if she was there. Just as Bucky reached for me I saw Elena burst from the trees behind Bucky and she whacked him across the back of his knees. He fell and she held up her pepper spray and started spraying it in his face. He yelled and struck out his arms. He knocked the bat out of her hand and then he grabbed her hand with the pepper spray and yanked it. Elena cried out and he hit her across the face. Elena yelled at me to get the bat. Bucky was cursing and rubbing his eyes with one hand but he lunged for me and hit me across my jaw. It hurt so bad I saw stars. I fell to the ground and I saw Bucky spin around and grab at Elena. He threw his arms around her legs and she fell. He had his hand on her mouth and was saying terrible things to her. His eyes were red and watering like he was crying. But I knew he wasn't crying. Bucky never cried.

"I wanted to get up and help Elena, but I couldn't. And then I saw someone else reaching for the bat near me. It was Drew. He had seen Bucky going into the woods. And Elena, too. He had the bat now and he brought it down crashing on the back of Bucky's head. Bucky crumpled over and Elena scrambled out from under him. Bucky was moaning, so we knew he would come to pretty quick.

"Drew looked angry as he helped us up. He asked us in his stuttering voice what we were doing in the woods. Elena said we had to teach Bucky a lesson. We had to make him stop. And he turned to Elena and said, 'You think a little pepper spray is going to stop him?' Then he stood there watching Bucky moaning on the ground and I could see him thinking. He was thinking hard. He turned to me and asked if I was all right. I said yes. Then he told me to run home and get some rope and some duct tape. And he told me to hurry. So I did.

"I came back with the rope and duct tape. Bucky was starting to writhe on the ground and was struggling to get up. He started cursing us and Drew grabbed the duct tape from me and taped Bucky's ankles together. Then he taped his mouth. He told Elena and me to help him prop Bucky against a tree. Then he told Elena to get the bat and if Bucky tried to get up to smack him with it. He told me to take the rope and tie Bucky to the tree while he duct-taped Bucky's hands. He said, 'Make it tight, April. Really tight.' I wrapped the rope around his middle and his shoulders and I pulled it as tight as I could.

"Then we stood there, looking down on him. He was fully conscious now and he was looking back at us with such hatred. Drew kneeled down. He said something like, 'I overheard your mother tell a friend once that you're afraid of the dark, Bucky. Bet you didn't know that I know that about you. She had a friend over and they were talking in your backyard. I was in my backyard and I heard every word.'

"Then he told Bucky we were going to leave him there overnight so that he could see what it was like to be surrounded by what he feared the most. Then he said this, and I've never forgotten it. He said, 'This is what it's like to be alone and afraid and unable to speak, Bucky. This is what it's like to be *me.*'

"Then Drew stood up and said we were leaving and that we'd come back for him in the morning if we remembered him. The next morning would be a Saturday. And we left. We got back to the street and it was just as peaceful and quiet as when we had left it. I told the others that Bucky would probably kill us all tomorrow. And Drew said he didn't care, he was already dead."

April paused and dabbed at a few stray tears that had gathered in her eyes.

"And I knew how Drew felt, I did," she continued. "I was afraid for him. And he had been so kind to me. I wanted to somehow convince Bucky to leave Drew alone. That what he was doing was killing him. I barely slept that night—I don't suppose any of us did—and the little sleep I had was filled with nightmares. I awoke at sunrise and I just had to see if Bucky was still there."

Tears began to slide down April's cheeks like rain on a window.

"So I got dressed and I went into the woods. And there wasn't a sound. Not a sound. I saw his feet first, through the trees. I saw that he was no longer sitting on the ground, but that his body was in some horrible half-standing, half-hanging contortion. I got closer and I saw he had one hand wrapped around the loops of rope that somehow now encircled his neck. The rope that I had tied around his shoulders."

April paused as if stricken. In her mind, Rachael saw the pictures Trace and Sid had drawn of Bucky gasping for air—and how she had been mesmerized by those drawings and not the others....

Then April opened her mouth and continued. "His mouth was taped. His eyes were...his eyes were open and wide, like they were popping out of his head. He wasn't moving. I knew he was dead. I knew he had strangled on that rope. But I said his name anyway. 'Bucky?' And he just stared back at me. He had tried to escape, tried to stand up, but the rope held him tight and the tree he was tied to was thick around its middle because it split into two trunks, so when Bucky stood and the ropes cinched up from his shoulders to his neck, they got tighter, not more loose. And he must have panicked and struggled against them, making them tighter and tighter...."

April's face had drained of color. She appeared to have almost forgotten Rachael was in the room. Then she seemed to remember. Her body made a startled movement and then settled.

"I don't remember doing this, but I sank to the ground and began to rock and cry," she went on. "That's how Santos found me."

"Santos?" Rachael said.

"Elena had awakened him and told him what we had done. He had told her to stay at the house and he would come into the woods and let Bucky go. When he found me and saw Bucky, he started saying something in Spanish. It sounded like a prayer.

"I remember asking Santos what we should do. And he didn't say anything at first. I told him what Bucky had done to me, what he had done to Elena and that Drew had saved me. Had saved us both. I told him I was afraid the police would come for Drew and arrest him. Then he quietly told me to go get a shovel. I left and came back with two shovels. It took us two hours to bury him. When we were done, Santos told me Drew and Elena didn't need to know what happened to Bucky. Bucky had run away before. Maybe everyone would think that he had run away again. And I remember saying, 'But this time he won't come back.' And Santos said, 'That's right, he won't.'

"So he went home and told Elena he looked and looked but he couldn't find Bucky anywhere. He told her he even peeked in Bucky's bedroom windows. And I went home and took a bath. I saw Drew going into the woods at about 9:30 that morning. He came right back out. I had to pretend I knew nothing. I was outside and he looked over at me with this puzzled look on his face. And I just shrugged my shoulders like I had no idea where Bucky was.

"Bucky's mother called the cops later that day and they came out and asked around the neighborhood if anyone had seen Bucky. We all said no."

"And Elena and Drew never knew what really happened?" Rachael said.

"No. But Drew…I always wanted to tell Drew that I had paid him back for what he had done for me. But I couldn't. And he kind of just grew up without me after that. It was like when Bucky left he started a new life. I was part of the old one. He barely spoke to me in the next four years before he went away to college."

Longing and regret coated April's words.

"You were in love with him," Rachael murmured.

April smiled. The first Rachael had seen since the woman arrived. "Always. From the moment he looked down on Bucky and me in that filthy cellar and told Bucky without so much as a stammer to let me go."

"He never knew?"

April looked away. "He never really looked my way again. And I was too shy to look his. No, I don't think he ever knew."

"Did you keep in touch with any of these people through the years?"

April shook her head. "No. I hadn't talked to any of them since high school. When the newspaper said that the police had been tipped that Bucky's body was there, Elena called Santos right away. She had thought all this time that Bucky had run away. Santos told her then what he and I had done. Neither one of them knew my married name but Elena got a hold of my graduating class president and the reunion committee. She eventually found me. By that time I had written to meet with you at the coffee shop, but Elena convinced me I shouldn't, that the police would never be able to piece it together."

"So you've not spoken with Drew?"

April's cheeks darkened. "No. I don't think he knows the truth."

Rachael cocked her head. "He may not know exactly what you and Santos did, but I think he suspects that someone went out of their way to protect him. He refused to answer our questions about who might have written the letters, April."

"I sometimes wonder how different our lives would've been if Bucky hadn't been in them. How different we would've turned out," April said, looking at her lap. Then she lifted her face to Rachael. "Do you have to call the police today? Right now?"

Rachael reached out and touched April's arm. "We don't have to do it today."

"I need to tell Jay. He'll be so angry with me. And hurt."

"You were just a child, April," Rachael said. "And you had been abused in a terrible way. You found a way to cope. It wasn't the best way or the right way, but no one will say they can't understand why you kids did what you did. And Bucky's death was an accident. God knows you didn't mean for that to happen."

April sought Rachael's eyes. "Does he? Does God know?" Her voice sounded childlike and afraid.

"He has always known, April."

"It *was* an accident," April whispered. "Like I told you from the very beginning."

"Yes."

"I knew you'd understand." April placed her hand on top of Rachael's. "I was right about you."

The sounds of footfalls and voices in the carpeted hallway outside the front door broke the quiet and the two women turned their heads. "You want to go find Mommy?" Rachael heard Trace say.

The sound of Trace's key in the lock echoed in the entry.

"It'll be all right," Rachael said to April, squeezing her hand.

The door opened and McKenna was suddenly crawling confidently over the threshold, eyes on the floor, intent on just placing one hand in front of the other.

THIRTY

Drew Downing sat placidly in the interview room with his arms folded across his chest as he listened to Will read April's statement.

Rachael sat between the two men, in a chair that was normally reserved for a suspect's attorney. She had moved the chair from the defendant's side of the table to the head of the table—where no one routinely sat. She didn't want to sit next to Will; she wasn't a cop. She couldn't sit next to Drew; she wasn't his attorney. But she wanted to be there for Drew's sake, and she had promised April she would try to explain to Drew why April had done what she'd done. This was the perfect opportunity to speak to him.

Will had agreed to let her be in the interview room partly because Rachael had been present when April gave her statement and partly because he said he owed her one. He had already rewarded her with a three-pound bag of M&Ms. She had grinned when he gave them to her, thanked him and then promptly placed the bag in the break room.

It was not murder and mayhem that took Bucky's life.

It was desperation and utter misfortune.

Will finished reading the statement out loud and looked up at Drew. "Do you wish to modify or add anything to your own account of what happened, in light of Ms. Madden's statement, Mr. Downing?"

Drew's outward countenance didn't waver. He spoke with calm assurance, other than the ever-present stutter. "When you w-w-were at my house, you asked me if I knew how B-B-B-Bucky ended up dead and buried in that lot. I told you didn't. I wasn't lying to you."

"All right," Will said.

"And you asked me if I knew who wr-wr-wr-wrote those letters and I told you I didn't. That's because I didn't."

"Can you corroborate Ms. Madden's statement?"

"If you're asking me if she and I t-t-t-tied Bucky to a tree, yes, I can corroborate that. If you're asking me if he tried to rape her in the cellar of that house, I can corroborate that, too. You want me to c-c-c-corroborate anything else Bucky did?"

"No," Will said. "We've just been lied to a lot these last few days. I just want to make sure we now have the truth."

"Yes. Now you have the whole, stinking t-t-t-truth about Ronald Buckett. About 25 years too late."

Will tossed April's statement on the table in front of him. "I wish you kids had just called the police when things got out of hand."

"They were out of hand from day one, Detective. When you live that w-w-w-way from the time you're ten, after awhile you just start to believe that's how life is. Unless you decide to make it different."

Will said nothing.

"Am I under arrest?" Drew asked.

"No. You're free to go."

"Will there be charges?"

Will turned his head toward Rachael.

"It's possible there'll be a charge of involuntary manslaughter, but my guess is you'll get a stayed sentence, if any," Rachael said. "Believe me, the court will hear how all of you were mistreated."

"You should probably retain a lawyer nonetheless," Will said.

"And the others? W-w-w-what about them?"

"Santos wasn't there when you tied Bucky to the tree and left him," Rachael replied. "There's a statute of limitation for his offense, but not for yours. April and Elena will likely face the same scrutiny as you—and will receive the same mercy, if I have anything to say about it."

"Mercy," Drew echoed, and then was silent. "Are we done?" he said a moment later.

"Yes," Will answered. "I'd say we're done."

Drew stood and turned to the door. Rachael stood as well.

"I'll walk you out," she said. She mouthed a goodbye to Will and he nodded once.

Drew was silent as they walked through the corridors to the main entrance. As they stepped outside, Rachael turned to him and touched his arm so that he would stop.

"April has never forgotten how you rescued her, never," she said. "It's why she and Santos did what they did when they found Bucky dead. She was afraid if they called the police, you would've been arrested. She wanted to save you like you saved her."

Drew looked out on the streets of St. Paul ahead and beside them. "Don't you think there's something terribly wrong with a world where broken children without a life-saving skill to their name have to save other broken children?"

The afternoon sun bore down on Rachael and she squinted as she looked up at him.

"Yes," she answered. "I do. It makes me mad. But it also fills me with hope."

"Hope." He said the word derisively.

"Yes. Unfortunately there are people like Bucky. But there are also people like you. What you did for April was very brave."

"And what I did to B-B-B-Bucky was very cruel." He turned to look at her, to challenge her.

"You didn't think it would kill him."

"But you're c-c-c-conveniently forgetting I wanted it to."

Rachael lifted her chin. "That doesn't mean hope doesn't exist."

Drew leveled his eyes at her. "Hope is a powerless w-w-w-word. You can't really depend on anything, Ms. Flynn. Life is just the like the weather. It's powered by a giant, unknowable force that c-c-c-can warm your face one minute and rip your house apart the next, without so much as one moral thought behind either action."

Rachael opened her mouth to disagree; to tell Drew that there were indeed some things he could count on. But Drew turned on his heel and began walking purposefully across the parking lot.

"Goodbye, Drew," she called after him.

He raised a hand in farewell but didn't turn. She watched as he got into his car and drove away, carrying, it seemed, his wounds and regrets in figurative suitcases that jostled in the back seat.

The afternoon sun was warm on her face as she stood there and watched Drew's car disappear into traffic. She turned toward the doors of the police station wondering if she should tell Will she was heading to Coon Rapids that afternoon. She had promised April she'd let her know how things went with Drew. Drew wasn't angry with April, not at all. If anything, the bond of their shared experiences was still sadly intact. But Drew was indeed angry. She wouldn't lie to April about that.

Rachael turned back around and stepped off the sidewalk onto the asphalt. Will didn't have to know she was on her way to see April. He was probably already hard at work on some other horrendous case where someone died who shouldn't have.

She got into her car, ready to head to April's house, but as she sat there with her hands on the steering wheel, she felt an intense pull to drive to St. Anthony Park first—to Willow Street and the collection of houses that lined its sidewalks—and one house in particular. She had to make sure there were no stones left unturned.

Rachael joined the Friday afternoon traffic and was soon pulling up along the curb by Santos's and Elena's old house. As she switched off her car and opened the door, she was greeted with the sounds of wood and steel becoming a future address. Work was progressing at a swift pace at the construction site at the end of the street.

She got out of the car and surveyed the little neighborhood. The former Valasquez home was closest to her. It had not taken Marisol long to retract her story once Will called her and told her April had confessed, and that he knew without a doubt that Santos and Elena were implicated. And Marisol had vehemently maintained that her children were victims first, last and always. Santos had also upheld April's statement when Will called him, albeit somewhat reluctantly. He had not known that the perverse threats Bucky had made to him about Elena had also been made *to* Elena, face to face. Santos had declared to Will that Bucky got the burial he deserved and that he'd gladly serve prison time for his sister or April in defense of what they had done. As of that afternoon, Elena still had not spoken to Will. Her husband had told him that letting her mother take the blame for what had happened was hard enough on his wife. Coming to terms with having a hand in Bucky's death was proving to be harder still.

Rachael looked past the former Valasquez home to Drew's old house and Bucky's right next to it. The sadness that overcame her made her look away. One life was gone and another seemed to be wasting away little by little. She said a silent prayer for Drew as she turned away from his house.

Her eyes lingered on the construction site for a moment—the place where Bucky died—and then traveled to April's house on the other side of the street, where April's parents still lived. She wondered what Mr. and Mrs. Howard thought about the events of the last few days, if they finally understood how much their daughter had suffered.

Rachael turned her body now to face the new house directly across from her car. She walked slowly across the street and then stood motionless on the sidewalk, waiting to see if a wave of troubling thoughts would sweep across her.

A sprinkler was dousing the lawn with a lazy arc of water. Piano music drifted out of the front room window. She knelt down and placed her hand on a patch of grass outside the sprinkler's half-circle path. The grass was cool to the touch but she felt nothing else.

Nothing at all.

She had been released. At least from this place.

Rachael rose, satisfied but not happy. She walked back to her car, finding herself anxious to tell Joshua that he had been right; she wasn't meant to get inside the Divine. She was meant to be open to its invasion.

And she also wanted to tell Josh that she was surprised at how empty she felt now that this task was done, now that she was walking away from a house, a street, a place that was suddenly very ordinary.

She was empty. Trace would say things were back to normal. Fig would say let's have some haggis and celebrate.

But she was instantly aware that she didn't particularly like feeling empty.

Rachael pictured saying as much to Josh, and as she did, she immediately imagined him saying back to her, "Don't get used to it." A tiny grin spread across her mouth.

She started the engine, checking to make sure she still had the directions to April's house in her briefcase.

Outside her car window and across the street, a light breeze began to stroke the petaled heads of hydrangeas sparkling in the sprinkler's path. The breeze skipped its way across the towering trees that shaded the new house—ancient elms that had stood there for decades. As she pulled away from the curb Rachael saw the branches yield to the wind and respond, in kind, to its caress.

RESOURCES ON BULLYING

Websites:

Raven Days *(www.ravendays.org)*

True-life stories from victims and former victims, plus articles, initiatives, and resources that reveal how to counter the devastating effects of victimization.

Bully B'ware *(www.bullybeware.com)*

A Canadian site that includes tips and strategies to deal with bullying, plus how to understand what makes a bully and what makes a victim.

Kid Power *(www.kidpower.org)*

Practical skills for dealing with bullies, for both kids and their parents.

Book:

Fried, Suellen and Paula Fried. *Bullies and Victims*. New York: M. Evans and Company, 1996.

ABOUT SUSAN MEISSNER

Susan Meissner is an award-winning newspaper columnist, pastor's wife, and novelist. She lives in rural Minnesota with her husband, Bob, and their four children. If you enjoyed *Sticks and Stones,* you'll want to read Susan's other novels, including her first Rachael Flynn mystery...

WIDOWS AND ORPHANS

When her ultra-ministry-minded brother, Joshua, confesses to murder, lawyer Rachael Flynn begs him to let her represent him, certain that he is innocent. But Joshua refuses her offer of counsel. As Rachael works on the case, she begins to suspect that Josh knows who the real killer is, but she is unable to get him to cooperate with his defense. Why won't he talk to her? What is Josh hiding?

The answer is revealed in a stunning conclusion that will have readers eager for the second book in this gripping new series.

Susan's other excellent novels include:

WHY THE SKY IS BLUE

What options does a Christian woman have after she's been brutally assaulted by a stranger...and becomes pregnant? Happily married and the mother of two, Claire Holland must learn to trust God "in all things."

A WINDOW TO THE WORLD

Here is the story of two girls who are inseparable until one is abducted as the other watches helplessly. Years later the mystery is solved—and the truth confirmed that God works all things together for good. Named by *Booklist Magazine* as one of the top ten Christian novels of 2005.

IN ALL DEEP PLACES

Acclaimed mystery writer Luke Foxbourne lives a happy life in a century-old manor house in Connecticut. But when his father, Jack, has a stroke, Luke returns to his hometown of Halcyon, Iowa, where he reluctantly takes the reins of his father's newspaper for an undetermined length of time. Memories of Norah—the neighbor girl who was his first kiss—haunt Luke to reflect as he spends night after night alone in his childhood home. Soon he feels an uncontrollable urge to start writing a different story. Norah's story. And his own.

A SEAHORSE IN THE THAMES

Alexa Poole intended to spend her week off from work quietly recuperating from minor surgery. But when carpenter Stephen Moran falls into her life—or rather off her roof—the unexpected happens. His sweet, gentle disposition proves more than she can resist and now she's falling for him.

Her older sister, Rebecca, has lived at the Falkman Residential Center since a car accident left her mentally compromised, vulnerable, and innocent. Now, 17 years later, she has vanished, leaving Alexa fearing the worst. After Alexa places a call to her twin sister Priscilla in England, Priscilla agrees to come home for a visit despite a strained separation from her family.

As Alexa begins the search for Rebecca, disturbing questions surface. Why did the car Rebecca was riding in swerve off the road killing her college friend, Leanne McNeil? And what about the mysterious check for $50,000 found in Rebecca's room signed by her friend's father, Gavin McNeil?

Coming soon in the
Rachael Flynn Mystery series...

DAYS AND HOURS

A single mother and recovering drug addict is charged with abandoning her infant in a downtown St. Paul alley, but assistant county attorney Rachael Flynn believes the young woman when she passionately insists her baby was taken from her while she slept. When the baby disappears three months after being returned to the mother and foul play is suspected, Rachael bitterly second-guesses her instincts. Did she make a horrible mistake in allowing the infant to be returned home?

Her colleague Sgt. Will Pendleton and the rest of the St. Paul police are convinced the mother killed the baby during a relapse while high on methamphetamines, and Rachael believes she failed the child in the worst possible way. But then another live, days-old infant is found in a dumpster in another part of the city—and another single mother claims her baby was taken from her. Rachael begins to reconnect with her earlier intuitions. Something is not right. Who would steal a baby only to abandon it, making it seem as if a troubled single mother was to blame? Where is that missing baby? And will she be able to see past the deception before another child is taken and abandoned, or worse, found too late?

THE BOOK CLUB FOR TODAY'S CHRISTIAN FAMILY

A Letter to Our Readers

Dear Reader:

In order that we might better contribute to your reading enjoyment, we would appreciate your taking a few minutes to respond to the following questions. When completed, please return to the following:

Andrea Doering, Editor-in-Chief
Crossings Book Club
401 Franklin Avenue, Garden City, NY 11530

You can post your review online! Go to www.crossings.com and rate this book.

Title _____ Author _____

1 Did you enjoy reading this book?

❑ Very much. I would like to see more books by this author!

❑ I really liked_____

❑ Moderately. I would have enjoyed it more if_____

2 What influenced your decision to purchase this book? Check all that apply.

❑ Cover
❑ Title
❑ Publicity
❑ Catalog description
❑ Friends
❑ Enjoyed other books by this author
❑ Other _____

3 Please check your age range:

❑ Under 18   ❑ 18-24
❑ 25-34   ❑ 35-45
❑ 46-55   ❑ Over 55

4 How many hours per week do you read? _____

5 How would you rate this book, on a scale from 1 (poor) to 5 (superior)?
_____

Name_____

Occupation_____

Address_____

City_____ State_____ Zip_____